Try a Little Tenderness:

A His-Love.com Novel

Try a Little Tenderness:

A His-Love.com Novel

Allyson M. Deese

and

Isaiah David Paul

URBAN CHRISTIAN

Urban Books, LLC
97 N18th Street
Wyandanch, NY 11798

ISBN 13: 978-1-62286-808-7
ISBN 10: 1-62286-808-0

First Trade Paperback Printing July 2015'
Printed in the United States of America

10 9 8 7 6 5 4 3 2 1

Distributed by Kensington Publishing Corp.
Submit orders to:
Customer Service
400 Hahn Road
Westminster, MD 21157-4627
Phone: 1-800-733-3000
Fax: 1-800-659-2436

Try a Little Tenderness:

A His-Love.com Novel

Allyson M. Deese

and

Isaiah David Paul

Acknowledgments

First and foremost, I give all glory and honor to God the Father, God the Son, and God the Holy Ghost. Without you, Lord, none of this would be possible. Jesus, you are the center of my joy.

I would also like to thank my parents, Dolores and James Deese, Sr., who supported me even when they didn't agree with me. Mommy and Daddy, I love you with everything I am and ever will be. To my brothers, Michael and James, Jr. and my sister, Quanda, I love y'all.

To my great-nieces, Kamylah and Makiyah, Auntie Ally loves you both so much.

To my extended family, I love you so much.

To my ace, my partner in crime and pen, Jay, your go-get-'em attitude and spirit has motivated me many a day, and I will always appreciate you for that. Your talent is immeasurable, and I look forward to the day that the rest of the world recognizes the gift that God has blessed you with.

I want to thank Linda R. Herman, my sister in Christ and of the pen. You've always encouraged me, even when I didn't want to hear it. I love you so much. It's past time for us to do another collaboration! It was so great to finally meet you and the family!

To my Auntie (Pokey) Beverly Peppers-Smith and my new friend, Ms. Doris Bennett, thank you so much for your help organizing the 2014 Asheville Literary Reunion. We couldn't have done this without you.

Acknowledgments

To the Literary Divas Spartanburg book club, thank you so much for your support! We love you ladies! See you soon!

To our thought-provoking editor, Joylynn M. Ross, thank you so much for your dedication and belief in our craft. We love you!

To Urban Christian, thank you so much for this opportunity to make a country girl's dream come true!

To my readers who've rocked with me from the very beginning, hard to believe it's been eight years! Look at God! To my new readers, thank you for taking a chance on me. I appreciate you too. Way too many people to name, but I have to shout out Mrs. Joyce Dickerson and her family. Your support throughout my career has been overwhelmingly amazing!

To my homie-apple-scrapple Charles Wallace of Massages by Chuck of Washington, D.C., thank you for all of your support from the beginning!

To anyone that I may have forgotten, please charge it to my head and not my heart. I do thank you.

God Bless,
Allyson M. Deese

Acknowledgments

First, I give honor to God, Jesus, and the Holy Spirit for everything, even when I don't deserve it. I appreciate You making this project come to fruition with my wife, Allyson. Without the Trinity, none of this would be possible.

Allyson, I love and appreciate you and the hard work we put in to make the project and our marriage happen. In it for the long haul.

Mr. Tyree, I remember the first time we spoke about me publishing a book. You'd just released *A Do Right Man* in paperback, and I was about to turn seventeen. I was on the humble because I had just talked to E. Lynn Harris again via e-mail (RIP) and your Uncle Joe Joe had to be the most patient man on earth. He answered twenty (plus) questions about how to get my book published and where I needed to take my literary career. I wanted to know more about the business of publishing and how you published yourself before signing with S&S. You gave me some advice out of the kindness of your heart, and it took me a long time, but I finally got it, and now I'm here. I pray you get to enjoy this book and see that my wife and I FINALLY made it to *this* side of the publishing game. Now I can say I've experienced almost everything.

To the Imes, Deese, Hagan, Simmons, Phelps, Tinsley, Peoples, and Odom families, I'm still writing books. I hate that I don't get to spend as much time with you all as I should, but do know that you are loved, thought of, and prayed for. My church families at The Lord's Church of Asheville and Restoration Church, we appreciate the love, prayers, and checking in on us.

Acknowledgments

Joylynn M. Ross, you've been rocking with me since I was at A&T. Before we were affiliated with one of the legendary street labels of all time, I was treated like family before I became family. For that, I am greatly appreciative. Mr. & Mrs. Carl Weber, the first time I saw *Drama Queen* by LaJill Hunt in Walmart I knew then I'd eventually get it together to join the Urban Books family. I respect the time and the patience in waiting on me to mature to truly appreciate this opportunity. I want to thank the three of you for the work you've done in helping make sure *Try A Little Tenderness* is the best book possible.

To our Urban Christian label mates, we're here. Shana Burton, Tyora Moody, Leslie J. Sherrod, and K. T. Richey, thank you for supporting and participating in the Asheville Literary Reunion. If it's the Lord's will for us to do this again in 2016, let's get that group picture together. To Dwan Abrams, Tiffany L. Warren, Shana, who knew that the picture Miranda Parker (RIP) took would foreshadow all of us being on affiliated labels. Rhonda, Sherri, and E. N. Joy, I hope y'all enjoy the *Woman's Revenge* series as much as I enjoy being able to contribute to them. I pray that y'all are pleased with the stories I'm writing.

To the old school Triple Crown label mates, K'wan, Nikki Turner, JOY, KaShamba Williams, Tu-Shonda L. Whitaker, Keisha Ervin, T. N. Baker, Trustice Gentiles, Joy Deja King, Kane & Abel, Jason Poole, and of course, Victor L. Martin—when we first came out, we were considered literary bastards. People had the nerve to curse us and told us to our faces we would amount to nothing. Over ten years later, I think about the impact we've had on all of those who came after us. We run this. Y'all accepted me because I did everything for Victor humanly possible with what I had, and y'all continue to show me how a real publishing family moves and acts. Toy and

Acknowledgments

Charisse Washington, for continuing to hold me to the dream and helping me with the store. Shannon Holmes for always being a wealth of wisdom and encouraging me to take my own path. And Vickie Stringer, with the ups and the downs, we've learned with and from each other. Continue to move forward.

Mrs. Wahida Clark, sister, mediator, I still have most of the letters you wrote to me while you were locked up. It is a pleasure and honor to work with you outside the walls.

For the alumni of North Carolina Agricultural & Technical State University, especially that Class of 2004, thank you for rallying behind my first novel and still showing love for the work I do now. For the alumni of Winston-Salem State University, my home away from home, the mentorship and camaraderie are greatly appreciated. And to the alumni of Western Carolina University, for making graduate school a wonderful experience, to you I say thank you.

A toast to the brothers of Alpha Phi Alpha Fraternity, Incorporated—especially Sherrod, Sam, Mike, and "POPS"—the journey continues. Onward and upward . . .

To the Vera Pathways students, continue to dream and to look forward as you leave the camps and regain control over your lives. Use this "second chance" wisely. And to the ladies at Swannanoa, thank you for answering some of the questions I had. I really appreciate it.

I know I may have forgotten some people. Charge it to the head and not the heart. Lord willing there will be a next time.

—Isaiah David Paul

Prologue

Let's Not Waste Time

"This is Mateo Valdez, and I'm calling to find out whether the Chase card provided to me can be used to pay for this room." Mateo spoke into the headset as he watched the couple in front of him get touchy-feely with one another.

Mateo looked up from behind the counter. He could see a few coworkers were helping other guests bring in luggage or cleaning various spots in the motel. He silently thanked God for the Dr. Scholl's insoles that made the Johnson & Murphy wingtip shoes he had been wearing for the past nine hours comfortable. The shoes were a far cry from the Timbs or the Jordans he rocked on a regular; they signified maturity beyond the three hundred dollar pair of shoes he was used to wearing.

"And you're calling from the Heaven's Inn motel in Asheville, North Carolina?" the customer service representative asked.

"Yes," Mateo replied.

"Mr. Valdez, I'll have to place you on hold while I find out what I can do for your customer," the customer representative told Mateo over the phone.

"What's taking so long with this room, man?" the woman at the front counter yelled so loudly that all of the patrons and workers of Heaven's Inn turned their attention to her.

He took off his headset and hung it on the screen of the Lenovo computer he was working on. Mateo rubbed the left side of his head. As he stood, he quickly scanned the lobby and met every eye that wanted to see what he was going to do next. He could hear the woman tapping her fingernails on the oak counter as if she were banging keys on a piano. "Ma'am," Mateo started his reply. He sounded like he had a frog in his throat. "We're waiting on Chase to approve the card your friend gave us as payment. When I attempted to process the card for payment, they gave me an eight hundred number to call to verify funds in the account."

Mateo tried his best not to go off on the woman and the nervous young man standing next to her. He'd only been saved for six months and found the temptation to get unprofessional hard to resist.

Mateo thought he recognized her, but he wasn't sure. He tried to remember the woman's name but kept drawing a blank. What he did know was that he wanted the woman and her "man for the night" out of his face.

"Chase needs to stop tripping and take this card." The woman at the counter continued to amplify her voice as if she were broadcasting the play-by-play in a football stadium. "I don't mess with no low-budget dudes, and Fredrick Acropocolips better not be no low-budget dude."

Fredrick looked at her, rolling his eyes before settling his view on her backside.

Yeah, she's tricking, Mateo thought as he picked up Fredrick's Chase credit card and verified that the young guy in the shirt and tie in the picture matched the man standing before him trying to get a room.

Mateo noticed that he and Fredrick were polar opposites. Fredrick was at least six foot three, wafer-thin and wiry, like the frames used for a cheap pair of eyeglasses. His extremely pale skin reddened every time his "woman for the night" opened her mouth to speak. Mateo was much shorter, five foot six, one hundred and fifty-six pounds of muscle.

Mateo looked every bit of the self-proclaimed thug he used to be. The extra-long white polo shirt he wore that bore the black inscription *Serve Them, Inc.* was a command and mantra of his spiritual mentor and boss, Minister Stanley Hammer. The logos for Heaven's Inn and the Christian Cab Company represented the spiritually guided businesses the man they called Hammer ran out of the motel. Mateo's black slacks hugged his waist appropriately, with the guidance of a belt—not barely hanging on, exposing the shape of his rear end. No one besides Mateo knew what type of underwear he had on.

However, this outer appearance and desire to serve God did little to change some of his ways. Mateo was and would always be a street dude.

"Godiva." Mateo finally remembered her name.

"Yes, Mateo." Godiva looked up and smacked her thick lips. Mateo knew he remembered her name. He tried not to stare at her lips, but those lips and her body called for him to rekindle the lust-filled night they had shared two years before Mateo found Jesus. Mateo's body was calling her curves and her nicely stacked five foot six frame, but he had to stay true to the promise of celibacy he took when he got saved.

"The customer service rep still has me on hold. As soon as he gets back to me, we'll be able to find out what our options are," Mateo informed them as he flipped the card in his hand like a quarter.

"Well, they need to hurry up. I got work to do." Godiva pouted as she put her hand on Fredrick's face and rubbed it like she was proud of her latest pet.

Mateo had shown growth. The old him would've pushed the computers, telephones, and other electronics used to facilitate business off the counter and handled his business with the loud mouth. If Mateo let his carnal rage have its way, Godiva would be screaming for mercy and calling his name like he was God.

That was not the Mateo he was striving to be.

Out of instinct, Mateo put his hand in his front left pocket. The knot he'd grown accustomed to carrying was gone. Instead, Mateo had to rely on his ability to read Braille and feel the denominations. He had $52.67. The $52.67 represented the direction Mateo needed his life to continue going in. The $52.67 was legitimate money made working at Heaven's Inn motel.

The money also had to last him until he got his next paycheck the following Tuesday.

Mateo enjoyed working at Heaven's Inn and not having to watch over his shoulder to make sure the FBI wasn't trailing the counterfeits he used to produce and peddle. When he swiped his pre-paid MasterCard, he knew exactly what was on it and how the money got there.

"Yo, how long before our room is ready?" Godiva talked over the customer service representative, who was returning to the phone line to let Mateo know whether the card could be used.

Mateo wanted to put his finger up to his lips to politely tell her to be quiet, but he didn't want to come off as rude. Instead, he sucked in his lips and gritted his teeth and tried not to tell Godiva that acting like a low-budget hussy wasn't going to make him get her into a room any faster. He also wanted to tell her that she wasn't *that good* to be charging anyone for her services. Yet Mateo chose to keep those two thoughts to himself.

"Godiva, I apologize." He let his lips loose quickly and returned them to his gritted stance after he asked the representative on the line to hold. "Until the bank can give us permission to bill these charges on the account, we can't use this card for payment."

Godiva started to ask another question, but a frustrated Mateo held up his finger. She pierced her eyes at him. Mateo put on a smile that would've made his dentist proud. He really wanted to say something smart, but the service representative from the bank was on the line.

Godiva paced back and forth and talked trash about Mateo and Heaven's Inn. Mateo's ability to remain meek was being tested. "Come here, Fredrick." Godiva gave him a hug from behind. "We may have to go somewhere else if they don't get their stuff together."

Mateo started to tell Godiva and Fredrick to take their business elsewhere. Instead, he tried to ignore them as they engaged in a heavy amount of public display of affection.

Even though Hammer frowned on such displays, a customer was a customer. "You should treat them the way God would treat them." Hammer was quick to remind Mateo and the other staff members of Heaven's Inn's policy.

So Mateo held his tongue and instead turned his attention back to the rep on the line. "I'm sorry about that. What were you saying?"

"Yes, sir, Mr. Valdez, are you still on the line?" Mateo heard the rep ask him.

"Yes, I'm still here. I'm waiting on approval to process this payment for eighty-six eighty-three at the Heaven's Inn motel." Mateo looked back at Godiva, who was allowing Fredrick to palm her backside. He remembered the days when he used to do that, publicly staking his claim on the female he was being intimate with at the moment. Grab her, pull her close, and kiss her on the lips or the neck. If he was up for it, he might've given her some tongue action. Then he would open his eyes and watch as the guys who looked on from a distance got jealous with envy. He got a thrill from seeing the looks on the other men's faces as they wished his girl was *their* girl.

"I'm sorry, Mr. Valdez, but Heaven's Inn cannot process this card for payment." The service representative interrupted his thoughts. "They will have to offer another form of payment."

"Okay, thank you, sir." Mateo confirmed that he understood what the representative asked of him and ended the call. He nodded his head at Fredrick. "You have another form of payment?" Mateo repeated the instructions given to him as he handed the man his card.

"You guys are bugging," Fredrick complained as he snatched the card from Mateo's hand.

Mateo closed his eyes and shook his head. *One more time, Lord, and I'm sending him to you in the next few minutes.*

Mateo forced a smile as Fredrick dug his hand into his back pocket and produced a black wallet. He put the card back into the wallet and pulled out five $20 bills and placed them on the counter instead of putting the money into Mateo's extended hand.

Mateo nodded. He thought it funny that Fredrick would pick a black woman to sleep with, but he couldn't put the bills into a black man's hands. It wasn't like his hands were dirty. Mateo decided not to address the implied racism being directed at him as he picked up the bills from the counter. He got his bill marker and confirmed that the bills weren't counterfeit. He counted out the man's change. "Sixteen dollars and seventeen cents is your change, and you're in room one twenty-four." Mateo put the money and room key in Fredrick's hand. "We hope you enjoy your stay."

"I hope this room is better than your service," Fredrick replied as he palmed Godiva's booty and pushed her ahead of him.

Godiva turned around and stared at Mateo. She winked at him and licked her lips, enticing Mateo to steal her from

Fredrick. The blood flow seemed to drop from his head to waist, almost transferring the decision-making role from his crown. Godiva was a beauty, and Mateo was tempted to oblige. Tall, dark, and stacked in the right places as far as he was concerned.

The flesh wanted to go after her.

Mateo sized Fredrick up again and decided the battle wasn't worth it. True, Godiva had curves in places that would make a man forget he was saved and entertain the lust demon, but Mateo was trying to stay focused on his walk with Christ.

God, help me not burst through these pants, Mateo pleaded. *I'm trying to stay saved, but that girl right there gonna make me show her something.*

Just as the thought to live with God crossed his mind, Mateo heard a commotion at the front door. Problem solved, prayer answered. His thoughts had been diverted.

The first man to walk through the door was his long-time nemesis, Turner Mustafa Spartenburg, and he knew why the man showed his face at the motel. Turner was trouble with a capital *T*. The man's first objective in life was to run Asheville like he was the gangster version of Adolf Hitler. With his father being a former powerful councilman and criminal lawyer and his mother a prominent sheriff with the local law enforcement agency, Turner was practically king of his own castle. He had both the county sheriff's office and the city police department in his back pocket. That made him a terror with a capital *T*.

To say Turner was spoiled was an understatement. As Turner thought it, so it happened, at least most of the time. Drugs, cars, women, men, money: if Turner wanted it, he got it. He didn't take too kindly to giving back things he'd stolen from people, nor did he let go of anyone who wanted to leave his circle.

A few months earlier, Hammer had gone to confront Turner about some property, specifically a green Kia Rio that belonged to one of the new Christians named Sonic that Hammer was mentoring. Sonic had just re-dedicated his life to Christ after being in a relationship with Turner, and Hammer went to help him get his stuff. Turner got jealous after seeing Sonic with Hammer and assumed that Sonic had been intimate with him . . . that maybe Sonic was leaving him to be with Hammer.

Turner bucked up to Hammer. Both men stood six feet four inches tall with physiques that could go toe to toe with LeBron James. Hammer's well-kept dreads were bound together with a rubber band, and Turner's French vanilla light skin complexion showed off the tight mohawk fade that resembled mountain peaks. Turner may have had youth on his side, but Hammer had experience on his side when he wiped the floor with him in a one-on-one square-off.

Hammer was upset with himself at the time because he'd allowed Turner to provoke him when he pulled his gun out and struck him. The Bible says to turn the other cheek; Hammer turned Turner's with his fist.

The gangsta wasn't alone as he walked through the doors of Mateo's place of employment. He'd brought his crew of ten troublemakers who knew how to shut down the club—and not in a good way.

Mateo recognized two of the guys. The dark-skinned African American guy, LeMarquise, was some punk he'd been fighting off and on for most of their junior high and high school years. Even though they both were twenty-seven years old, the rivalry was still apparent. Mateo and LeMarquise were evenly matched at five feet six and one hundred and fifty-six pounds of muscle. Santos was the lighter, Dominican dude. He was so sneaky he'd steal the oxygen out of water and leave you with hydrogen if you weren't careful.

Surprised but alarmed, Mateo's defenses went up. He'd had many fair fights with the two of them in the past, but he knew this one wouldn't be.

"If it isn't that punk Mateo." LeMarquise opened his big mouth. "I thought that crazy uncle of yours would've had you leaking by now."

Mateo thought it was a low blow for LeMarquise to bring up his child-molesting uncle. Before Mateo got saved, he'd messed around with his uncle's new wife, who was fascinated with the phallus between his legs. In some ways, this was payback for his uncle raping his sister. When his uncle found Mateo and his wife getting down in their bed, he chased Mateo throughout the Kenilworth area of Asheville to the front door of Heaven's Inn. That was how he met Hammer and got reacquainted with Jesus.

"And I thought you would've learned not to speak unless your elders are talking to you." Mateo moved from the behind the counter. As LeMarquise, Santos, and a few of Turner's hellions drew close, Mateo held his ground. "What's up?" Mateo greeted him.

He looked over to see Hammer coming into the lobby from the office behind the counter. Mateo could see the disappointment in his mentor's eyes. They were supposed to minister and spread the Word. At that moment, Mateo was more content in expanding his reach and landing a blow to LeMarquise's jaw.

Some of Mateo's and LeMarquise's previous fights flooded his mind. If they weren't fighting over some girl, they were fighting for bragging rights over who whooped whose butt.

LeMarquise wasted no time getting the confrontation started by calling Mateo a slew of offensive names that were derogatory to Mateo's African American and Mexican heritage, and soon, Mateo landed with a right across the jaw. LeMarquise spit out some blood, looked over at Mateo, and said the ultimate Spanish curse toward his mother.

"Oh yeah?" Mateo got animated and rushed toward LeMarquise. Santos punched Mateo, and the blow landed on the right side of his face. Mateo quickly retaliated and sent punches to both LeMarquise and Santos.

Mateo was holding his own considering he was out-numbered two to one. He would go at it with LeMarquise for a little while, and when LeMarquise got in a bind, Mateo would find himself rumbling with Santos. When Santos needed some help, he and LeMarquise would double team him.

Mateo could see the other eight guys and Turner had Hammer and a few of the other employees held up. Turner and three of the guys were jumping on Hammer, and the rest of the guys were giving the two coworkers a fit.

A hard object struck Mateo from behind, and the next thing he knew, he was on the ground, trying to avoid the raining fists that were landing all over his face and chest. Feet fell next, and he felt more than four.

Accepting defeat was difficult, especially for a fighter like Mateo. He curled his body as tightly as he could as his assailants multiplied faster than roaches. Raid couldn't shake these jokers off. He heard a loud, familiar popping sound and prayed to God he hadn't broken a bone or something.

Heaven's Inn was under attack, and Mateo felt guilty for not being able to save it or himself. He could hear Turner yelling at Sonic, and a few more gunshots made their presence known in the room.

Mateo felt a burning sensation in his calf. It felt like his leg was on fire. He bit his lip and tried not to curse as he reached down to stop the blood from leaking from his leg. As he looked up, he felt his head being forced forward from a forceful blow from the back, and he saw the soles of one of his attackers' boots moving closer to his face. That was the last thing he saw.

Chapter One

Breaking News

Six Weeks Later

Whoever it was that decided that a big-boned, street-smart sista who once lived in Winston-Salem's Cleveland Avenue Apartments deserved her own talk show must've lost their mind!

Amirah smiled when she looked out of the makeshift studio she'd converted from the spacious conference room at her church, Gospel United Christian Center. One hundred and fifty faces stared back at her and her guest, Thursday Jackson, as they discussed her situation.

"I can't believe Armaad would do this to me." Thursday sobbed after her ex-boyfriend revealed some startling information.

"I didn't do nothing." Armaad got up and walked off the stage.

Amirah kept a straight face while she exhaled a sigh of relief. *The Amirah Dalton Show* was supposed to be a Christ-centered talk show that dealt with love and relationships. Thursday and Armaad were two seconds from bringing the action Jerry Springer was better suited for.

"Yes you did!" Thursday shouted as she got up to go after him. Her honey-blond wig struggled to stay on her head as she shook it violently. "You slept with that nasty chick Tarsha"—Thursday pointed to the extremely pregnant woman in the front row of the audience. Tarsha shook her head and crossed her arms over her protruding belly. She looked like she was getting ready to pop at any moment—"after you told me that you were done with her trifling tail. Then you got the audacity to tell me you and her used to be married!" Thursday continued as she began to run off the stage.

Amirah jumped up and ran after her guest. "Thursday, let's sit down and talk about this. You don't need to chase—"

"Don't tell me what I need to do!" Thursday snapped as she turned around and put her finger in Amirah's face. "You're not the one that laid up here and had three babies with this man. I did." As her finger moved up and down, she continued, "You're not the one he proposed to after we made love on his mother's fifty-year-old dining room table. I did. And you're not the one he gave chlamydia and syphilis to three times. That was me. Thursday Honesty Denyla Jackson." Thursday, huffing and puffing, went and sat back down in her chair after she'd made her point.

Amirah shook her head. *I'm sorry,* she told God silently, hoping that the Lord got her message. When she let her producers talk her into doing a show where her guests could learn to forgive their exes, she envisioned a show with more mature guests—couples who were trying to get Jesus back into the center of their relationships. These people were supposed to be screened before they walked into the church.

Amirah intended to brush the blunder under the rug and hold up like a champ in front of the thousands of people who she knew would be talking about her in Asheville by the next morning. She had to think about what the students she had to face on her day job as a high school teacher at Shiloh Christian Academy would think. To say she was embarrassed wouldn't begin to describe how she was feeling. Over and over again, Amirah was determined that she was not gonna cry, but even Mary J. Blige couldn't comfort her tears.

"Baby, I'm sorry." Armaad kneeled before Thursday, his soft, gentle hands trying to wipe away her tears.

"You know you sorry! But this is good, boo! Real good." Thursday smiled and tried to laugh. "Thanks for the misery."

"And we'll be back after this," Amirah yelled as that song by Monica echoing Thursday's last words began to play in the background. Amirah kept note of how good the sound people were. In the back of her mind, she was making mental notes on how she was going to clarify the format of her show to her new staff.

"Yo, Thursday, you need to drop that punk!" she could hear Chris yell in the background. Chris was Amirah's crazy friend that some people thought looked like a man. Chris sported a low fade, and her hairline was sharp. Her hardened pecan-colored skin betrayed her twenty-nine years of age—yet that didn't stop dudes from trying to talk to her.

Amirah knew for a fact that Chris wasn't a lesbian, but anyone else who didn't know would be hard pressed to tell. On the outside, Chris looked like a regular thug on the block with her oversized T-shirt and pants that weren't even pulled up to conceal her boxer shorts. It was when she talked and the mercury that moved in the way she walked that let everybody know what the deal was.

"Why don't you shut up, playa?" Armaad yelled and jumped up as he began running into the crowd. Chris met him halfway.

"Hey, hey hold on!" Amirah yelled in the mic. "You can't swing on a female. We are about to go on air in a few minutes."

"Man, this show is so fake!" Tarsha yelled as she got up from her seat. She glared at Armaad. "Armaad, let's go! I got to be in class in an hour. I don't have time for this mess!"

"Go on and go!" Amirah encouraged Armaad. "I don't even want you to honor your contractual obligation and stay on the show." Amirah was ticked and had no way to hide it. She knew this wasn't the vision of the show, and she almost called off the whole thing.

The spirit inside of her wanted to do the same thing, but Amirah wasn't a quitter. She promised herself to see this idea to the end and then use clips of this show to remind future staff why ideas like this didn't work.

"And if I weren't pregnant, I'd be *contractually obligated* to whoop your tall, Medusa-looking fat—" Tarsha hurled the insults with hopes of inflicting mental harm. The harshness of her voice felt like jabs as Amirah studied Tarsha's stern face as she called her everything but a child of God. "You know what? I changed my mind. I don't even know why I mess with Armaad anymore, let alone have babies with him. I'll leave by myself." His ex-wife/current side chick angrily grabbed her things and left as fast as she could.

God, this is not what I signed up for—Amirah was in mid-prayer when she was told by one of the producers she had fifteen seconds to fix her face and get ready to continue her live taping.

The audience watched as Tarsha got up and waddled off. Armaad came back and lowered his lanky, oak-colored frame next to Thursday. The two of them looked like total opposites. Give Armaad some glasses and a high top and he'd look like a darker version of Ron Johnson from *A Different World*. Thursday, in turn, moved her chair away from him. The only person who was semi-cool with the situation was the slightly effeminate pretty boy that

Armaad had been creeping with. He cheesed and waved from the audience like he knew he was going to be asked to come on stage.

"*Ya lo ves, ya lo ves. Ya lo ves amor esta vez te olvide.*" The irreplaceable hit anthem by Beyoncé played in the background. It was a surprise that half of the audience still knew the words to the Spanish version. The song was so old.

"All right now, we're back on *The Amirah Dalton Show*. If you are just now tuning in, let me say this is not normally how we do things on this show." Amirah wanted to scold her staff before the live studio audience. She could see the pastor's wife standing at the back door with her arms crossed. The big green hat she wore with green, black, and gray feathers did a poor job of hiding the look of disdain on her face. Amirah definitely wasn't looking forward to the end of the show. She could hear the chastisement from the church leadership for how the taping of this episode turned out.

"We are here with Thursday Honesty Denyla Jackson, and she has sent her man, Armaad, to the left. And I see someone thought it was cute to put these boxes with his name on here to the left—wait, am I being punked?" Amirah stopped reading the cue cards and addressed the crew.

The producer shrugged her shoulders. She looked at the boxes that were stacked three high with Armaad's name splashed across the center. Amirah shook her head and resisted the temptation to yell "Cut!"

"I want to remind you that it is okay to come on *The Amirah Dalton Show* to air out your differences, but when you come on the show, we are going to do a better job of representing Jesus than what was displayed today. If you have an issue you need to address, call me at 828-555-7118 or visit us online at AmirahDaltonShow.com.

Thank you for watching our show, and have a blessed day."

Amirah could take no more as she brought her hand across her neck and pretended to cut it off. Thursday got out of her chair and stormed off, leaving loose papers flying a few inches off the floor. Amirah could feel the tears roll down her face and onto her suit jacket. She never pictured that she'd be as thoroughly embarrassed as she was, and she was tempted to cancel the rest of the season.

As Amirah walked toward her dressing room, she felt free and was sure that she could overcome the unnecessary and embarrassing drama she would endure for the next two weeks. Two weeks would be all that was needed for the drama to die down in Asheville. Sure, people would be able to rewind and play the clip over and over on YouTube—but she wouldn't have to face anyone from out of town.

Amirah looked at her phone and noticed that Chris had called and was trying to reach her. Thursday brushed past her. A strong whiff of the Tommy Girl body spray left its mark, invading Amirah's nostrils.

"Girl, I'm gonna have to call you back." Amirah talked to the phone and rushed to catch up with Thursday. The woman was cursing at the same fast pace she was walking.

"Thursday, I just want to apologize. This was not what I intended when I invited you to be a part of my sh—" Amirah may not have been done talking, but Thursday thought she was.

"You knew I'd get embarrassed when you brought me on the show with Armaad," Thursday vented as she reached deep down to her pinkie toe, drew up *all* of her strength, and as if she were one of the Williams sisters, used her hand like it was a racquet. Thursday exhaled loudly as her hand connected to Amirah's face and followed her to the floor.

The crew members got excited, and the crowd yelled the way Chris Tucker and Ice Cube did on *Friday*. Ironically enough, they were taping on a Friday. The camera was all up in Amirah's face, catching her eyes blink as she faded in and out, feeling the after effects of that blow. The cameraman pointed the camera at Thursday and called after her. Thursday promptly threw up the inappropriate finger and walked out with her sparkling stilettos, satisfied that she did not break her nail in her confrontation with Amirah.

Chapter Two

Order in this House

"I can't believe that chick slapped me!" Amirah vented as she stormed to her dressing room. The first lady wasn't too far behind her, as were a few members of her production team. Amirah took a seat in front of the mirror and leaned forward to get a good look at her face.

"Please tell me what that was about," the first lady demanded as she took a seat next to Amirah.

Amirah looked closer in the mirror. Her lip was a little puffy and her face was swollen on the left side, but other than that, she was okay physically. "I don't know, Mrs. Slate. I can't explain what happened or why I feel like someone on my staff deliberately tried to set me up, but I do know that this is *not* how this ministry is supposed to work."

Amirah continued to inspect the damages done to her face. She was glad that Mrs. Slate wasn't caught up with her title or position at the church. She didn't have to "First Lady this," or "First Lady that." Mrs. Slate would suffice.

Mrs. Slate wasn't scared to get her hands dirty as she got up and helped Amirah as the tears continued to fall from her face. "We all make mistakes, and unfortunately, this is one of yours."

"I bet you want to cancel my show, don't you?" Amirah asked from the comfort of Mrs. Slate's shoulders.

Mrs. Slate lifted Amirah off of her thick frame. She never got down to the slender one hundred and thirty-five pounds the doctors and most vain people in society thought was ideal for her five foot four inch frame, but she was happy because she'd birthed and raised four of the children she had with pastor, plus the two they adopted. She was used to nurturing people, and Amirah found that she was no exception.

"Now why would I do that?" Mrs. Slate instinctively wiped the tears from Amirah's eyes like she were her own daughter. "Everyone makes mistakes, and now you'll have an opportunity to fix yours. At Gospel United Christian Center, we focus on uplifting and motivating people through the Word of God. We have no reason to cancel your show. Normally, your show is part of the outreach ministry that shows the world exactly what we are."

"I bet they are Instagraming and creating memes of me being slapped—"

"Let them insta-meme you," Mrs. Slate cut her off. "Yes, I was upset, but I will be even more frustrated if you don't lead the damage control and restore order on your show."

After a few seconds, Amirah realized that Mrs. Slate was right. She picked up her smart phone and sent a group text: Meet me at the studio in one hour. She was going to find out who, where, what, when, and why did the show go the way it had. Amirah intended on restoring order on her show.

There was an uncomfortable silence as Amirah and the crew watched Amirah land on the floor for the umpteenth time on the local news station. Her worst fears had come true—someone had wasted no time getting the footage on

YouTube and tagging her Twitter account. Thursday was on Twitter and Facebook talking about how she was glad she finally got her chance to beat up Amirah and couldn't wait for another opportunity to do it again. Thursday took it so far as to issue a challenge for a rematch.

Amirah had never met Thursday before. She couldn't possibly understand what she'd done to piss Thursday off. All Amirah knew was that she thought she was trying to use a Christ-centered version to mend Thursday's relationship with Armaad. Amirah also heard rumors that Armaad and the dude that came with him got into a physical altercation, and both of them had to go to the hospital for minor injuries. Tarsha had tried to commit suicide and lost the baby in her attempt. She was still in the hospital trying to recuperate.

"Lord have mercy on you," one of the crew members said after they watched the footage.

Mercy was one of the motivators for the founding of *The Amirah Dalton Show*. Amirah had always faced rejection in one way or another. She was considered a little thick at five feet ten and one hundred and eighty-six pounds. Amirah had always been a reject in one way or another. She was too fat to be in most beauty pageants and too small to be considered a "big girl." She was too poor to be in social organizations like Jack & Jill or the Links. Never welcomed in the poetry slams because as well as she could write her own material, she could recite others with the best of them.

The worst offense was when some trifling chick she used to call her friend stole her manuscript. This "friend" watched her labor over that book for nine months. Amirah sent the book to her with the understanding that the "friend" would review it and get it back to her. She made two or three minor changes, submitted the book to the publisher as her own, and when the book became a smash hit in the beauty salons and the black-owned bookstores, the "friend" got *her* name on the *Essence* bestsellers list.

Amirah tried to take that chick to court, but her "friend" used her advance and part of her royalty check to get a good lawyer, and their money always kept her from getting anywhere to pursue her case. Because of her "friend," Amirah had severe trust issues, and she stopped writing altogether. Thoughts of completing other manuscripts came to mind, but every time she thought about it, she grew bitter.

The Amirah Dalton Show was a therapeutic release from that dream. She took the concept she put in one of her unpublished manuscripts and built the show around a Christ-centered version of *The Oprah Winfrey Show* and *The Rikki Lake Show*. When she first brought the idea to her outreach ministry and the leaders of the church, they were skeptical, until she showed them the footage she did of the pilot show she filmed in her living room.

Amirah amazed the church leadership with the fact that she took the money she got from her ex-boyfriend, who was trying to make a name for himself hustling on the streets, and invested it in cameras, equipment, and wardrobe. When she got the job at Shiloh Christian Academy as a teacher, she saved every extra dime she could get her hands on and put money on his books and in an account that belonged to her ex-boyfriend's mother to ensure that she paid back the money.

Aside from the church, Amirah's first advertisers were businesses owned by former and current drug dealers. It wasn't ideal, but she took the money knowing where it came from. After her first season, Amirah gave internships to high school students around the Asheville-Greenville-Spartanburg area. Through her show, Amirah helped them to gain exposure and be prepared when they studied communications- and broadcasting-related majors in school. Her students, in turn, worked for local affiliates as production assistants or in other areas.

Amirah even looked out for the black college students from around the state by giving them the kind of experience they would never receive at a television station. Of course, she *worked* those interns, but in the end it all paid off. A few of them were now popular disc jockeys on R&B and hip hop stations nationwide; some of them appeared on television stations in their neighborhoods, and one of them was even on BET.

That's black star power.

After doing her show for three years, Amirah had helped twenty-two students achieve their dreams of working in broadcasting and film. Two of her students had success as independent filmmakers who produced a variety of web series on YouTube and were making serious money from the advertisements their shows garnered. She and her friend Aja also owned a local children's entertainment company and would often dress as clowns and perform around town. So, in her eyes and those of her pastor's, the wicked money she took from the drug dealers was well invested in children to keep them from idolizing those same people.

Amirah's fan base came from those who knew her as a no-nonsense teacher at Shiloh Christian Academy in Asheville and those who remembered the fearless around the way girl who grew up near the old Atkins High School, which was now Winston-Salem Preparatory Academy @ Atkins. In her old stomping grounds, Amirah was still hood. When she went to visit her old neighborhood, she still talked to the old ladies and men who sat on their porches and saw any and everything that went on. Amirah was legendary for the boldness she possessed in walking up to some of the most dangerous drug dealers and hustlers and asking if they would quit selling on her block. Folks thought she was crazy, but every now and then she'd get a couple of them to move if they saw her walking down the street.

Amirah was the one who called the police when the neighbor's music was up too loud or if they were partying way too late. Amirah *was* Neighborhood Watch because she watched everything from the comfort of her living room or bedroom window. In Asheville, she was no different. So, she shocked everyone when she went to North Carolina Agricultural and Technical State University and majored in business education instead of criminal justice. Amirah became a teacher instead of the police officer some swore she was imitating.

Amirah's first guests were some of the very people she used to see hustling on the block—those who turned their lives around and went to school or became advocates in her community. She got her best ideas from interacting with everybody.

Before she was on YouTube, Amirah made use of the public access television networks in Winston-Salem and in Asheville. When there was money for it, she did special shows on the local channels to draw attention to issues she felt were important. Once she built her channel on YouTube and made costly improvements on her Web site and became active on Facebook, Twitter, and other social media avenues, Amirah became a hood celebrity.

Naturally Amirah had a love/hate relationship with most of the influential people in the community. The church leaders loved when she paid tithes and offerings, even though she didn't belong to their places of worship. Amirah saw that some religious leaders in some churches really wanted the fame and power associated with being men of God to elevate themselves, not Jesus. The civic organizations didn't mind inviting Amirah to their functions to bring her audience to their causes, but in the same breath and oftentimes at the same event, they'd let her know they thought her show was trash.

Amirah's love for the hood ran deep, and the hood loved her back. She took the mothers in the area out on Mother's Day and let them thoroughly enjoy themselves. Amirah arranged for children whose parents didn't have a lot of money to have memorable Christmases, and she gave a lot of money anonymously.

Amirah prayed that all of the hard work and positive influence that she had in the community hadn't gone down the drain with the backlash of recent events that occurred on live television.

Chapter Three

Miss Me with That

Mateo banged on the rust-colored door that led to Sonic's room. He could hear the traffic pick up as people made their way on Tunnel Road. Heaven's Inn was like most motels on the strip, built in the sixties with a one-story L-shaped layout. The light blue paint on its exterior was the only thing modern about the building. A neon green sign featuring a teepee and the word *motel* in the middle of it drew in spectators who were hoping for a good quality room with cheap rates.

Mateo could see Sonic's white 1996 Toyota Corolla with a gold trim still parked in the space in front of his room. Its smooth tan interior was well kept, and Mateo and Sonic got a lot of compliments and a few offers from Toyota fanatics who were in awe that the car looked like new. Mateo remembered when they picked out the car eight months ago, before he started working at Heaven's Inn. The car belonged to an older man in Greenville, South Carolina, and he only drove it to church, the grocery store, and to see his grandkids in neighboring Spartanburg every now and then. Since Sonic had the car, he'd only added ten thousand miles to the fifty thousand the Toyota had when he purchased it.

Mateo was sure the other guests at Heaven's Inn heard him, but he didn't care. He turned around and could see the cars moving around in the parking lot and that

Tunnel Road was getting busier as morning traffic started to pick up.

Ever since Mateo, Sonic, Hammer, and the staff from the motel were beat down and shot at six weeks ago, Mateo spent part of his days as his friend's unofficial bodyguard. Of the three of them, Mateo recovered the fastest. He was in and out of the hospital in two days. Sonic and Hammer's injuries were more severe, their stay lasting almost a week. Still, Mateo had a funny feeling where the bullet had entered his leg. His steps were a little slower, because even though the bullet didn't hit a bone, the flesh wound was still tender. He walked with a limp as a reminder of his earthly wound.

Mateo put his face to the door, hoping to hear some Kiki Sheard or J. Moss blaring from Sonic's laptop. Not one heavenly note could be heard, but the melody from Katy Perry's "Dark Horse" echoed loud and clear from one of the cars that passed by. Mateo knew that Sonic couldn't have gotten a ride to work. Mateo was a little frustrated because he figured he could've stayed a few extra minutes in bed if he hadn't gone down to check on Sonic.

The growl of his stomach reminded him that he hadn't eaten anything all morning. He walked back to his motel room to see what he had in the refrigerator. It was bare. He didn't get paid again until the following Tuesday. That meant no going to the local café or fast food restaurant for a quick breakfast. Mateo shook his head at the realization that once again, he'd have to eat the continental breakfast served by his employer. Like him, the four other people on staff that rotated between front desk and janitorial duty all lived in one of the rooms at Heaven's Inn, and Hammer was helping them all obtain some form of stability before they moved out into the "real world."

Mateo gave the quaint efficiency he called his room a once-over. The modern Asian-style décor shined as he noticed clean dishes on the counter of the kitchenette. The updated bathroom reeked of the bleach he'd cleaned it with earlier. To his left, Bibles, daily devotions, and older Victor L. Martin, K'wan, Joy Deja King, and Dutch novels were stacked neatly on the edge of a sand-colored desk. A table-sized calendar with his schedule and other important appointments took up the bulk of the tabletop. The two Sealy queen-sized beds were identical, with red sheets under comforters with a black, red, and silver design. The bed was made military-style, just like he would have to make the others in a couple of hours. The curtains, which complemented the comforter, concealed his room from the outside world. Dirty clothes that he had to take to the laundry down the street were over-flowing from the basket—but not one article of clothing touched the floor. Shoes neatly lined the wall. In the bathroom, an array of personal supplies lined the sink. His personal stash of dollar-store cleaning supplies were at the bottom of the sink, and the door that connected his room to another room of similar size was bolted shut. Mateo and Sonic had a room in between theirs that was usually empty, but many of Heaven's Inn's twenty-four rooms were occupied by the night's end. They spent so much time in each other's rooms that they could've been roommates.

While none of the other maids and janitors stepped into his room, he always made sure it was neat, just in case they did. Satisfied that his room was presentable, Mateo headed out the door. He walked on the sidewalk that led to the entrance of Heaven's Inn and saw the man he was looking for had just taken a seat in the front lobby. Sonic had taken a bite of the turkey bacon on the plate of food in his lap. While watching him chew, Mateo noticed

Sonic got a space to fill in what used to be a missing bottom front tooth. A clear cup with orange juice in it was at his feet.

Another couple entered the lobby and took a seat on the plush green couch with their food. Sonic's plate of turkey bacon, boiled eggs, a bagel, blueberry muffins, mixed nuts and fruit were about to topple the Styrofoam plates. Aside from a few patrons sitting at one of the tables, the dining area was empty.

Sonic's navy blue spikes gave him the look of a punk rocker instead of a man of God. He rocked the spikes because he had the same name as Sonic the Hedgehog, and before he was saved, he thought the hair helped him embody the character. Liking all things Sonic, the drive-in restaurant that bore his same name was his favorite place to eat.

Mateo looked at the white Christ-centered shirt that was ripped at the sleeves and the dingy, grayish-colored jeans that did a horrible job of concealing Sonic's wafer-thin frame. His iced-coffee-colored skin, compliments of having a black father and a white mother, looked beaten.

"Sonic, what happen—" Mateo expressed concern for his friend but was interrupted by the couple's thunderous laughter. Mateo looked at the television monitor and could see they were being entertained at the expense of a full-figured, well-kept woman being backhanded by a slender woman who resembled the rapper Trina. Mateo shook his head at their lack of maturity.

"Sorry. I had to spend some time with God." Sonic could barely be heard over the laughter and his chewing on a bagel. Sonic picked up the napkin and wiped the cream cheese from his mouth before taking a sip of orange juice. "I woke up early and went to the top of Town Mountain Road and got a breath of fresh air and some peace and quiet. When I got back, I was hungry and decided to get something to eat."

Mateo had been to the top of that mountain before too, mainly to get into some mischief, but he could relate to what Sonic was saying.

"That's all right," Mateo replied as Sonic picked up the juice and made room for him to take a seat. "I just wanted to make sure you were okay."

"I'm sorry I kept you worried," Sonic apologized and offered Mateo the two blueberry muffins. "I took the last two, and Hammer already said we didn't have any more until tomorrow."

"Thanks." Mateo unwrapped the muffin and stuffed it in his mouth, wiping the excess crumbs off his face. "You're like my little brother now. I always got to watch out for you."

"Just for a while." Sonic finished his bagel and continued drinking his juice. "You'll eye me like a hawk until some fine lady comes around and steals your heart. Then you'll be following her around like a puppy."

"No, I won't." Mateo unwrapped his second muffin and gave it the same treatment as the first one. "I haven't been with a woman in over seven months. Ever since my crazy uncle tried to put some hot lead in my butt for messing with his second wife."

"Wait—" Sonic looked confused as he pulled his drink away from his mouth. "Tell me that story again."

"I told you about how my mother's sister's ex-husband had left her for some younger chick. Well, back when I was younger, my ex-uncle's wife caught me relieving myself on the side of the house and been jumping my bones ever since. He didn't like that so much, so one day, he caught me in the bed with her. I was doing my thing, and he hit me in my back with a frying pan. Then he went to cursing out his old lady, and when I came to, I beat the breaks off of him." Mateo took the package of mixed nuts and ate some.

"I wasn't saved then, and I gave him the whooping Madre should've given him for raping my sister when I was younger. After that," Mateo continued, "I ran as far as I could, but that old fart was quick. I got to the bowling alley off of Kenilworth Road before you get to Tunnel Road, and this fool started shooting at me. I knew Hammer's motel wasn't too far from where they lived and if I could make it there, I'd be safe. I ran into the motel, and Hammer saved me just like I thought he would."

Mateo hated talking about the woman, his ex-uncle, or any of his twisted family secrets, but Sonic was as close to Mateo as his brother, and eventually, he'd tell the man everything. If nothing else, he did it so Sonic wouldn't feel like a freak.

"Sounds like your family is equally as twisted as mine," Sonic confided as he continued to nurse his juice. They looked ahead and saw that the breakfast line was going down. The two of them decided to raid the place for some more food.

Mateo looked around to see if Hammer was in the vicinity. He was about to grab his first plate after sampling Sonic's. Seeing that Hammer was nowhere in sight, Mateo added a few extra eggs and an extra carton of juice for his daily supplement.

"Man, look," Mateo started as they returned to their seats. "All you gotta do is continue walking the path you are on. We pray together when we can, but you're taking trips to the mountains to be one with God and to have your own prayer time. You are doing a lot more than most people are doing right now. If I didn't know any better, I'd think you were the next Moses."

Sonic chuckled, and Mateo felt good seeing his best friend laugh a little. The plate of food went down like the breakfast snacks that Sonic had shared, and the two men relaxed for a while. Upon finishing, Sonic gathered their trash and put it in the trash bin.

At that moment, Hammer rounded the corner. He grinned when he saw Mateo and Sonic together.

"I didn't know you were coming with us." Hammer addressed Sonic as he took a seat on the loveseat next to Mateo.

"Us where?" Mateo looked at him like he was crazy.

"I see not only do I have to work with you on your personal skills, but I gotta help you develop a strong memory as well." Hammer sounded disappointed. "We got a meeting with Pastor Cummings in the next hour about what we are going to do for the house we're building for Habitat for Humanity next month. Then you gotta clock in after a while too."

The meeting had slipped Mateo's mind. He looked at Sonic and then looked away.

"I'll be there. What time do we need to leave?" Sonic offered.

"*Now,* gentlemen." Hammer got up and motioned for Mateo and Sonic to do the same. "Time waits for no man, and we have too much work to do to be procrastinating."

Mateo and Sonic got up and followed Hammer out of the motel. Mateo hadn't expected ministry to involve so many meetings about what they were going to do. He thought people just got up and did it. He started to ask Hammer about that, but Hammer's phone rang. He immediately began discussing a meeting with a minister from Winston-Salem who wanted to start a street-based ministry in Asheville.

From hearing Hammer's part of the conversation, the minister piqued Mateo's interest. During his stint in prison, he'd heard of several guys ministering to other inmates and offering an encouraging word, but the message never seemed to reach him. Now that he was saved, Mateo wanted to meet other men who'd been locked up and given their hearts and souls to Jesus.

Mateo was more interested in the meeting that Hammer was talking about than going to another boring church meeting, but he also knew that Hammer was selective about which people he connected. At the moment, Mateo was stuck going to the meeting at the church. He knew to pocket his questions about the minister for another time.

Chapter Four

Worship Warrior

Mateo followed the older, well-built man inside a humble, frail storefront. "Madre used to go to these huge, castle-like cathedrals that always felt cold and stuffy. Some of them had dragons on the outside of them and stuff."

Mateo continued talking to Hammer and Sonic about his past experiences with the Virgin Mary, wearing crucifixes, hearing mass in Latin, and other prominent fixtures of the Roman Catholic churches. For a while, Mateo didn't mind the fact that he seemed to be talking to himself, until he didn't feel the older man's presence in front of him. He could see Sonic out of the corner of his eye.

"Yo, old man, where are you at?" Mateo was disrespectfully loud enough to be heard outside. Suddenly, he felt a powerful grip on his neck, turning his stocky, compact, action figure–like frame a hundred and eighty degrees. Sonic gasped, and for a moment, Mateo thought Hammer had laid hands on him too. When Mateo faced the older man, he realized two things: one, the older man didn't have as much gray hair on his face as Mateo thought he'd have, and two, Hammer was still in good enough shape to whoop his tail if he needed to.

"Son, I'm old enough to be your father. You will show me some respect." Hammer was firm and blunt. It reminded

Mateo too much of Abuelo, and in the back of his mind, he figured Hammer and Abuelo had met somewhere in their past. "Remember, I'm Hammer. Please don't make me lay hands on you in my house of worship, son. You understand where I'm coming from?"

Mateo looked Hammer over again and quickly straightened up his act. "*Sí, Señor*."

"*Bueno*," Hammer escorted Mateo and Sonic into his office. "You said you wanted to be in ministry and that you needed to be around people that would keep you outta the streets, right?"

"Yeah," Mateo mumbled. "Something like that."

"Well that *something* is a group very near and dear to me, and the man who's traveled two and a half hours from Winston-Salem to help you and some of the other hotheads be a part of this ministry is like a little brother to me. I adopted him when we both were serving time in prison, and he's made me proud. You will not give him or me a hard time, or you and I will be taking a trip back to the sixties, you understand?"

"*Comprendo*." Again, Mateo was obedient as he nodded his head to indicate that he understood. "How'd you change into a suit so fast?" he asked. "Just five minutes ago you were in an oversized shirt and a baggy pair of jeans."

"We came here so I could change clothes, since I'll be speaking at another event later tonight, and so I can keep an eye on you. Let me remind you: where I come from, we move fast and don't waste time." Hammer shook his head. "Also we speak when we're spoken to and show our elders some respect."

Mateo was surprised at how quiet Sonic had been. Normally, Sonic had a few comments of his own to share. Mateo continued to listen to Hammer talk about being a man of God. Hammer had Mateo's attention at first, until he noticed one of the framed pictures of hands praying had a light reflection. Being vain, Mateo stopped and checked his reflection. His naturally curly hair made him appear to have Jheri curls, due to the excessive amount of mousse he'd applied to his hair.

"And we act like men." Hammer finished his statement.

"I am a man, dawg. You just don't know."

"Son," Hammer gritted, "I'm gonna tell you one more time. I'm not your dawg, your homie, your man. You are staying in the motel I own out of the kindness of my heart because I like to see young men like you turn yourselves around and get your act together. I've taken time to mentor you so you can develop into a man all of us can be proud of." Hammer exhaled. "But you are really testing my ability to be meek, kind, and gentle. I declare that must be the sole purpose of why God put you in my life."

"No, I told you God led me to you because He knew you'd show me how to be a better man." Mateo restated the very statement he'd told Hammer well over seven months ago, when he needed Hammer to save him from his uncle who was trying to gun him down after accusing him of impregnating his wife. Mateo wasn't the only man his uncle's wife was messing around with, and for Mateo's benefit, a paternity test ruled him out from being the father. Still, the rumors followed and continued to be spread all over Asheville.

"Thanks for reminding me." Hammer led Mateo out of his office and down a short hallway that led to a classroom filled with other men around Mateo's age, from all walks of life. From the ones wearing suits and ties to a few who had mohawks, multiple earrings in each ear, and leather vests and pants, they were all standing around or talking amongst each other.

Before Hammer could get another word in, he heard a gavel bang on a podium three times, and then the room was silent. Rahliem Victor, leader of the Street Disciples Ministry, was standing before them. Shockingly, he had on a red-and-white Winston-Salem State University basketball jersey that exposed all of the tattoos from the base of his jawline to the tip of his wrists. The only tattoo on his left hand resembled a wedding band.

"Welcome to the first Street Disciples Ministry of Asheville meeting." Rahliem addressed the men in front of him. "I'm glad to finally see this ministry expand to Western North Carolina."

Mateo looked around and noticed that the group of men clapped. While he wasn't skeptical, he was concerned with how Rahliem was going to turn what appeared to be a group of misfits into a well-oiled ministry that served God.

"There are about fifteen of you in here. The first group in Winston-Salem had about nine when we first started." Rahliem continued. "And we worked with all kinds of people. We have former adult video stars, drug dealers, and murders."

"Well, in Asheville you'll be working with ex-cons and weirdos," Mateo blurted out, and the whole room chuckled.

"And if they're willing to follow Jesus, then we can make use of every one of them," Rahliem replied confidently.

Rahliem continued telling the history of the group and the expectation that the new members be hearers and doers of the Word. Once Rahliem was done, everyone was handed a plastic bag that contained a miniature Bible, a travel-size flashlight, a pack of black ballpoint pens, and a couple of business cards. The business card that stood out to Mateo the most was the one for His-Love.com. It read: *Created by God's people to encourage the spreading of God's word and the fellowship of men and women in Christ. A Christ-centered networking and relationship site.*

The words grabbed a hold of his spirit and piqued his interest. Mateo pulled out his Samsung Galaxy and added the site to his favorites. He quickly registered, using the name SenorCristoAmor and answered a few personal questions about himself. He held the phone in the air and took a picture of himself. Satisfied with the way he looked, he uploaded his picture on the Web site.

"Ay, man."

Mateo turned toward the husky Southern drawl that had gathered his attention. He had to look up to see the blue-eyed, orange-and-purple-mohawk-wearing young man standing before him. "'Sup," Mateo replied and then returned his attention to his phone.

"You nervous about getting out into the streets and spreading the word of God?" the man asked.

"Naw, what I got to be nervous for? I stay in the streets." Mateo was cocky, and the last thing he wanted to admit was that he had a slight concern about not knowing what he was doing.

"I'm just saying, after we do this training, we gotta step out of these four walls and represent God. By the way, my name is Marvel. What's yours?"

"Mateo," Mateo quickly answered as he looked for Hammer. He was ready to leave, and he had no intention of staying around to get acquainted with Marvel or anyone else.

"You looking for love?" Marvel peered over and took a peek at his phone.

"Marvel is it?" Mateo tried to wave the young man off, to let him know he was overstaying his welcome. "I'm about to leave and meet up with some people. I'll have to catch you another time."

"No problem, brother. Let me get your number so we can stay in touch. Maybe we can study the Bible together."

"A'ight cool," Mateo replied and spit some numbers real fast to get the young man out of the way. Mateo thought about the question Marvel had asked him. He wasn't sure if he was looking for love. Mateo loved the idea of being on another social networking site that seemed Christ-centered. He went back to His-Love.com and downloaded the app for the site on his phone. He figured if he saw the app on his phone, he'd keep up with it and remember to read a scripture a day, since they advertised sending a verse and devotional daily to their members.

"So how do you feel about the ministry?" Rahliem asked as he approached Mateo. Mateo had been so caught up on checking out the Web site that he hadn't even seen Rahliem coming. He knew he was slippin' and had been out of prison too long if he couldn't tell when someone else was approaching him. That was the second time in less than ten minutes.

"Man, I think this is a good thing and something that will keep me out of trouble."

"How long you been saved?" Rahliem asked.

"About seven months or so. I'm still getting used to being out of the joint and rocking with the Lord. I got a church home, but I'm still looking for myself."

"Well, it's a ride worth taking if you're willing to stay the course. And our ministry is not limited to the members of Guiding Light Ministry Center. We welcome members of all churches."

"I'm willing."

"Well, we'll be meeting again on Tuesday. And Mateo?"

How did he know my name? Mateo wondered. "Yeah."

"Bring a copy of your Bible too. We'll spend some time going over the Word we will be spreading."

Mateo nodded his head. "I'll be there."

Just like that, Rahliem had moved on to the other attendees. Mateo got a buzz on his phone. The His-Love.com app was working, and already he had a woman who was interested in getting to know him. He was tempted to take her for what she was worth, but he knew in his heart of hearts he couldn't just jump out and get into anything. Jesus wouldn't like that—and he hadn't finished creating his profile yet. He glanced at the profile and decided to deal with it and the potential date another time.

Chapter Five

Sick of the Sorries

"Amirah, I hope you are hearing me," Mrs. Ingle pleaded.

Even though they were in Mrs. Ingle's spacious mini-suite that served as her office as principal of Shiloh Christian Academy, Amirah felt claustrophobic. Normally, Mr. Maddison, the Assistant Principal of Instruction and Amirah's direct supervisor, would be in attendance at any disciplinary meeting, but he was out of town. That meant Amirah had to deal with Mrs. Ingle all by herself.

Mrs. Ingle wasn't imposing; at least her five foot two frame didn't incite fear upon first sight. Her choice of earth-toned eye shadows, foundation, and lipstick only highlighted the features that enhanced her natural beauty. The short, lightly tinted Afro emphasized the sharp cheekbones and her almond-shaped eyes. With those features, one could easily to assume that Mrs. Ingle was in her early-to-mid forties. Aside from a prior conversation with Amirah, Mrs. Ingle rarely told anyone she was closer to sixty.

Mrs. Ingle was the first to remind anyone that she wasn't always a saint. Mrs. Ingle had five children by three different men, none of which were by her third husband, Pastor Ingle. In fairness to her, her first husband died when he fell from a ladder cleaning the Jackson Building in downtown Asheville, and her second marriage was annulled when she later learned that the man was still legally married to his wife in Colorado. She didn't know who her third baby daddy was, nor was she interested in tracking down one of the fourteen men it could be.

"You are wasting your talents with that television show, and you have been called to preach the Word of God. That's why you got the show in the first place. When are you going to feature Jesus on your show?"

Pastor and Mrs. Ingle had been trying to get Amirah to head her own church since she walked through the doors of Shiloh Christian Academy three years ago. They'd leave brochures for seminary schools in her mailbox and introduce her to influential seminary educators in the area.

"Mrs. Ingle, that is not fair. God is always welcomed at my show. I'd never turn Him away." Amirah defended her show. "What happened last Friday is not a representation of who I am and what I'm about. I thought you knew me better than that."

"I know that." Mrs. Ingle relaxed a little. "But I want you to look at the number of messages on my phone system."

Mrs. Ingle turned the phone around so that Amirah could see them. Five hundred sixty-two messages were left for Mrs. Ingle. Another had just come in, making that 563 messages. Amirah knew she had an uphill battle to convince Mrs. Ingle not to force her to cancel her show in order to keep her teaching job.

Unlike Mrs. Slate, who appeared nurturing and under-standing, Mrs. Ingle would be harder to please. Mrs. Slate didn't care about social media, but Mrs. Ingle had a personal profile and a fan page on Facebook and actively participated on her own and the school's Twitter accounts. Mrs. Ingle taught a well-respected seminar on LinkedIn and its benefits in business twice a year on campus and at two of the local community colleges. She also advised students and staff on the best practices to develop professional accounts.

So the question wasn't *if* she saw "the video," but how many times?

"I'm sure that once I get back in the studio tomorrow I'll be able to clean this up. Instead of doing a new show, I'm going to clean house and start the search for new staff." Amirah tried to convince Mrs. Ingle.

She wasn't impressed. "That's what your lips say, but what does your heart say?"

"Mrs. Ingle, please—" Amirah didn't want to beg. She hated the idea of begging anyone to do anything for her. "I have a show next week with Donte Longstocking. This show was already on the schedule."

"Donte Eugene Speaks," Mrs. Ingle corrected her.

"I've forgiven that man. I'm sure he has forgiven me for putting him on blast and criticizing his decision to follow God and join a church ministry." Amirah conceded, "I was wrong to tell people it's all fake and a ploy just to gain sales for his movies."

"Well, you of all people should know that one can't sell pornography at church." Mrs. Ingle got up from her desk and walked around to the side Amirah was sitting on.

Donte Eugene Speaks, aka Donte Longstocking, was a five foot ten, sexy chocolate track star cutie with a Barry White-esque voice. He became a local celebrity and a national adult video star when he produced a series of webcasts and homemade movies featuring himself physically penetrating women of all shades, shapes, and sizes. Unbeknownst to Mrs. Ingle, her students, and most people around her, Amirah appeared in a few of his *Fabulous and Thique* videos—a concept he stole from the comedienne Mo'Nique. The videos featured him doing his thing with the big girls. Amirah knew what she was doing when she signed up for the flicks, but she also knew that she'd need to practice discretion. Folks didn't know Amirah was in the videos because she always wore shades and had a lot of extensions added to what was then a short hairstyle.

After doing those videos and hearing an insensitive comment made by Donte, Amirah worked hard to grow her own hair and lose the weight. It was during that time of reconstruction that she found Jesus and worked to get her life together, as well as getting some of her immediate family members, including her mother, saved. The seven years that had passed played a role in the reason why people didn't recognize her from the videos. Her use of a fake accent and the extra hundred pounds she had carried then aided in her disguise.

"Well, Donte isn't the only man at the church, and besides, it's your fault for laying up with him and doing whatever it was you may have done with him on film," Mrs. Ingle chastised while giving her a hug.

How did she know? Amirah started to ask, but there was no way she was going to confess to being in an adult flick to her boss.

The better question was what was *she* doing watching it?

"It wasn't me," was the best denial she could come up with. Amirah and Mrs. Ingle had the best relationship a superior and an employee could have, and she didn't want to ruin it by lying.

"We're not perfect, and if I thought you couldn't have a life beyond sex and pretty boys, I wouldn't have hired you. But you really need to give this ministry a chance. I can see where your idea of doing the show with Donte could give you some room to clean up the situation. It is a risky move but one I know you can handle and do right.

"I want you to look at it this way." Mrs. Ingle reached behind her and pulled out the iPad, which was well protected in a special case that blended in with the books on her desk. She turned it on, and in a few seconds, she had a video clip of a young female preacher with fiery red hair giving a fiery word that commanded the attention of the congregation. "This young lady used to be a well-known porn star. Don't assume that because there are a lot of old people like me that go every Sunday that that is all church is. There's a young man in Winston-Salem that was just up here this past Sunday recruiting members for his growing Street Disciples Ministry that I think deserves more time on your show. Donte's younger brother—that Christian rapper—The Revelation would benefit greatly from the exposure your show could give him. And Lord forgive me, but if I were your age and unmarried, I'd give both of them a run for their money."

Amirah shook her head. She didn't want to admit that Mrs. Ingle was a cougar, and she definitely didn't have the courage to call her one to her face. After all, Pastor Ingle was at least five years younger than Mrs. Ingle. "After I interview Donte, I'll see about getting Rahliem and The Revelation on my show. Some of my students listen to his music. Maybe we can get him to visit the school."

"I'll tell you what—" Mrs. Ingle pulled up a writing app on the iPad. "We'll talk about finding you the right seminary school another time. I can help you bring The Revelation to Shiloh if that's really what you want to do. Right now, let's focus on you getting your act for your next show."

"I already have it worked out. Plus, Donte's done a great job cleaning up his image, and I'm sure he can help me too."

"I won't make you quit the show in order to keep your job," Mrs. Ingle promised.

Amirah breathed a sigh of relief.

"I already have some of my people doing damage control. Shiloh Christian Academy will help you with all the resources we have available to us. That's one of the blessings of being a private school: we have more freedom and flexibility to fix things and call on the Lord to help us, too. But your show can't get sidetracked like this again, or it will put you in a position to leave it behind—or find another school to teach at."

"Yes, ma'am," Amirah answered. She was glad that Mrs. Ingle and Shiloh Christian Academy were going to help her with damage control. Gospel United Christian Center had already released statements condemning her attack, and after she found out who was behind the prank, she began digging through resumes to find replacements.

Chapter Six

Old Things New

The scent of the Axe Instinct body spray filled the air as Mateo moved the small black can across his frame. He looked in the mirror and his whitened smile reflected back when he saw his spiked hair maintaining its form at the top and the sparkle of the small diamond stud that clung to his left ear.

Mateo had decided to get dressed in Sonic's room as opposed to his because Sonic had a run-in with Turner a week ago. The one day Mateo hadn't met up with Sonic at his job, Turner confronted Sonic and started beating on him behind the restaurant. It seemed that the violent and abusive relationship would never evade Sonic. If it weren't for a coworker who happened to be taking the trash out, Sonic could've ended up in the hospital. Ever since then, Mateo always made sure he knew where Sonic was at all times, and when they were together, Sonic stayed in plain sight.

"Mateo, what's wrong with you?" Sonic complained as he coughed while ironing some khakis in the middle of his room. "We're going to Bible study, not to some club or a house party."

"Wait a minute." Mateo turned around to face his friend. "Do I say anything about you wearing that God-awful wave cap every time you step out of the door to go somewhere, or how you always poppin' Tic Tacs like you have intentions of catching the next female in sight?" Mateo thought it was cool how his friend was trying to turn *all* aspects of his life around.

Sonic rolled his eyes, easily irritated. Mateo knew that questioning the fact that Sonic wanted to leave his homosexual ways behind would get under his skin. "Mateo, seriously dude, we are just going to the Street Disciples meeting to get the Word and continue our study on the Book of Acts, not for you to find the next woman you want to be with."

Mateo dropped the plush green towel that had been covering his midsection and picked up the black slacks that were still in the packaging that had come from the dry cleaners earlier that day. He reached in his bag and pulled out a gold rope necklace. "Bruh, I've picked up many a woman after Sunday service." He put on the necklace while simultaneously slipping into his onyx-colored wingtip shoes. "Besides, I'm trying to remain celibate. Been that way for a few months now. Don't tempt me and make you regret it when I'm entertaining my guest in my room."

Sonic shook his head as he set the iron down to put on his khakis and to reach for the white button-up shirt he was going to wear. Mateo had just finished buttoning his sky blue shirt with the matching silver-and-black tie that he'd gotten from an urban clothing store earlier that day as well. He reached for the mint-flavored bottle and pressed the spray twice in his mouth.

"You are so vain." Sonic quickly put on his clothes so that he could be ready when Mateo walked out the door, because they both were going to ride in Sonic's car to the Guiding Light Ministry Center. The church was about a mile from the campus of W. E. B. DuBois College in Asheville, North Carolina on Merrimon Avenue. They would be meeting with some students from the nearby campus of University of North Carolina at Asheville to study the Word and fellowship.

"Whatever, bruh."

Sonic shook his head and pressed his lips shut. He knew it was pointless to argue with Mateo. He knew every word Mateo spoke about his previous reputation to be true, and Sonic, being the ex-homosexual, had no right to judge.

Mateo and Sonic had been prayer partners since Hammer brought them together almost eight months ago. Sonic had taken Mateo with him to church many Sundays, because it would be another two weeks before the suspension on Mateo's driver's license was lifted. Mateo was still working off the time he got for a DUI a few years back.

They left Sonic's room, and Sonic suddenly reached for his pocket. "I think I left my key inside."

Mateo smirked. "Don't worry. I have mine." He reached into his pocket and dug out the plastic card with the Pizza Hut advertisement on the front. Mateo and Sonic heard a car honking as they were leaving Sonic's room. Sonic's car was at the end of the parking lot closer to the street. Sonic had taken to parking the car in different locations to avoid the risk that Turner may find it and do some damage.

Just as they pulled off from the motel, Mateo's phone dinged, alerting him that he had another notification from His-Love.com. This was a message from a Dijonaye96, whose profile said she was only eighteen. He tried to think of a polite way to tell her that he wasn't interested. He was proud of himself, because the old Mateo would have met the girl, had his way with her, and then never called her again.

Amirah pulled into the closest space near the church so that she and her two friends, Marjorie and Aja, wouldn't have to walk very far.

"Why didn't you park in the back?" Marjorie asked from the backseat. "I would've been fine walking."

Amirah looked at her friend from the rearview mirror. "We always park in the back, because we are usually late and have to walk the farthest. This is a reward for getting to the Lord's house on time."

"Oh, really?" Aja reached up to turn the rearview mirror in her direction so she could make last-minute adjustments to her makeup and to make sure no loose strands of hair had come apart from her bun. "So God's gonna start giving bonus checks if we have a quarter of good attendance? I could use one of those checks right now."

Amirah turned and looked at her friend. "Aja, you know going to church is not about getting something material. It's about gaining something that will benefit you spiritually and keep you grounded in the Lord."

"Amirah, stop turning my words around." Aja attempted to put the mirror back to its position. "I'm just saying that I spent up all of my tax refund check and I could use some financial aid right now."

Amirah shook her head. "Did you tithe any of that money?"

"Did you tithe yours?" Aja shot back.

"Yes, I did. I gave about seven percent. I know it's not the full ten, but I've been working my way up to that since I gave my life to the Lord a few years ago."

Amirah was telling the truth. She'd been having financial problems since having to bury her mother this past summer. She was still sorting out her mother's affairs with some of her business partners when she returned to her job as a teacher a few weeks ago.

"Well, when I get some money or find a man with some money, then I will tithe. Until then, may God have mercy on me."

Amirah could see Marjorie shaking her head in the back.

"Hey, isn't that Sonic and that fine Blatino getting out the car?" Aja shouted as if they were outside.

Marjorie took a quick look in their direction and then moved away. "They look nice today."

"When are you going to ask Sonic out?" Aja looked in the mirror and licked her lips like a seductress. "That boy is fine, and you know you like him. That's the only reason I haven't asked him out yet is because I know you like him."

"Because the Bible says that a *man* who finds a *wife* finds a good thing," Marjorie quipped. "It's Sonic's job to ask me out on a date. I'm not going to chase after no man. Girl, bye. This is 2015, and when a man wants me, I'll be just fine, because this fabulous and thick madam don't need a man. Besides, I want to make sure he has his past out of his system completely before I give him the time of day. And he's gotta stop dying his hair blue."

Amirah unlocked the door so she could let her friends out. For a brief moment, she caught herself thinking about Mateo, but she detested the idea of leaving the Bible study just another one of his harlots. Amirah had heard stories about how Mateo got around, especially with women who either left church or their social club gatherings. She knew how he would purposely pretend like he'd come from a meeting or be at church just so he could spit game and talk the women out of their undergarments.

"Well, I came to hear the Word and to talk about how Paul and Silas managed to overcome being in prison." Amirah got the girls refocused on the mission at hand. She stepped out of the car, and soon all three of them were closing their doors at the same time.

"Hello, ladies," Sonic greeted them as he and Mateo reached Amirah's car. He hugged each of the ladies. "I managed to bring a guest with me."

Mateo shook each of the ladies' hands, but he lingered when he shook Amirah's. Amirah felt her heart beating faster when Mateo's hands slipped into hers. She'd always heard about how fine Mateo was, but she had never been this close to the man. She noticed the sharp goatee that outlined the shape of his chin, and how it matched his mocha-colored eyes. She also noticed the slight limp every time he took a step. Amirah wondered if it was an act or if it was natural. Normally, she didn't find non-African American men attractive, but she did enjoy the interracial romances she discovered on her mother's bookcase, and she did like Miguel's latest album. Before she got saved and holy, she did think Mario Lopez was cute.

"Nice to meet you." Amirah gathered her thoughts.

Amirah couldn't believe they made Hispanic men this dark. Then she remembered her studies in undergrad about the Moors conquering Spain, and it made sense. Amirah reflected on some of the comments her professors had made about the Africans not getting their due for preserving the European culture, and the resentment some Africans have toward them for trying to annihilate them.

"We'll have to sit together and study the Word. See what Jesus is talking about." Mateo smiled as bright as a hundred-watt bulb.

Amirah shook her head. She felt that Mateo didn't mean it and didn't entertain the thought. Together, the ladies, Sonic, and Mateo headed toward the entrance of the church. Aja pulled Amirah to the side.

"Girl, you better be careful. You know Mateo is a player, and you don't want that," Aja warned as she spoke quietly in Amirah's ear.

Amirah could feel Aja pulling on her arm. "I know. I came here to study the Word. I know where my priorities are."

Aja smiled and Amirah instantly felt convicted for how she had answered her friend.

"I'm sorry, Aja. It's just that right now, I'm not trying to think about a man. I got to stay focused on school, the show, Jesus, our business, and whatever He'd have me to do."

"Okay. I was just warning you. Be careful."

Amirah and Aja caught up with the rest of the group. Amirah observed the way Mateo and Sonic acted like gentlemen as they interacted with the other members of the Bible study. Amirah saw Mateo look at her, and when she felt herself looking too long at him, she turned away and opened her Bible so she could make sure the notes she wanted to discuss with the group were available. Once she found her notes, she looked them over and then hugged one of the girls who'd come up to greet her. They'd taken a seat near the front and excitedly waited for the leader of the Bible study to continue their study on Paul.

After the lady took her seat, Amirah looked back at Mateo and wondered, *What if?*

Mateo nodded his head every time Minister Soulja Harmon emphasized certain points in his mini-sermon. He admitted to himself that Minister Harmon was impressive for a twenty-year-old communications major who accepted his call into ministry early in life.

The minister reminded him of one of the boys he used to hang with back in the day. The way Minister Harmon carried himself gave the impression of a young street soldier. Mateo saw the way members of the congregation followed him as he paced the pulpit. His voice was bold, and the Bible verses felt like daggers with flame tips as they took root in Mateo's soul.

Mateo hated how just earlier Sonic had planted a seed that reminded him of the lust he used to have for women, and how he used to displease God with the women he led astray in his bedroom—the women who would worship him while they did their pretzel-bending exercises while forgetting about the Savior they had professed to love just hours before. Mateo loved the attention he got in the bedroom and felt that was the ultimate highlight of being a man.

Back when his mother was active in the Catholic Church, Mateo used to go in his own mind, thinking that he was god and that he knew the way. After meeting with Hammer and taking his salvation seriously, Mateo was beginning to change not only how he felt about God, but how he saw himself being left out of His Kingdom. Mateo began to confess within himself that he did not have a heaven or a hell to put anyone in and started to take this visit with the Lord seriously.

For the first time in his life, when Mateo heard Minister Harmon pray about escaping strongholds and dealing with the battle of spirit verses flesh, Mateo felt convicted. When he'd stray from the prayer to Amirah, he couldn't get the tall, full-figured beauty out of his mind. Being that he was a few inches shorter than her five foot ten frame, she was definitely among one of the tallest women he'd ever pursued. He enjoyed the thought of what it would be like to take her down like Chris Brown. At the end of the prayer, his thoughts changed to how he could show her the godly man he had the potential to become.

"But at midnight, Paul and Silas were praying and singing hymns to God, and the prisoners were listening to them. Suddenly there was a great earthquake, so that the foundations of the prison were shaken; and immediately all the doors were opened and everyone's chains were loosed." Amirah read Acts 16:25-26 aloud, and at that moment, Mateo felt convicted. He knew in his spirit that Amirah was serious about her work and mission to serve God. There he sat, lusting after her as if she were one of the women in his old collection of dirty magazines. He blinked his eyes for a minute, and when he opened them again, he no longer saw the pretty face that had a body stacked with thickness in the appropriate areas to his liking. He saw a woman of God that he wanted to get to know on a more spiritually intimate basis. The conviction continued when he realized that Amirah was worth more than the one night stand his flesh saw her as.

The rest of the study was a blur. He didn't remember what the rest of Acts 16 was about, but at that moment, he was dealing with a bigger, deeper purpose. Mateo heard a voice say, "No one comes to the Father except through Me." He thought that he was in the presence of a ghost when he saw Minister Harmon stretch out his hands and welcome sinners to the congregation.

"You are never too young to give your life to Christ," Minister Harmon continued. "If you don't know today whether or not your name is in the Book of Life, then this is the chance of a lifetime. Come, give your life to Christ today, because you may not get another opportunity once you walk out of the door."

Mateo watched as two young men lifted their frames from the seats closest to him. Like Tyson Gay at the Olympics, they rushed to the stage as if they were doing the last lap of a relay. Mateo closed his eyes, and tears flowed from them like honey dripping from a hive. Mateo looked around and was surprised to see Sonic praising God and shouting "Hallelujah!" from his seat.

"That's the power of God right there. We got two souls around my age giving their lives to Christ and accepting the free gift of salvation." Minister Harmon kneeled down to pray with the two men.

Mateo turned to his left and didn't see anyone, but on his right side was a woman he'd almost had an intimate encounter with shortly after his salvation. The initial walk with Christ was a challenge for Mateo and one that would tempt him to backslide. He recognized the woman, remembering that he'd met her at a charity event before the end of the prior school year. He didn't remember her name, but he remembered all of the foul and cruel things he'd said to this woman.

"I'm sorry," he said. *I pray she'll forgive me*, he thought as he reached out for a hug. He was surprised when the woman hugged him back.

"God is so good!" Sonic could be heard yelling.

Mateo felt good that while he may not have known the Bible nor could he quote scripture the way a few others at the study could, he was on his way to building a relationship with the One whom he could trust the most.

"I forgive you," he heard the lady say as they let go of their embrace.

Minister Harmon walked around and gave Mateo and every other person without one a small Bible, and he encouraged them to come to Gospel United Christian Center to hear him preach the upcoming series. For the first time, Mateo made a promise he intended on keeping.

Even though he was enjoying his work at Guiding Light Ministry Center, he saw himself visiting Gospel United Christian Center on a more frequent basis.

Chapter Seven

What To Do

Amirah and Aja were shaking their heads as their green-and-white clown wigs bounced from side to side as they did their routine to André 3000's "Hey Ya!" They had practiced the routine for a couple of hours prior to their performance at a young lady's sixth birthday. The girl's mother, Ms. Parker, attended Gospel United Christian Center with them on Sunday mornings, and it was their performance at the birthday party for the pastor's daughter that got them the business they had today.

When Amirah wasn't teaching at the local high school, and her friend Aja wasn't working as an accountant, they owned and operated the Stars & Glory Entertainment Company. They dressed as clowns and performed at different occasions, usually at birthday parties and other gatherings for children under the age of eleven. After their first year in business, they were considered for a local minority business award, and even though they didn't win, they were happy to be recognized. They were well known and respected for their wholesome routines that usually were performed to hip gospel music, but every now and then, they'd do a routine for a secular song.

They pulled out Polaroid pictures and encouraged the kids to get up and shake it like André told them to. Then they reverted back to the '50s and '60s style dancing, and they were doing a good job at keeping the younger kids engaged. Amirah and Aja looked around the backyard at the kids and smiled, as they could see that they were finishing another successful birthday routine.

Something next door briefly caught Amirah's eye. A girl with a pink top on was opening the window and holding back the white lace curtains. Amirah didn't think much about what she was seeing at first, so she put her attention back on the kids. Once their routine was finished, they escorted the kids back to the picnic table, where they sang the Stevie Wonder version of "Happy Birthday" to the sweet little birthday girl, Maliyah.

"And let's thank Amirah and Aja for a wonderful performance," Ms. Parker instructed before she cut the cake and began serving the children. The round of applause brought a smile to the girls' faces. They picked up the props and materials that they used for the celebration and they began putting away their things.

"That was a wonderful performance," said Mrs. Gourdine, the jubilant wife of one of the deacons at the church.

"Thank you," Amirah replied as she looked at the older, plump lady in her bright orange business suit and matching hat that was accentuated by an orange-and-white lace ribbon tied into a bow at the top.

"Do you have your calendars with you?" Mrs. Gourdine continued. "I would like to book you ladies in about a month for my sister's daughter's party. I know you don't remember Renessa, but she's the deaf child I bring with me to church every now and then."

"I'll get that for you." Aja handled her part of the business. She left Amirah with Mrs. Gourdine, who asked a few questions about the routines and the music and the costumes. Usually Amirah and Aja tried to accommodate whatever requests the parents asked for, because that was their secret to keeping satisfied customers and more referrals.

Amirah was getting ready to respond to one of Mrs. Gourdine's questions when she noticed a pair of Air Jordan's hanging out of the window of the house next door. She also recognized the older gentleman, who bore a striking resemblance to the father of one of her students, turning his key in the front door.

"Oh, gosh. I know that Xen is not hanging out of Rasheeda's window," Amirah thought out loud, shocked by what she saw at one of her student's home.

"Excuse me, what did you say?" Mrs. Gourdine brought her attention to her conversation.

"I apologize, ma'am. I was distracted." Amirah tried to bring her attention back to the business at hand. "Aja is on her way now, so we can work together to come up with some ideas for your niece's party."

"Hey, Mrs. Gourdine, here's the calendar." Aja stopped in her tracks when the boy hanging out the window caught her attention. When her jaw dropped, Mrs. Gourdine noticed what was drawing Aja's and Amirah's attention away from their conversation.

Xen's loose-fitting light blue jeans were hanging off his butt, and he was struggling to pull them up as he was working his way out of Rasheeda's window. All three of them could see the crack of Xen's behind and his well-defined backside, as he was losing the battle to keep it all together. Xen dropped into the bushes, ripping his shirt on the way down. Amirah shook her head. Her students had embarrassed her yet again.

"That boy ought to be ashamed of himself," Mrs. Gourdine started. "If you come in the front door, you ought to leave out the same way." All three of them noticed Rasheeda closing the window and fixing the curtains. "She didn't even look down to see if the boy was okay."

They continued to watch as Xen jumped up and dusted himself off. He quickly fixed his pants, adjusted the belt, and bolted out of the yard. Rasheeda's father exited the door and was running down the street not too far behind him.

"Ha! Serves him right," Mrs. Gourdine continued, the only one being entertained by the situation. "I hope he gets caught."

Under normal circumstances, Amirah would've gone along with that statement, but the last time she suspected that Xen and Rasheeda were playing "grown-up games" in the school bathroom, she got in trouble with Mrs. Ingle for not reporting it.

Aja redirected the conversation back to the business at hand, and Mrs. Gourdine pulled out her cell phone and got her sister on the phone. Once they agreed on a date, they rejoined the birthday party.

Amirah couldn't help but wonder whether Xen made it home safely, or if he had to face the consequences of being in Rasheeda's room. She knew she would find out the answer if Xen showed up to her class the next day. She said a quick prayer that he made it home safely and that she'd see him in one piece. Though she couldn't praise him for his actions, Amirah couldn't bear the thought of something bad happening to him.

Chapter Eight

Stackin' Paper

"Man, I didn't think you were going to make it!" Sonic yelled out of the car window when he pulled up to Mateo's room. Sonic's room was only two doors down.

Mateo took a step back and looked over at his boy. He had been waiting on Sonic to arrive for the last twenty minutes. He looked out the window periodically, then gathered his things and left his room once he saw Sonic pull up. Sonic sported a tapered-faded crew cut that showcased three different shades of blue going from dark to light. His dark blue sleeveless jacket hoodie blended in with his baggy blue jeans.

"I decided to try something different," Sonic suggested as he spoke over the upbeat 21:03 tune booming from his stereo.

"Different . . ." Mateo opened the door and slid into the seat. "Right." Mateo put on his seatbelt then turned around and looked at all of the clothes that Sonic had piled up in the backseat of the car. Grunge wear, leather vests and jackets, and ripped designer jeans floated on top of a sea of shoes and boots.

"You should've let me try on some of this stuff before you threw it in the back seat." Mateo turned around and watched as Sonic backed out of the space and got onto the road.

"Man, please." Sonic turned the radio up a few notches. "I tried to get you to try on some of this stuff, and you complained about how you didn't want to look like a punk rocker."

"I don't want to look like a punk rocker," Mateo defended as he rolled the window down a little bit. "I'm just saying that some of this stuff would look fly in my closet, that's all. Anyway, where are we going?"

"I was on Craigslist and I found this little spot in Greensboro that said they would give me a few hundred dollars for all the pieces I have." Sonic smiled as he backed out of the driveway.

Mateo smiled too. He knew what time it was, and they needed to get that paper.

"Will that be enough to remove the *T* from your back?" Mateo questioned as they got on I-240 East heading toward Swannanoa.

At one point in time, Sonic had a tramp stamp with Turner's name right above the formation of his rump. He also used to have nipple piercings and a slew of tats commemorating Turner's gang, favorite quotes, and lifestyles. That was how Turner branded Sonic as his property.

Since they had broken up for good almost eight months ago, Sonic had gone through the painstaking task of getting a total body transformation. First, he removed the set of nipple rings with spinners. Then he removed the navel ring and one of the tats with Turner's name from his neck. Throughout the process, Sonic also started working out at the YWCA near his job, where he'd managed to add fifteen pounds of muscle to his still lanky frame.

"Nah." Sonic shook his head. "But it's enough to get me that much-needed appointment with the urologist to make sure that Prince Albert I used to have healed the way it was supposed to."

Mateo squirmed in his seat as he remembered that Sonic did tell him he was pierced down there. Just the thought of it made his stomach turn.

"I told you it didn't hurt as—" Sonic started to make an excuse.

Mateo cut him off. "Sonic, you have a high tolerance for pain. I only want to deal with the kind that comes with making babies with my wife."

"Speaking of wife, how are things going on His-Love. com?" Sonic asked as I-240 merged into I-40. Their destination was still about three hours away.

"I'm good. Some women have hit me up. I haven't found anyone that I want to spend a few minutes talking to. I did connect with some online book clubs, though."

"Really?"

"I wish I'd brought a book with me. I found this book, *Brother Word* by Derek Jackson, that I meant to download on my Nook reader." Mateo told him, "I wanted to get the paperback but couldn't find it in the stores anywhere."

"Reach in my glove compartment and grab the Green Dot card." Sonic grabbed a can of sparkling water that was sitting in the console. "Go ahead and load the book on your phone."

"Naw, man." Mateo turned to him. "You don't have to do that."

"Mateo, if you don't get that card." Sonic started to reach into the glove compartment. "I appreciate you traveling all over North and South Carolina so we can dump all this stuff Turner gave me or I bought when I was with him. You take very little money, even when you have to look over your shoulder to make sure we are both squared away. Buy the book."

Mateo reached into the compartment and was surprised to see the card on top of the manual for the car and the registration.

"I always keep the card in the car in case of emergencies," Sonic reminded him.

"I still think you should keep it in the room," Mateo countered.

"I change the location every so often. I only keep it—" Sonic started.

"To get gas in the car, a motel room, and to buy some food if you need to," Mateo finished for him. "I remember."

"I'm not going to lie to you—I used to think those cards were the devil, the way they take fee after fee and will put you in the negative to take their fees." Sonic continued as Trin-i-Tee 5:7 could be heard in the background. "But I learned to save money that way. I learned how to put aside money for tithes and offerings, my living expenses, and everything else."

"How?" Mateo couldn't believe what he was hearing. He'd heard all the horror stories about how the companies that issued prepaid cards charged so many fees that they wiped the users out.

"Well, when I was with Turner—even before I was with him—I always had a job, so I always had access to credit cards." Sonic continued as J. Moss followed his protégés with an upbeat track, "Turner would give me the money to pay them off, and I shopped like a king. Without Turner, I had no way to pay for the cards I was using, so I weaned myself off of them when I knew I was going to try to leave Turner the first time.

"As I started buying the prepaid cards, I noticed that some of them didn't charge as much to keep the cards as others. I also knew it would be a while before I came up with the money to pay Bank of America, Wells Fargo, BB&T and PNC all the money I owed them, so I called the banks one by one and started paying off the ones that had the lowest balances. Once one bank got paid off, I'd work on the next bank. BB&T was nice enough to let me keep my credit card with them provided I maintained my checking account. That's when everything really picked up for me financially.

"When I first got on with Burgers & Fries, they were still giving everyone paychecks every week. Then they went with this system where they would direct deposit to a company-issued prepaid card. As long as I worked at Burgers & Fries or a job where I get direct deposit, the company waives the monthly charge. When I get money for selling stuff, I deposit the money to my BB&T account, and then I transfer the money from the BB&T account to the prepaid card.

"At the bank, I found that they would allow me to electronically pay the credit cards, so instead of paying by money order, I saved money making electronic deposits to the bank. I had a nice banker who talked me into putting five hundred dollars into a certificate of deposit. Once I got saved and joined Guiding Light Ministries, I found out that the church allowed people to pay their tithes and offerings via PayPal.

"Now when I get paid, I pay the church first via PayPal, then I pay the bills, and I move some spending money to the prepaid card. That's how I was able to amass a few hundred dollars on the Green Dot. It took discipline and sacrifice. Getting rid of debt is part of the reason I'm getting rid of the material things that remind me of my relationship with Turner. But I'm here."

Mateo felt like he was listening to a walking insurance salesman. Everything his friend said made sense, but he needed to see it on paper too. "Can you help me with that?" Mateo inquired as he noticed that they were almost in Statesville. "I don't have a problem spending before I get it, but I need help making my money stretch," he said, pulling his phone out of his pocket.

"Yeah, no doubt," Sonic assured him as they got off the exit, "I'm going to get some gas and something to eat. You want anything?"

Mateo nodded his head. "We'll see what they got."

Once Sonic pulled up to the pump, Mateo got out of the car and headed to the bathrooms. His phone buzzed, and he saw he had a message from His-Love.com. He put the phone back into his pocket and walked to the urinal and handled his business. When he was done, he washed and dried his hands and then walked out of the bathroom.

He took the phone back out of his pocket and opened the His-Love.com app. He smiled when he realized he had another inquiry and a new message just that quick.

Got any pics that show what you are working with?

He couldn't believe that people were on a Christ-centered Web site and still sending provocative messages.

Mateo shook his head. He'd deleted those pics a long time ago, and he wasn't interested in going back into the bathroom and whipping it out so he could take some new ones. That wasn't what he'd gotten on His-Love.com for.

The Devil stay *trying to get me in some mess,* Mateo thought as he deleted the message and blocked the sender.

Mateo walked to the gas station cooler and grabbed a few fruit drinks then went through the snack aisle to get some turkey jerky and some cake snacks. As he got to the register, he looked at the cashier and noticed that she had no problem blatantly licking her lips at him. The old Mateo would have taken her back to the bathroom and had her calling his name, but Mateo was committed to trying to meet the right girl the right way. He couldn't do that if he was letting his little head do all the thinking.

Mateo paid for the items and left the store clerk in her lustful thoughts. She kept blowing kisses and looking him up and down, letting it be known that he could get it. Mateo refused to take the bait.

Mateo walked back to the car and noticed that Sonic was nodding his head while sitting in the car. Fred Hammond's rock version of "He's Able" came on, and Mateo could see how Sonic got crunk.

"Man, you won't believe this," Mateo said as Sonic pulled off and got back on the Interstate. "That store clerk was making passes at me."

"CeCe?" Sonic smirked.

"How you know her name?" Mateo asked. "I didn't know you came off this way often."

"Yeah, I know CeCe. She used to be one of Turner's girls."

The thought of that repulsed Mateo. It was a good thing he didn't give into the temptation or else he'd have run up in something that had been around the block.

"She lives near her parents' farm a few miles out." Sonic filled him in on her business. "Turner wanted her to get an abortion when she got pregnant, and she refused. Word on the street was that she put the boy she had by him up for adoption, and she stays out in the country because she knows Turner won't come back this way to try to get her."

"Wow, Turner's one sick dude!" Mateo exclaimed, pulling out his phone again once they crossed into Davie County. That left them getting to Greensboro in an hour.

Mateo and Sonic spent that hour bobbing their heads to the beats and singing along with the *WOW Gospel* collection. Mateo also got into *Brother Word*.

When Mateo looked up from his phone, he found Sonic on Battleground Avenue. He was amazed at how busy Greensboro was for an early afternoon. They turned into a '70s-inspired thrift shop that promoted disco and world peace.

Sonic and Mateo grabbed the clothes from the backseat and walked in to the checkout counter. A young woman who looked like she could've been on *The Wonder Years* greeted them. Mateo noted that her long brown hair was covered with a thick, neon orange headband. The matching polyester blouse and skirt were just as bold as the candy corn–decorated stockings that concealed her legs. Her head rocked and body swayed to a lesser-known Jimi Hendrix track playing in the background.

"Sonic." She smiled as she came from behind the counter and kissed him on the cheek. "I see you've brought a friend."

"This is Mateo," Sonic said.

"I'm Dandelion—but my friends call me Dandy." She shook Mateo's hand. Dandy reached for one of the pairs of leather pants Sonic had placed on the counter. "My God, these clothes look better than the pictures." Her husky, British-sounding accent commanded attention. "I think you need to get a new camera. I'll see if I can get you some more money."

Dandy thumbed the rest of the clothes, and then she pulled out her iPhone from her clutch.

Mateo followed Sonic out to the car to get the rest of the clothes. "Where in the world did you find this place?" Mateo grabbed the clothes and made it back into the store.

"I used to want to own a store," Sonic announced as he held the door open while shuffling a lighter load to his right side. "A Vietnam era/Civil Rights Movement–themed store. Those were two major issues surrounding America in the late sixties/early seventies. I used to tell Turner all the time that if we could travel back in time, I would've gone back and fought with the Black

Panther Party for Self Defense. I always found those men intriguing.

"I also liked the soft rock and the disco that came from that time period. My mom was a big Janis Joplin fan. When I started researching gospel music in the seventies, I was amazed at how much the songs written during that time period had light disco undertones."

"Okay, soul man." Dandy interrupted their conversation. "I got the old man to let go eleven hundred."

That brought a smile to Sonic's face. Of all the tats he had to remove, getting rid of the *T* from his tramp stamp was one of the most expensive. Plus, Mateo knew that Sonic didn't have any health insurance, despite the passage of the Affordable Care Act. That meant Sonic's planned trip to the urologist was going to set him back a couple thousand.

"Thank you." Sonic acknowledged her. "And tell the old man thank you too."

Dandy nodded her head and smiled as she put the clothes in bags and labeled them. Sonic pulled out the Green Dot card, and Dandy went through the process of sending payment to his account. "If you got any more clothes like this, give us a call." Dandy smiled at the customer who was coming in. "That way, I can make sure I get you fair value for the stuff you have."

"Thank you." Sonic accepted the card with a receipt attached to it.

Mateo smiled. He liked the idea of Sonic getting more money and having a secure place to unload his stuff. "So when do we come back?" Mateo asked when they got outside the door.

"Give her six to eight weeks. That ought to be enough time to get rid of some of the clothes. I'll look through what I have and see what else I can spare."

"Next time, let me look at the stuff first," Mateo insisted as they got back in the car.

"Okay." Sonic smiled as he opened the door. Without another word, Sonic started the car and they were headed back to Asheville, North Carolina.

Chapter Nine

Train Them Up

Amirah smiled when seven new crew members walked into the makeshift studio at Gospel United Christian Center. Four of the crew members were selected from a group of students who had expressed interest at Shiloh and came highly recommended by Pastor and Mrs. Ingle. The other three were students at Mars Hill University and came highly recommended by the school's faculty and leaders in the community.

The staff that had survived the massive layoff were finishing setting up the studio. Mrs. Slate was also assisting, as she had promised to stay for the day's viewing.

"All right, can I have everyone's attention please?" Amirah called for everyone to gather and pointed to the seats up front. She could see Pastor Hughes opening the door and her guests, Donte Speaks and Rahliem Victor, peeking their heads in. She also saw a face she didn't recognize, one whose sharp features bore a slight resemblance to Usher.

"First, I want to apologize Pastor and Mrs. Slate and the rest of the Gospel United Christian Center for the misunderstanding we had during the filming of my last show." She looked at each of them. She could see Pastor Slate sitting next to Pastor Hughes, and both men were smiling at her.

"Next, I want to lay a few ground rules so that we don't have that kind of misunderstanding again." Amirah's voice got firm, and she noticed that some of the new hires straightened up quickly. "First, my vision for *The Amirah Dalton Show* is one where we help people solve everyday issues out of love. We agree—we agree to disagree—and we settle things in the spirit of Christ."

Amirah stopped, giving time for her words to sink in, and then she continued, "*The Amirah Dalton Show* is a Christ-centered show. We don't judge and condemn people like they do on the court shows. We don't let random people who don't know if they are the daddy, or if they don't know who the daddy of their babies are, act crazy like they do on your typical talk show.

"It is the expectation that I treat every guest that comes on this show with dignity and respect. I take God's first two commandments *very* seriously. I love Him with all my heart, and I love my neighbor as myself. And let me tell y'all, I can't love my neighbor if I'm directly or unintentionally setting him or her up for anguish.

"So having said that, from this moment forward, everyone here has a clean slate. If you are a new hire, study the first shows and not the one that ended up being parodied all over YouTube or on the evening news. In the future, guests who can't act right will be asked to leave voluntarily, or they will be assisted out."

Amirah saw the look of seriousness on the faces of the crew. She felt confident that from that moment forward, any missteps would be random and not feel like sabotage.

"Now, before we leave, let us say a quick prayer." Amirah grabbed the first crew member's hand, and others stood up and followed suit. She led them in a spirit-filled prayer and felt peace within her soul.

When she opened her eyes, the man who was trailing Donte and Rahliem was in her face.

"I'm King Dunlap." The man extended his hand and smiled. Amirah could tell he was dangerous just by the look in his eyes and the strong grip with which he shook her hand. "I do security work for Donte and Edris, and I just wanted to let you know that some of the misfits that were at your show last week will not be let in the building or get anywhere near the taping of your show."

"Thank you," she responded. When King mentioned Edris's name, she'd almost forgotten that was The Revelation's real name. In the back of her mind, she made a mental note to make sure to add King to her list of thank you cards she planned on mailing after the show.

"I'll be in and out of the studio and around the campus making sure that everything is handled and that you have a productive show. We can't wait for WorldStar to show clips of this episode like they showed clips of the last one."

Amirah thanked King again, and then she went on the stage and got ready for final preparations for her show to start. Once her music came on, she smiled at her cameraman and was pleased that the music team had selected an upbeat and encouraging song from Dave Hollister. Amirah looked out in the studio audience and was pleased to see a large number of members from her church as well as other congregations in attendance.

"Welcome to *The Amirah Dalton Show*." Amirah was excited as the song was ending. "Today's guests are three young men who are changing the way we view gospel music and street ministry. What I like about these brothers is that they aren't afraid to admit to past flaws and help even the most unlikely of souls find their way to Christ.

"First up, we have Rahliem Victor, founder of Street Disciples Ministries, which just set up a branch of the ministry here in Asheville, North Carolina. To his right is Donte Speaks, former adult video star, community activist, and business manager for gospel singers and Christian rappers. Speaking of managers, one of his most familiar clients happens to be his younger brother, The Revelation."

"It's good to be here." The Revelation commanded attention.

The audience seemed to be excited. Amirah made eye contact with Mateo and smiled. She was happy to see that he was sitting with Hammer and Sonic and a few other members from the local churches. She found herself drawn to him, but she couldn't explain why.

"Today's show"—Amirah focused back on the audience—"is about moving past scandalous situations. As we all know, two weeks ago our show moved away from our usual platform and got mainstream.

"As the past week went on, I was hurt, a little frustrated, and I felt betrayed by those who I thought were on my team. I took a tumble—I took a fall—but unlike Humpty Dumpty, I got up and with the help of Jesus Christ, I will continue rising and moving onward and upward toward the light He has for me."

The chorus of *amens* came from the crowd, along with a round of applause.

Turning to the camera and facing her studio audience, she said, "Regardless of who may or may not have been at fault, I want to take a moment to apologize for Thursday Honesty Denyla Jackson, Armaad, and the other guests that came on the show last week. My intention was to provide a platform where you guys could seek healing and see how our Lord and Savior works. I did not mean to create or involve you guys in a circus. I should have had better control of my show, and I should have cut it short the moment I got uncomfortable with the direction the show went. I also apologize to my loyal viewers, who come to us because they want something wholesome that they don't get on other television shows."

Amirah took a seat next to her guest. "Donte, I think I'll start with you. Most people in this audience know of your past. I need help in moving forward. I'm not ashamed to say it. Given what you've seen and know of my situation, what do I do to move forward?"

Usually, Amirah commanded the stage and kept the flow of the show moving forward. This back step was an effort on her part to move on. She saw no shame in asking other godly people for help and direction.

"First, I think you have it easier because the majority of your audience has never seen you naked," Donte pointed out.

Amirah chuckled. *At least they don't know it's me,* she thought.

"But in all seriousness, you have to decide that you are going to be about God's business." Donte pointed in the direction of the audience. "*This* is your ministry, and you affect a lot of lives with how you present your ministry."

"I want to add that so many celebrities have bounced back from worse," The Revelation mentioned. "Everyone got to see you fall down, and the part of this journey you are going to enjoy is watching everyone else watch you get up."

"I definitely agree with that point," Rahliem jumped in. "When I started Street Disciples Ministries, I heard about the work that Donte was doing to change his image while he was a student at Gilbert State University. I watched and studied him, as I knew he was watching me, being that I'd only been out of prison a few short years since starting this ministry."

"A lot of people think that you can't change when you come out of prison or have a public fall from grace," Amirah pointed out, "so that meant that you had an uphill battle getting men to join your ministry."

"No," Rahliem quickly answered. "The opposite is true. I have a harder time keeping those who are interested in joining the ministry engaged with meaningful projects to do in the community. I get requests all over the country to start ministries or partner with similar organizations to spread the word about picking up your cross, no matter what it is, and going into the streets to minister the Word as if we were Christ."

That made Amirah happy. She knew she could pull forward and get past the misunderstanding and the hoopla caused by her last show. She was convinced that her pastor, employer, and church family weren't the only ones praying for her.

Chapter Ten

My Favorite Book

Amirah made her way to her favorite restaurant, David's Table, despite the heavy traffic coming off of I-40. She had left the filming of her television show. She was pleased with the more positive turn the show had taken and had faith that her new crew would not embarrass her like the last group did.

Rahliem, Donte, and The Revelation continued giving her a boost and the support to move forward with her mission. The Revelation did an impromptu performance and surprised everyone in the audience with copies of his current CD, and Amirah got the exclusive that he was working on new material that he thought would be released before the end of the year.

She thought about whether or not Thursday, Armaad, or the other guests would've accepted her apology, but she didn't dwell on it. Moving forward meant accepting that the mistake had been made and moving forward and keeping a watchful eye to ensure that the same mistake wasn't made again.

Amirah had a decent commute to get from Gospel United Christian Center, which was on the south side of Asheville. The church was almost in Arden, one of the smaller towns in the metropolitan area. David's Table was in downtown Asheville near the courthouse.

Amirah stepped out of her 1992 Mercury Cougar wearing a brown, traditional-styled Alexander McQueen business suit with some white Reebok tennis shoes. She went to the trunk of her car and pulled out the brown pumps with two-inch heels she'd worn during taping. After changing her shoes, she walked into the restaurant and found the members of the local chapter of Essence of Prayer Book Club sitting at their traditional spot, the middle round table, with their copies of *Let the Church Say Amen* on the tables and various e-readers nearby.

David's Table was a Christ-centered, full-service restaurant that specialized in soul food and Creole dining. The restaurant's owners attended her church and were very active in ministry. The décor was West African–themed with kente tablecloths with Ashanti and Christ-centered statues placed at each end of the napkin holders. Amirah could smell the turkey and dressing, cooked greens, baked macaroni and cheese, and other specialty dishes as she made her way to the group's table.

"Amirah, girl!" Sarai yelled like she was outside.

Amirah looked at Sarai sideways. She knew Sarai knew better to address her like that. It was cool though. Truthfully, Amirah had forgotten that Sarai was a member of her book club as well. She was a young, first-year teacher who'd just graduated from Winston-Salem State University. Having graduated from North Carolina A & T, Amirah appreciated being around another HBCU alum. School rivalry jokes aside, Amirah found Sarai a pleasure to be around.

"Amirah!" Various members of the group joined in. All fifteen of them either stood or walked up to her to give her a hug. That was one of the reasons she loved meeting with this book club; they always welcomed her with open arms.

"Hey, ladies." Amirah tried to greet them all.

"Ooh, I love what you've done with your hair." Aja touched a strand. Amirah's micro braids had been twisted and curled, giving her a look similar to what the R&B singer Brandy had when she first came out. They highlighted her high cheekbones and emphasized her glowing, almond-colored skin.

"Thank you, thank you." Amirah accepted the compliment. "I try to change the style every now and then because just wearing my hair down can be plain sometimes."

"So what are you trying to say about my hair?" Marjorie jumped in and showed off her newly shaven head.

"There's nothing wrong with going natural," Amirah confirmed. "In fact, under all of this weave, I'm still kinky the way God designed me to be."

"Well, let's get the meeting started," Marjorie said as she stood up at her spot at the table. "Ladies, how are we doing today?"

"Fine" and "good" were the common responses from the group.

"Good. Today we are going to discuss ReShonda Tate Billingsley's classic novel, which I hear was filmed a while ago and is awaiting release."

The ladies clapped upon hearing the news. "We haven't had a faith-based novel get turned into a movie or a television special since T. D. Jakes did *Not Easily Broken*," Sarai pointed out.

"I know," Marjorie said, "which is why this is a big accomplishment for us. We need to support the movie regardless of the format it comes out in, because that's how we let the decision-makers know that we want to see our stories on the screen."

The ladies nodded their heads in agreement.

"Today, we are going to briefly discuss where we are in terms of the book, but we will hold off any major discussions until the next meeting. First, we are going to partake in a project based on a book we read last month. We are going to sign up individually and collectively as a group to a Christ-centered networking and online dating site."

"Oohs" and "ahhs" were heard throughout the table.

"The site that won the votes two weeks ago is called His-Love.com, and I like the fact that the site already has a book club on it. For those of you who are married, we gave you plenty of time to go over your participation in this activity with your spouses. If you didn't agree this was best for your household, then look on with another member. Now, before we register and talk about the positives and the negatives of online dating, how many of you have profiles on this site?" Marjorie asked.

Only Aja and another lady raised their hands. "Cheaters," Marjorie mumbled, which brought out a few chuckles from the members. "Okay, I'm just kidding. But I'm glad this will be a group experience for most of us who are single. If you are married and your husband is comfortable with you participating in this site for social media purposes, please put marital status on your profile when you register so that we don't give these men the wrong impression. If you and your husband said no or you decided that spiritually this is not a site you can participate in, feel free to look on with another book club member."

Amirah took note of the disclaimer. She could see how, on the outside looking in, one of the women's husband would take his wife participating on His-Love.com the wrong way. Even with its Christ-centered focus and direction, the last thing she wanted to see was someone's relationship in trouble because they joined the site.

"Did either of you find someone online?" Marjorie addressed the group. Amirah noticed that Aja half-heartedly raised her hand. "Would you care to share?" Marjorie continued.

Aja slowly rose from her spot at the other end of the table. "First, I want to say that we should be proud of His-Love.com. It is founded by a young African American lady who wanted a dating service and networking site that not only reflected His values and would be Christ-centered, but would encourage men and women of God to mix and mingle in a safe environment without the temptations of taking on worldly values. I particularly like the daily scriptures and the links to a few popular daily devotionals that come into my inbox daily."

Aja pulled out her iPad and showed everyone the site with her profile on it. Then she minimized it to show the His-Love.com app. "Next feature is the app, which you can synchronize to your smart phones, your laptops, and PCs and other devices. This is cool, because once I make a connection, the app updates all of my devices, which makes it convenient."

"Have you met someone?" one of the ladies asked.

"Actually, I have. I can't believe I'm saying this, but I've reconnected with Alyssia's father, and we've been talking for a few months now."

"How is that going?" another of the ladies asked.

"Actually, it's going very well. It was kind of bumpy when we first met, because I was only seventeen and he was much older. I wasn't the Christian lady back then that I am today, and he wasn't Prince Charming either. But once we got past that, we have not only learned to co-parent our daughter together, but we have seen our relationship grow by leaps and bounds. His-Love.com gave us a chance to start over and to meet the way God intended." Aja sat down amid applause from fellow book club members. She was still blushing.

"So when are we gonna meet this fine, handsome man?" another lady asked.

"When the time is right," Aja promised. "If it's God's will, of course."

"Thank you for your testimony." Marjorie shared a knowing wink. "I can't guarantee you will find a match as it appears that Aja has; however, I do want our trip to His-Love.com to be one that we can take together among friends.

"When we read *Diamonds* by Serita Evanovich," she continued, "we learned about the benefits and the dangers of connecting with people we meet online."

"I love that book," Aja interjected. "Serita did a good job at demonstrating how we present ourselves to the public and work hard to show our best sides, yet we often we forget that like diamonds, we are rough, imperfect creatures that have to be harvested and polished."

"I agree," Chris jumped in.

When Amirah heard her voice, she had to look around, because she had forgotten that Chris came to the meetings every now and then. "I look rough on the outside," Chris admitted. "I like men, but I have a hard time connecting with them. And before y'all suggest it, I tried the long hair, makeup, and glam thing, and that didn't work for me."

Amirah noticed a few smiles. She was happy to see that people weren't judging Chris.

"But seriously, I'm an introvert," Chris admitted. "Unless it's time to pop off and beat a chick down, I'm quiet as a mouse. When I'm behind the monitor and pounding the keys, that's where I'm the most comfortable. I'm not really a people-person. I can reveal as much as I want without having to show people what I look like."

"And that's the good thing about this site," Marjorie pointed out. "You don't have to show anyone what you look like right away. A lot of people choose pictures or other images for their profile picture."

"That's good," Chris said.

"Yeah, but when are we going to get to meet her?" Aja asked. "And is her husband okay? Because the last time we talked to her, he had to go to the hospital."

"I haven't talked to her lately," Marjorie answered. "We are still on to set up that interview with her, because everyone's been talking about *Diamonds* since it's been out. But back to the profiles—who'd like to be our guinea pig and create one for the group to see?"

No one raised her hand, and Amirah felt comfortable enough to give it a try, so she stood and volunteered to go first.

"Thank you, Amirah. We are going to finish our light appetizers that the waiters are starting to head our way to serve, and after that, we will watch Amirah create her site while we each create our own."

The waiters placed various snacks of cheese and crackers, fruit, and mini turkey sausage links on the table. Amirah pulled out a dollar bill from her purse and tipped the waiter. After Marjorie led the group in grace, the members of the group ate and discussed some of the short stories that they were reading on their e-readers.

Amirah sat at the computer and looked at the projector, which showed the form she had just filled out with her personal information. She chose the name AmirahIsLoyal because *loyalty* was what her name translated to in Arabic. She put in her leopard-print flash drive and selected one of the professional pictures she'd taken a while back as her profile picture. It took almost five minutes, due to the moderators verifying her information, but soon afterward, her picture was on the site, ready for the world to see.

Amirah headed to the main screen and was about to select her location when she was interrupted. "Y'all see that there are ten thousand women registered for the site, but only four thousand men. I don't like the odds of this already."

"Now, don't look at it that way," Aja spoke up. "Some of the 'women' on the site are groups and churches, and by default, the sex of a group is a woman. There are still more women on the site, but a few of the groups send postings and party invites. Some present business opportunities as well. Think of this as the Christ-centered versions of LinkedIn and BlackPeopleMeet.com rolled into one."

"Oh . . ." Some of the ladies felt put at ease.

Amirah continued with her registration, and she placed Asheville, North Carolina as her city to view. She was amazed at the diverse group of men and women online. It was expected that Asheville would have the most members, because the lady who founded the site lived there. Amirah began to view some of the men online, and she had to admit that quite a few of them were appealing to the eye. Almost every man had a face shot, as the site didn't allow body shots or private pictures. Those who didn't show their faces had Christ-centered pictures or a shadow with a cross in the middle to indicate they hadn't uploaded a picture.

As the information session wound down, Amirah got her first piece of mail: a friend request from TaxTithress. Noticing that she was a woman, Amirah almost rejected the request, until she saw Aja's profile picture when she hovered over the name. Amirah accepted that request and the one from Marjorie and other ladies in the group as they got the hang of the site. Amirah took a peek at Aja's page and saw that she linked with M. E. D. T. H. O. D. Man, whom she presumed to be Alyssia's father.

Amirah would've explored someplace else, but one of

the managers had come to the room to let them know that the next group who had reserved the room was ready to use it. The book club members quickly disconnected their laptops or shut down the computers they were using. They also agreed to discuss ReShonda's book at the beginning of the next meeting and to track their progress on His-Love.com as well.

Chapter Eleven

Power Moves/Struggles

Mateo stared out of the skylight in the business room of Heaven's Inn. The motel used to be owned by a wealthy businessman. When the owner realized he had no heirs who shared his vision, he helped Hammer move his business to the motel and financed the transfer of the motel to him as well. The man stayed on as a consultant for a year, during which Hammer got the vision from God to use the property as the basis for his business and ministry. The motel served as a hub for Hammer's more popular and well-known business, The Christian Cab Company.

As Mateo walked up to the window to take a peek outside, he saw that a small fleet of Lincoln Navigators, Continentals, and Cougars graced the parking spaces before him. Mateo almost got lost in Joshua Rogers singing "Rain On Us" in the background.

Mateo was supposed to be looking for another job. One of the conditions of being able to stay at Heaven's Inn was that he would seek outside employment at the end of his first year. Hammer wanted to see everyone become self-sufficient and begin to show that they could manage on their own. Hammer hoped that the long-term employment with one of his firms would entice other employers to give the individuals he helped another chance. Plus, Hammer and the church helped those employed seek housing elsewhere and often were able to get the employees discounts through the ministry.

After filling out the long and tedious online applications for department stores and convenient discount chains, Mateo wanted to fix his hazy eyes on a new sight. In the back of his mind, he thought about asking Hammer to let him drive one of the cabs to tide him over, but that would mean he would have to give up his employment with the motel and rely on tips for most of his income. On one hand, Mateo knew he could be a charmer and found the idea of making money via tips a challenge. On the other hand, he was still working on paying off the restitution due for his DUI charge, and he couldn't afford to go without the guaranteed income his hourly rate at Heaven's Inn afforded him.

Mateo's conviction on check fraud, identity theft, and larceny further limited his choices. Every major fast food chain had already rejected him, in part because he'd stolen from two of those employers when he was a teen. Word about Mateo's klepto ways had traveled fast, especially since some of his former coworkers moved on to other fast food joints. Ingles, the grocery store with a dominance in the Asheville area, also rejected him for employment. Some of the mom and pop stores and janitorial services weren't willing to cut him slack, even though they needed someone who could speak Spanish fluently.

Traces of lavender and vanilla competed fiercely for dominance from hidden oil jars near the back of the room. The cream-colored walls were lined with trophies and awards the motel had won since being under Hammer's ownership. Recognizing the profile from a major publication chronicling Hammer's success after getting out of jail left Mateo inspired and gave him the thought that maybe one day, he could own a string of businesses too.

Keep your lives free from the love of money, and be content with what you have, the Biblical verse he saw framed against the wall reminded him. Mateo thought it difficult when he didn't have a job aside from being a motel attendant, but just as quickly as the thoughts of failure and frustration crossed his mind, Mateo thanked God for Jesus, a place to stay, some food to eat, a sane and clear mind, and a desire to right his wrongs.

Mateo sat in the plush office chair and started to play Spider Solitaire on the computer, but closed the program after only a few minutes. Mateo decided to check his Gmail account to see if he'd received a response from the previous applications he'd turned in. The new messages were the typical, standard form rejection e-mails he'd received every day since he started the e-mail account.

Mateo was beginning to dislike the computer and the technology that came with it. He smiled when saw the messages from His-Love.com; one letting him know that he been added as a friend and another letting him know there was a message in his inbox.

As Mateo got further into his search on the Web site, he shook his head when he looked at some of the profiles on His-Love.com. Some of the women had directed him to links to adult sites and chats. Fortunately for him, Hammer had that kind of material blocked on the computers Mateo had access to. Good thing, too, because Mateo couldn't say at that moment that he wouldn't have given into the flesh and acted on some of those impulses. It wasn't that he didn't trust Jesus; Mateo didn't want to put himself in a position to be tempted.

A couple of the women were genuinely interested in praying for him, inviting him to noonday prayers, Bible studies, special church events, and of course the dozens of invites that flooded his box to attend someone's Missionary Pentecostal Baptist AME Zion Church of God in Christ.

"You better be filling out job applications and not trying to look at some adult video site!" Hammer yelled from the doorway.

"No, old man. I'm on His-Love.com."

Hammer stepped into the room. Mateo moved his chair to the side so that he could show Hammer that he was, in fact, on the Web site that he said he was on. Hammer pulled up a chair and sat in front of the computer and scrolled up and down the inbox. He, too, shook his head at the subjects of some of the notes that were left for Mateo.

"What you got that makes these women act like they are on the *Desperate Housewives of Atlanta* or something?" Hammer asked as he clicked on the HOME icon and then to the MY PROFILE icon. "Man, look at your pictures. You look like the thug you try to pretend to be."

"Old man, I'm more of a thug than you think I am," Mateo responded cockily. "I might be saved and still trying to learn God's way, but I'm not a stranger to the streets."

"Boy, when check fraud and identity theft count as hardcore crimes, then you can talk to me about the streets." Hammer blew him off.

"If you're so bad, what did you get arrested for?" Mateo challenged.

Hammer always avoided the question every time Mateo or Sonic brought it up. Word was that Hammer was a hustler and could move stolen merchandise faster than one could light a match. For the right price, Hammer would sell anything, including himself. The way Mateo heard it, Hammer had gotten pulled over one night in a Durango when a signal light failed to flash. Not having a valid driver's license or insurance on the stolen vehicle, Hammer did the only thing he could do: he beat the arresting officer to a pulp. He would have gotten away if another officer hadn't pulled up and shot him in the butt.

Hammer was quiet, as he knew that Mateo was thinking about the gossip. He continued to look at Mateo's profile, and then he got up and walked away from the computer. "Hurry up, Matthew. The other patron who needs to use the computer is waiting on you to finish. You can't be on this site all day."

"Old man, that's not an answer."

"Boy, get to my age and then you'll get an answer." Hammer turned off the overhead light as he headed out.

"And my name is Mateo!" Mateo blew him off, turned on the desk lamp, and continued looking at the site. He looked at the NEW MEMBERS section and noticed quite a few ladies he was physically attracted to. One of the members that stood out was AmirahIsLoyal.

I like a woman who is loyal, Mateo thought. "I'm gonna have to see how loyal she is for myself." Mateo clicked on the link that led to her profile. He was intrigued that the profile picture was the Amirah that he knew, holding a cross and an apple with a verse that instructed teachers to be careful of what they taught. He clicked on some of the other pictures that showed Amirah speaking in front of crowds or leading instruction in the classroom.

"Amirah may be the woman I need to keep me out of trouble, keep me grounded." Mateo was talking to himself.

"Found someone?"

Mateo turned around and saw Marvel walking in with a backpack on his back. Hammer was supposed to train him to operate the meter and drive one of the cabs that day. The wild orange-and-purple dye was out of his head, replaced with his natural, sandy-blond color. The crisp white button-up and green-and-gold tie made him stand out in a crowd like a sore thumb.

"No. Just checking out the site to see what's on here," Mateo said. "May leave the women on here alone and get myself together first."

"Man, at least the women are checking you out on there. I've had my profile up a few days and either I've been ignored, blocked, or the women flat out tell me they aren't interested."

Mateo tried not to pass judgment. He was the last person to speak on one's character, but he lived in the world for most of his twenty-seven years of life, and he knew that almost all women, saved or not, wanted their men to have certain characteristics.

"Let me see your profile." Mateo surprised himself with the offer to help. He looked Marvel over again, and he knew that if his pictures represented his presentation, he may have a solution to the problem.

Mateo stood up and offered Marvel his seat. Marvel logged Mateo's profile off and pulled up his own. Mateo looked over his shoulder, and just as he suspected, Marvel's presentation was a reflection of the way he looked. In one of the pictures, he was throwing rocker signs, and in a few others, he looked like the stereotypical punk rocker with the hair, the outfits, and the attitude to match.

"You don't have anything representing Jesus on your profile," Mateo offered. "Everything is about your past as a punk rocker or biker or whatever it was you were into."

"Dude." Marvel was offended. "Half of those pictures were taken at Christian rock concerts. Look at the shirts."

Mateo moved closer to the screen and maximized one of the pictures. Sure enough, *Jesus Lives* was in the center of the shirt in grunge, hard-rock lettering.

"Well, then we need to emphasize that." Mateo pulled up a photo imaging program that allowed him to manipulate and highlight certain aspects of some pictures. "If I can't tell these are Christian shirts, I'm sure the ladies can't either."

"Aw, look at the blind leading the blind." Mateo heard a sarcastic voice behind him. When he turned around, he smiled from ear to ear when he recognized Sonic standing behind him. Gone were the piercings in his eyebrows, nose, and ears. His face had healed nicely. Save for traces of navy blue hair coloring at the tip of his hair, Mateo hardly able to tell that Sonic was into grunge rock.

"I'm not blind." Mateo stood up and gave Sonic a hug. "Marvel, this is my boy Sonic. We got saved together a while ago, and now Sonic works for a call center in town and a fast food restaurant."

Mateo watched as Marvel and Sonic shook hands. "I know you," Marvel said.

"How so?" Sonic looked over Marvel's shoulder to see what Mateo was working on.

"Everybody knows you used to belong to Turner Mustafa Spartenburg."

Mateo saw the way Sonic tilted his head, acknowledging that the man was correct.

"I wasn't trying to bring up any ill vibes. I used to buy drugs from one of his boys. They kept me high." Marvel apologized. "I just know what time it is, and I know what the man is capable of. I knew you were his main boy."

"I used to be his; I'm not gonna lie about that," Sonic conceded as he lifted up his shirt. A few hard bruises that looked like welts from an extension cord graced a spot under his left nipple and on his right abdomen. They stood out on an otherwise flawless canvas. Sonic turned around, and Mateo could see the first three letters of his nemesis' name on the man's lower back.

"It used to say *Turner*, didn't it?" Marvel questioned.

"Yeah, I used to walk around with my tramp stamp in pride. Now I just want walk around and spread God's word in peace. The bullet wounds on my chest, my right leg, and my jawline are the price I paid for my freedom.

Every couple of weeks, when I can stand the pain, removing that bastard's name helps me step into my own more and more each day."

Sonic lowered his shirt. It had been nine months since Mateo had seen how much Sonic had healed. He also noticed there were no traces from where Sonic's nipple and navel rings used to be. The physical transformation into the man of God was happening before his eyes.

Mateo's mind flashed back to the price they had both paid for Sonic's freedom. Turner's main man renounced his sexuality, which meant no more favors for him, and Turner couldn't stand it. Most people who got out of Turner's gang left in a body bag, or they were made quadriplegics.

Mateo had images of men stomping on him, being shot, and the mandated bed rest. The new exercise regimen that was recommended during his stay at the hospital held him to the fire to maintain his health. The mouth guard that he wore when sleeping worked to realign his upper teeth. They were heavy, physical prices, but they were worth it to help Sonic stay in line with his new Christ-centered values—and away from an abusive relationship.

"Ay, man, we'll have to work on your profile a little later." Mateo began logging off the His-Love.com Web site and putting the computer into sleep mode. "I got to get ready to go put in some job applications, and I need Sonic to take me."

"A'ight, man. Thanks a lot. And I'll have to get up with y'all later," Marvel said as the three of them headed out of the computer lab. *I hope that this is the beginning to having some friends who are striving to be grounded in God, just like me,* he thought.

Chapter Twelve

Prototype

Amirah opened her metallic pink Toshiba laptop and entered her password. She waited for her machine to load up, and then she went to the Google Chrome browser and found His-Love.com in her favorites. She heard a ringing that sounded like a doorbell, and she noticed she had three messages.

The first message was a friend request from Marjorie, and the second one from her as well, inviting her to the Essence of Prayer Book Club group that she started on the site. She accepted both requests, and then she opened a third request from SenorCristoAmor.

Amirah was nervous because she saw that the green light next to his name indicated he was online.

Wow, my first request from a guy, Amirah thought. *I hope he's not a creep or a weirdo.*

Just when she was about to click on the link, she heard someone call her name. Amirah looked up and noticed that Mrs. Ingle was waiting at her classroom door.

"Oh, come in." Amirah minimized the screen on her computer.

"We're still waiting on Xen's parents to come for the parent-teacher conference." Mrs. Ingle walked in and took a seat closer to the desk.

Amirah looked at the time on her laptop. Xen and his parents were a good fifteen minutes late. She looked at the stack of reports she'd finished grading for the business law class she taught.

"I hope they show up." Amirah put the folder that had some of Xen's latest assignments to the side.

Xen was one of Amirah's problem students, and he was struggling academically in all of the classes. Amirah was also Xen's homeroom teacher, and she took great pride in making sure the ninth graders she advised had a good start at Shiloh Christian Academy. She loved working with Mrs. Ingle, as she took great pride in helping her teachers stay grounded in the Word and becoming great educators.

A few seconds later, Howard Amber, Xen's geometry teacher came in and had a seat. She noticed how casually dressed he was in a collared, checkered Rocawear shirt, loose-fitting Dockers, and some work boots that added two inches to his five foot eight frame, making him and Amirah the same height.

"I see our wonder child isn't here yet." Howard was clearly upset. "I'm beginning to wish I hadn't cancelled our math club meeting for this."

"Mr. Amber," Mrs. Ingle started to chastise, but two more teachers walked into the room. Xen's English teacher, Ms. Josephine Diamond, looked like she was going to work on the sales floor of a department store, and his gym teacher, Sarai, was casually dressed in a white-and-green polo that had the school's logo on the right side, some cream-colored slacks, and matching white-and-green tennis shoes.

"We have to be understanding with our parents. Everyone can't take off from work and just get up and go to a parent teacher conference. Employers change their minds as often as the parents do." Mrs. Ingle continued, "I am thankful that you are here."

"No worries," Sarai responded. "I like to meet the parents of our students."

Nothing else was said as Amirah and the other teachers waited. Her room was chosen for Xen's parent teacher conference because it was the closest to the office and the most spacious. Howard got up and went to the computer nearest to Amirah's desk. Pretty soon, Spider Solitaire filled his screen, and Ms. Diamond took the seat next to Howard. Sarai pulled up a chair and sat next to Amirah.

"Have you gotten any requests from His-Love.com yet?" Sarai asked. "I didn't do a profile yet because my husband and I haven't had a chance to talk about it yet."

"I don't really expect much from it, but a few friends and maybe a nice guy or two to talk to," Amirah responded as she noticed ten more minutes had passed and no Xen or parents.

"Let me see how you did yours," Sarai asked.

Amirah maximized her screen and showed Sarai her profile. Being nosy, Sarai pointed at the avatar next to the message. "Ooh, who is this cutie?" she whispered discreetly. Sarai had clicked on SenorCristoAmor's picture, and Amirah was amazed that Mateo's picture covered her whole screen.

Amirah admitted to herself that Mateo was attractive. He had an edge on him that spelled *B-A-D B-O-Y*. Mateo's head was tilted at a right angle, showing off a tight bald fade at his temple. His goatee was sharp and symmetrical to the angles of his face. His eyes drew her in like an orb, and if Amirah believed in witchcraft, she would've believed that he'd cast a spell on her.

"He does look good," Amirah finally allowed herself to admit as she clicked on the link that displayed his message.

I love a woman who is loyal. That is a perfect attribute to a Proverbs 31 woman.

"I know he's not trying to spit game over the net." Sarai got excited.

"Girl, I know you aren't over here lusting over this man," Amirah teased. "Don't you have a man?" Amirah pointed to the ring on her finger.

"I can admit that another man looks good." Sarai defended herself. "I'm not lusting after him, although I do admit"—she clicked through the other pictures on his profile—"I can see how it would be easy for someone like you to fall into temptation."

Amirah shook her head. "You are something else."

Amirah was about to type her message when Xen walked in with his parents. Xen had recently shaved his head bald and looked like a nomad with his loose-fitting hoodie, baggy pants that fell past his bottom, and his obviously oversized and tattered name-brand boots.

His father didn't fare much better. Amirah was surprised at how short the man was. The two of them looked like they shared clothes. Xen's mother appeared to be an inch or so taller, but not much. Their slender figures made Amirah wonder if they had eaten anything in the last few days.

"Let's get this meeting started," Xen's mother said. "I got to get back to Walmart in an hour."

It was then Amirah noticed the bulky name tag that hung at the hem of her dark blue shirt.

"Okay, let's get started," Mrs. Ingle said.

Amirah joined the other teachers as she stood up and introduced herself to the boy's parents. She looked at Xen and noticed the young man had stared off into space, a common problem in her classroom. She looked at the boy's father and noticed that the trait seemed to run in the family. This was a prelude of just how this conference was about to go.

Chapter Thirteen

Out into the World

Mateo, Marvel, and Sonic walked into an old warehouse in the River Arts District, which was situated near Downtown Asheville. They could see five other guys sitting at a table near the entrance. They each took seats and waited in silence.

Not a moment later, Hammer and Rahliem came in and handed each of the guys a drawstring backpack filled with copies of *The Upper Room* and other daily devotionals.

"When I started this organization," Rahliem began, "we used to go the corner of Dr. Martin Luther King, Jr. Boulevard and New Walkertown Road. The Muslims would be selling their copies of *The Final Call* and their bean pies, and we would be passing out the Word. With the celebrity status the first group had, we had our work cut out for us, but we persevered, and now we are here."

Mateo remembered that Rahliem had mentioned that one of the guys used to do adult videos. He could imagine the problems they had keeping the females at bay. Admittedly, he didn't think he was ready to handle that kind of temptation.

"The difficulty you guys have here is that this is a city that prides itself on 'Keeping Asheville Weird.'" Rahliem stopped and looked at each young man in the face before continuing. "A lot of 'nontraditional folks' walking around. You can't tell who's a man or who's a woman. People look like they stepped out of secular rock and gangster rap concerts."

Mateo looked at the guys, and he could see they were taking it all in.

Rahliem continued. "There is no street corner here for you to stand at. You guys have to go out into the world, in front of the hookah bars and the gay and lesbian clubs and the atheist hangouts, and get the Word of Jesus Christ out there."

"Can we pass these devotions out at our jobs?" Sonic asked.

"Yeah, but that is too easy just the same," Rahliem responded. "We want you to meet and interact with the people. Show them what Christian men look and act like. There is no mistake that all of you look different, and if I were to judge you based on what you look like now, I'd say that each of you could minister to a different crowd."

"People are going to listen to the Word coming from me?" Marvel asked.

"If it *is* the Word being spoken, everyone will listen eventually. All God called you to do is to be the messenger. He set no criteria for what you had to look like."

Mateo saw himself being an active part of this ministry. He loved to talk to people, and back when he used to hustle bootleg CDs and DVDs, it wasn't nothing for him to walk up to a stranger and try to sell him something new.

"I want y'all to read the devotional first and then talk to those around you. A house that prays together, stays together. Once you get your families into the Word, your work will multiply, and you'll find that you'll be leading your own crews of disciples bringing men and women to Christ."

Mateo liked the sound of that. As Rahliem closed out the meeting, Mateo thought about how he could get out and spread the Word. Walking up and talking to people wasn't a problem. He just didn't want to come off like a Jehovah's Witness when he did. He could see the desire to have the same level of boldness, but he wanted it to be for the Lord.

"I see you are staying out of trouble," Rahliem told Mateo as he approached him.

"I got to," Mateo answered. "I'm too pretty to go back to jail."

Rahliem laughed and shook his head. "Well, now you have too much work to do for the Lord. If you stay busy doing His will, there'll be no time for trouble."

"Amen to that," Mateo co-signed. "I'm still job hunting. I do a little work at the motel, but I'm supposed to find some outside employment."

"Ask and ye shall receive; seek and ye shall find; knock and the door shall be opened up to you," Rahliem responded biblically. "It's not just a cliché; it's a lifestyle. Normally I don't quote outside of the New King James, New International, or the Amplified, but I love how the English Standard Version says, 'Be watchful, stand firm in the faith, act like men, be strong.' Also, my brother, 'And if we know that He hears us, whatever we ask, we know that we have the petitions that we have asked of Him.'

"I don't just believe the words I hear and speak; I know them to be true because I know the Man who inspired the creation of the Word to be true. So I never walk around with fear, anger, or resentment, because I always have God and His Word to stand on."

Mateo let the words sink in. He especially liked the *stand firm in the faith, act like men* part. He knew he believed what he read, but admittedly, he had to start acting on it more.

"Your job will come faster than you so desire." Rahliem gave him hope.

As they exited the warehouse, Mateo remembered he had to drop Sonic off at work. Maybe he could start there.

Mateo could feel his stomach growling as he inhaled the scents from the fast food joint he was sitting in. Grilled beef almost made him wish he was a meat-eater, but Mateo had committed himself to being a vegetarian since he'd lost seventy-five pounds from his former obese frame. He'd worked hard over the last two years to get and keep his weight in order, and he didn't want to go back to eating the foods that he knew would cause him to blow up bigger than the Michelin Man. Every now and then, Mateo had a relapse and crashed on some muffins or a soft pretzel, but most of the time, he was on point with his self-imposed diet.

"Keep still," Mateo told himself as he focused on filling out the application to Burgers & Fries. This was his third application with the fast food chain in several months. He hoped that with Sonic putting in a word for him, the manager would have mercy and give him a part-time job.

Mateo checked over his application several times before he stood up. He pulled up his pants and tightened the belt that he was wearing, making sure that he wasn't sagging. He tucked in the teal polo shirt and pulled out his phone. Using glare from the screen as a mirror, he made sure that he didn't have any food in between his teeth and that he looked good. He checked his recently trimmed nails to make sure there was no dirt underneath.

He knew the manager probably wouldn't be able to smell the fragrance coming from the shea butter–based lotion he was wearing. He also was happy that he didn't have sweaty hands and that the application was flawless.

"Can I turn this in to the manager?" Mateo stepped in front of the cashier. He looked at the young lady, who, judging by the way she went heavy on the eye shadow and the lip gloss, had to be a teenager.

"Sure, hold on a minute," the young lady responded as she put her hand over the microphone. "Doug, come up here please?" The young lady turned back and faced Mateo. "He'll be with you in a moment."

Mateo saw Sonic being set up at the drive-through window. They gave each other a head nod.

"'Sup, chump," a voice behind Mateo said.

Mateo turned around and tried to hide the anger that covered his face. Turner smirked and flexed.

"'Sup." Mateo added some bass to his voice. "What you want, Turner?"

"I want to know how you enjoying my toy over there." Turner licked his lips at Sonic.

Mateo shook his head. He didn't have time to engage Turner in a war of words. Mateo saw that Turner was flanked by two goons on his left and right side. One of the taller guys had a smirk. Mateo recognized him as being one of the guys who'd participated in jumping him a few months ago. The other guys of various shapes and sizes weren't so recognizable.

"Sonic's not a toy. He's a grown man. And I don't get down like that."

"Whatever, dawg." Turner tried to intimidate him.

"Whatever, punk. You can leave me alone." Mateo stepped back a little to give him some distance. He wanted to make sure that this time, five people couldn't jump on him at once. He planned on knocking out the short dude who was about his height and worrying about the other four when they struck him.

"How about you—" Turner started to say something until he was interrupted.

"Yo, didn't I tell you to stay out of my store, thug life?" Doug, the manager of Burgers & Fries, came from behind the counter. Mateo turned around to see that another employee had followed Doug from behind the counter as well.

"Man, if you don't get out of my face, I'm gonna dribble you like a basketball," Turner threatened as he got in Doug's face.

Turner looked down at the shorter man and smirked. Turner only had a few inches on Doug, but the two of them wouldn't have been unevenly matched if they went toe-to-toe. Mateo was impressed that Doug held his ground.

"I guess you would get close enough to spit on me," Doug replied casually, drawing laughter from the growing crowd. "Now, I'm gonna tell you one more time: Get out of my restaurant or I'm calling the police. You don't work here anymore."

"Man, whatever." Turner rolled his eyes and gave his boys a signal to turn around. "I'm gonna see you around, Doug—and you, Mateo. Both of y'all gonna get it, 'cause it seems like neither one of you learned your lessons the first time."

Turner left, and he bumped into two city employees on his way out. One of the city employees grabbed the other to keep him from confronting Turner. Seeing the ruckus he caused, Turner laughed as he stepped into a large, white Nissan Titan. Turner and his goons were making their grand escape as the bass in the truck announced their departure.

It was ironic that iLoveMakonnen's "Tuesday" was shaking the truck on a Tuesday.

"Mateo, right?" Doug called his name, redirecting his attention to the goal at hand. Doug extended his hand to Mateo.

"Yes, sir," Mateo replied, giving him a firm grip.

"Come on to the back. I'll give you an interview and we'll see what we can do for you."

Doug took the application from the counter and looked over it as he headed to the back. Mateo turned to Sonic, who gave him a quick smile before handling an order. Mateo followed Doug to the back of the restaurant.

"So you one of Hammer's boys?" Doug shut the door behind them and gestured for Mateo to take a seat.

"Yeah, he's cool." Mateo noted the organized clutter. Applications and company papers floated over pens and paperclips. The large print wall calendar was buried beneath the mess.

"I like what that man is doing with his ministry at Heaven's Inn. I see you been with him for about eight months now."

"I appreciate him helping me get on my feet."

Mateo didn't know where the interview was going. He didn't expect to have to answer so many inquiries about Hammer.

"Man, look." Doug leaned forward over the desk. "Everyone needs a hand up and a hand out. I'm a convicted felon too. Been clean for eight years. Fortunately, in North Carolina, these felonies fall off after seven years. Man, the whole process is like serving time for a habitual felon in a state prison. Once the felonies dropped off, it took another year for the corporate managers to consider me for a shift leader position. I run this place now."

"Folks don't work at one job for eight years anymore," Mateo replied.

"Not unless they're felons," Doug replied. "Then we have to work ten times harder than the clean-cut guys to show we deserve a chance. And that's what I want to give you, a chance to get on a good foot and show that you can be one of the clean-cut guys."

That made Mateo smile. "So when do I start?"

"We'll get you in here on Friday so you can see how it goes down," Doug answered as he straightened up some of the papers and moved objects where they belonged. "This will give my boss time to make sure that your criminal background check is complete. If you've left off a felony or a misdemeanor, you need to come clean now, because if something else shows up, I won't be able to consider you for the job."

Mateo took the application back from Doug. He scanned it over, and he was confident that everything was truthful. Mateo handed the application back to Doug and shook the man's hand.

He felt like things were moving up. Two jobs meant he had no business getting in trouble. Mateo felt like he could save up enough money to get his own apartment and a car in six months to a year. In order to accomplish this, Mateo was going to focus on showing he could be a clean-cut guy too.

Chapter Fourteen

Do As I Say . . .

"I can't believe Xen's parents wilded out like that," Sarai said after the police came and escorted Xen and his parents out of the room.

Amirah looked at the school desks that were turned upside down and on the side. Two of the computer monitors found their home on the tile flooring, and pieces of the screen were found on the floor. Howard was picking up some of the other chairs, and Josephine was comforting Mrs. Ingle.

"I can't either. But some parents can't accept when their child needs help, and we did what we could by suggesting that he get a tutor for math and possibly take the remedial math course so that the *F* he's about to get in geometry doesn't damage his GPA." Amirah restated Mrs. Ingle's position, the one that had made Xen's mom try to snatch her up like they were on the street. His father would take out his smart phone and walk around Xen's mom like he was a cameraman, screaming "WorldStar!" every time she started yelling and screaming. Xen's mom lifted up four computer monitors and threw them to the ground as she ran her tirade before Howard and Sarai were able to block her path.

Xen looked embarrassed to see his parents acting like fools. He had his head down, and when his mom continued yelling and screaming at Mrs. Ingle and Howard, he was the one trying to get her to calm down.

After the room was as close to normal as possible, Mrs. Ingle told the group of Xen's teachers and school counselors that they would meet briefly on Monday morning to discuss a plan of action.

"I can stay a little while to make sure y'all get to your cars okay," Howard offered.

"I'm good," Josephine replied. "My husband is waiting on me, and we'll take Mrs. Ingle home." She gave Howard a hug and headed out the door. "Y'all call me to make sure you got home okay." Josephine hugged Sarai and Amirah and followed Mrs. Ingle outside.

"I can defend myself, but maybe you can be Amirah's bodyguard," Sarai suggested as she headed out the door.

"I'm fine, Howard, but thank you," Amirah replied.

"Please call Mrs. Ingle and make sure y'all let her know y'all got home okay," Sarai said at the door. "You know her and pastor are going to be worried sick about you until they hear from you."

"I know," Amirah confirmed. Being one of the older staff members, Josephine served as mentor to numerous teachers at Shiloh, Amirah included. "I promise I'll call."

Amirah watched as Sarai and later Howard exited her classroom. One of the janitors came in shortly afterward and swept up the mess and disconnected two of the monitors from the computers and took them to repair. Fortunately, her first class of the day was second period, which would be almost two hours after the school day started. Amirah had been assured that the monitors would be replaced before her class started on Wednesday.

Amirah sat at her desk and exhaled. She was still excited and slightly nervous after the unexpected confrontation with Xen's parents. Her spirit caused her to have discernment about his family, and she immediately bowed her head in prayer. After getting her message to the Lord, she lifted her head and went to shut down her laptop so that she could leave.

She noticed that the His-Love.com window was still open. She clicked the REFRESH button and noticed more friend requests from various women in her book club, including Sarai. SenorCristoAmor's profile showed that he was still on online.

I hope he's not one of those player types, Amirah thought. *But we're only talking online. It's not like I'm going to meet him in person.*

She reread his message—I love a woman who is loyal. That is a perfect attribute to a Proverbs 31 woman—before deciding to enter one of her own.

Thanks for the compliment. I'm waiting on God to send me a David-type of man because I believe that is the kind of man He has set aside for me.

Today's been a little crazy, but I know God will allow me to get through it. What kind of day are you having?

She pressed SEND and almost instantly wished she could delete the message.

Why did I tell him that? Amirah questioned herself. *I don't know this man and he does not know me. He doesn't need to know what kind of day I'm having.*

Amirah went through the HELP section to see if there was a way for her to retract the message, or edit it so that the part about her having a crazy day could be taken out. She didn't want to explain to a stranger how the mother of one of her students was on a warpath.

After seeing that her message wasn't retractable, she resolved to log out of her profile. Before she could click on the LOG OFF button, she noticed that SenorCristoAmor had sent a reply. Curious, she opened it.

***

"It's funny you said you had a crazy day. I had one too." Mateo spoke into the Samsung Galaxy, using the phone's speech-to-text feature as he left Burgers & Fries. He was a little excited because Doug had decided to try him out on a part-time basis, allowing him to work fifteen hours a week and giving him a quarter more than minimum wage. He was also thankful that Sonic had put in a good word for him as promised.

Mateo stepped into the Lincoln Continental that he had borrowed from Hammer. As he clicked on the seatbelt, he heard the buzzer and felt his phone vibrate, indicating he had a message from His-Love.com. He checked it and saw that AmirahIsLoyal had responded to him.

> David confronted his challenges head on. I figure this is what I'm going to have to do as well. I hope you are the type of man that doesn't run from obstacles.

"Why does she talk about David so much?" Mateo let his thought drift above the *WOW Gospel 2013* album playing in the background. Mateo Googled "David" and "The Bible." He'd heard a little about David, but didn't know much about him other than he was the kind of man who had a deep love and passion for following God.

I don't have that kind of relationship with God yet, Mateo admitted to himself. *I'm still a baby in Christ. She sounds like she wants a pastor or a deacon.*

Mateo looked up David's bio in Wikipedia and was impressed to hear about David's heroics. That David was a wise leader, and though he fell short of the glory of God and fell into temptation, David was a man after God's own heart.

> I can't be David, but I do strive to share many of his good characteristics.

Mateo put his phone in his pocket. He wasn't going to lie to impress Amirah. He didn't want to be vain, because he was trying to do something different. Before he got saved, Mateo liked women who were proud of their bodies, kept their facial appearances on point, and smelled good. It also helped if they were passionate like him.

As he drove down busy Patton Avenue in five o'clock traffic and headed back to Heaven's Inn, he saw a beautiful young lady walking down the street wearing a Subway uniform. She was the kind of woman his flesh was used to. His loins let him know they had been awakened, and he thought about the fact that it had been almost eight months since he'd known a woman intimately.

He pulled up to a stop light as he thought about how the last woman he "knew" was married and had him believing that he was possibly the father of her baby. Even though the baby wasn't his, he knew the job at Burgers & Fries was important so he could take care of himself. VaShawn Mitchell was singing about how his situation was turning around for him, and within seconds, the light turned green and Mateo's fleshly desires yielded to the will of God as he sought his way home.

Mateo felt the buzzing on his phone, but he decided not to text and drive. He'd read the message when he got home.

Chapter Fifteen

No Cookies

Amirah was wondering if she'd scared him off when she didn't get an immediate reply from SenorCristoAmor.

She had made it to her quaint, one-bedroom loft that she could barely afford with a teacher's salary in West Asheville, even if she didn't tithe. She had changed from the heels she was wearing to the comfortable New Balance sneakers and walked the three flights of steps. Upon opening her door, she inhaled the powerful scent of lavender, immediately calming her nerves.

She put the oversized bag that had papers that needed to be graded on the floor. She placed her laptop bag on the dining table, pulling out her Toshiba and connecting her charger to her laptop and the outlet on her wall. She hit the power button to restart her computer, and while her computer was booting up, she went into the kitchen and pulled out the vegetable tray with diced zucchini, squash, mushrooms, onions, red bell peppers, and spinach that she had planned to use for the homemade soup she wanted to have with her turkey sandwich and corn chips for dinner. This was a normal meal for her. She'd take it for lunch, and at times, eat it for breakfast.

Amirah wasn't too fond of cooking, a trait that she hoped didn't scare away any potential husband. Of course, she tried to bake cakes and whip up desserts, but to no such luck. The dough either got too hard to pour into the baking pans, or she failed to measure some ingredient correctly that would cause the savory treat not to rise to her expectations.

She had a Crock-Pot, and she knew how to cut meat and vegetables. And Amirah was patient. In three hours or less, her food would be ready, and in that time, she typically graded papers and got a good portion done of whatever book she was reading for the book club.

Amirah logged into His-Love.com, and she noticed that SenorCristoAmor had not responded to her last message. She opened it again so she could remember exactly what she typed.

What profession are you in? I'm a high school teacher.

She hoped that she hadn't gotten too personal, but then again, she didn't see the harm in finding out where the man worked. She'd already disclosed and shown through various pictures that she was a teacher and clearly, she enjoyed her job. She really didn't care where he worked, as long as it was legal. When she was younger, she was attracted to the bad boys, the kind of young men who lived dangerously and by the gun. A near death experienced changed her life and helped her maintain her course to finish her studies and become a teacher.

Admittedly, Mateo looked like the kind of men she used to attract. She could sense in her spirit that he was the type of man who had experience with the streets, but she also reasoned that if he hadn't made some changes in his life, he wouldn't be on His-Love.com. Plus, after she met him in person and got to know him better, if he wasn't the kind of godly man that she knew she needed in her life, she trusted the Lord would give her the discernment to leave him alone—and that this time, she would listen.

She was excited when she heard back from him hours later. In her mind, as she spread a thin layer of mayonnaise on her honey wheat bread and carefully folded the sliced turkey breast over the tomato and lettuce she'd already placed on the other slice of bread, he would reveal his true colors.

I work for a motel and I'm hoping to start a job part-time at a fast food restaurant.

Amirah didn't know if that was what she was supposed to expect or not. She had heard whispers in her church group that she was expected to marry a professional like herself. Asheville was a tourist town, a large one at that. Chances were, SenorCristoAmor probably made good money offering well-to-do travelers a quality service and clean places to rest their heads as they traveled from one place to another. Those types of concierges were tipped well for their knowledge and their professionalism when it came to pitching the best that Asheville had to offer. Amirah figured that he probably worked in a fast food restaurant in the winter months to pay the bills from December to April.

"If he works two jobs, he doesn't have time to be in these streets," Amirah told herself as she finished her plate and went back to the dining table.

Would you like to get up somewhere? Mateo quickly responded, not giving her time to respond. She was surprised at how blunt he was.

Was it too early to meet him? She asked herself. Amirah wasn't sure whether Mateo was trying to be blunt or aggressive, but even though they knew each other in passing, she didn't want to come off easy since they just started communicating through His-Love.com. She heard of some of the things people did when they met someone online, and when Amirah was out in the world, she was guilty of some of those things too. She knew the reputations girls had from meeting men from Facebook, MySpace or BlackPlanet. She wasn't a ho and not into doing some ho-ish activity either; yet she knew that at some time, they would have to spend time together in order for her to decide whether to take their relationship to the next level.

She needed to find out what Mateo's true intentions were. If this was a booty call, he definitely could forget it. The question was how could she tell? Of course, she expected His-Love.com to be different and not be a breeding ground for such behavior. Then again, Amirah was trying to live the simple Christian lifestyle. She wasn't about to give it up.

Where do you want to meet at? she typed. In Amirah's mind, if Mateo suggested a motel, then she knew that all he wanted was the precious jewel between her legs. She wouldn't dignify that with a response, and not only would she block him, but she would report him to the administrator of the site so that his profile would be removed.

If he suggested somewhere scandalous like a parking lot or at some vacant park, then she knew he wasn't just any kind of freak, but one of those super freaks that Rick James sang about.

She didn't get down like that.

Why don't we meet at Barnes & Noble at the Asheville Mall? Mateo suggested. And bring your laptop. You do have one, don't you?

Amirah could rock with that. She hoped that he really had an interest in reading and didn't suggest the bookstore because he thought that would be the best way to get into her pants. If nothing else, Amirah at least knew she could stick to literary questions when she first met him, and if the conversation steered toward certain erotic or sex-related books, she could leave him there and be safe.

Yes, I have a laptop, she typed, and I'll bring it with me. When do you want to meet?

Let's try tomorrow? Mateo quickly responded.

Tomorrow sounds perfect, she typed.

She looked over his pictures again. One thing she didn't like about His-Love.com was that they didn't ask personal features like height, weight, smoking or non-smoking status, or other physical questions. Fortunately for Amirah, she already knew he was shorter than her and had a respectable build, and as far as she knew, he didn't smoke. At least, he didn't smoke cigarettes.

I've decided to meet him one-on-one, she thought as she continued eating her meal. *I hope this isn't a mistake.*

Chapter Sixteen

Making Moves

"Ay, Sonic, you still got that laptop you trying to sell?" Mateo barged into Sonic's room.

"Yeah, man. I hope you not asking me to borrow it. I'm still trying to get a couple of bucks off it."

Mateo nodded his head. He knew that Sonic had been selling some of the more expensive gifts Turner had given him during their courtship. Sonic and Mateo had a system. Every so often, Sonic would list an expensive item on Craigslist, eBay, Half.com, or Amazon, or he would post the item in one of the local online papers. Potential buyers would speak with Sonic on one of the prepaid phones he had, and once it was agreed to make the transaction, Sonic would wait in a nearby gas station, convenience store, or at a church, while Mateo would exchange the products.

Turner knew that Sonic and Mateo were pawning off his love gifts, sometimes for pennies on the dollar. He'd sent his boys a couple of times to retrieve the items, but each time, a police officer would intervene. Even though both of them had restraining orders against Turner, the hood rat still found a way to come after them.

Sonic used the money from the sales to get rid of the tramp stamp tattoo that still haunted him. He'd already told Mateo he'd keep the other tattoos that decorated his skinny frame.

"I know you need the money. Look, I'm meeting Amirah at Barnes & Noble tomorrow," Mateo said.

"And you lied and told her you had a laptop?" Sonic cut him off.

Mateo scrunched his mouth and shook his head. "Give me more credit than that player. I asked her to bring hers. Besides, while we're talking, I'm going to fill out some job applications and stuff."

"Wait a minute." Sonic got on the floor and pulled out the metallic MacBook that he was selling.

"I'll give you five hundred for it." Mateo dug into his pockets and pulled out three Ben Franklins. "But I can only give you three hundred now. I just paid Hammer rent, and it will be the end of next month before I can give you the balance."

Mateo saw that Sonic was contemplating the offer. Then he reached out and took the money. "I'll let you have it for the three hundred. You do help me out without taking a dime, and if this is your best offer, then I'm not going to milk you."

Mateo gave Sonic a hug. Sonic was the closest thing to a best friend that Mateo had, and he looked at the taller man like the younger brother he never had. The gesture proved that their bond was becoming as thick as blood.

"So you and Amirah finally gonna have a sit-down?" Sonic sat back on his bed and pulled off the black-and-silver Burgers & Fries T-shirt. The shirts were very popular for their Christ-centered messages and grunge rock designs. Mateo realized that Marvel had a similar shirt as well. "I'm gonna wear that shirt Doug gave me a few days ago. I can't believe we gotta pay fifteen bones a piece for these jokers."

"Aw, don't be like that." Sonic changed into a red-and-white basketball jersey and some matching New Balance sneakers. "We gotta support the ministry that the owners of Burgers & Fries are trying to spread to the masses. A lot of people who wouldn't get the message otherwise hear it when they come to the restaurant. They get it when they listen to the Christian rock and the gospel rap that is rotated on the XM stations at each of the sit-down location, the T-shirts they sell, and the devotions they give away at the top of the month."

When the first Burgers & Fries opened in Asheville, Mateo had no idea that the chain restaurant was part of a ministry. He just went there for the grilled chicken sandwiches, the curly fries, and the frothy shakes that came in many fruit flavors. That was another guilty pleasure he gave into while on his self-imposed diet. It wasn't until he started working at Burgers & Fries that he realized the company really took the ministry seriously. Mateo was familiar with how many major companies claimed to have Christian principles and had seen a lot of local business owners advertise that their businesses were owned by Christians. He figured that was more a selling point to get into the older church ladies' pockets.

"Besides, we get the hottest black-and-silver shirts because those are only available to the employees. Everyone else can get their shirts in any color they want except black and silver."

Mateo thought about his last work day at the restaurant and saw how it made sense. He could wear any blue or black jeans he wanted, but he had to have on one of the Black and Silvers, as they called it. The alternative was to wear a solid black shirt and apron, which meant the employee worked in the back and cleaned the restaurant. Not wearing the Black and Silver could also cause the employee to get sent home early.

"Well, that's what's up. I appreciate you looking out with the laptop," Mateo said as he got up and headed to his room. "We got any sales lined up today?"

"Naw, but I got enough money saved up to get the U and the R off my back. Thanks, brother." Sonic was excited.

"No worries, brother. No worries. That's what we are here for, to look out for one another."

Mateo excitedly exited the room and headed down to his own room. He was beginning to like the idea of having his own laptop and not having to use the public ones in the business room. He'd played with it before when he was in Sonic's room last week, so he was already familiar with all the features. He'd been toying with the idea of getting an iPad, and that was what the money he'd given Sonic was saved for. With the laptop, he could do more.

Mateo realized that it wouldn't be a bad thing to be mobile. A part of him had a desire to start his own business, but he had no idea what kind of business he'd start. With his criminal record, he knew it would take forever for these unforgiving folks in the Blue Ridge Mountains to extend him a hand. He thought being fluent in Spanish, he'd be able to get a job easily, but that was not the case.

With the MacBook, Mateo got on the Web and downloaded the Kindle app from Amazon. He logged into his account and made sure he could see all of the books he "1-clicked" that were free or ninety-nine cents. He wanted to catch up on some of the Christian fiction books he'd started to get into, but he'd be lying if he were to say that he didn't read a little street lit or some suspense novels every now and then.

Mateo looked at the time at the bottom of the screen and knew he needed to be heading out the door. After making sure his book needs were taken care of, he turned off the MacBook and headed to his destination.

Chapter Seventeen

The "First" Night . . .

Amirah was pleased that the Barnes & Noble at the Asheville Mall had a moderate amount of business. The two-story store was exciting with Nook demonstrations and other electronics and gadgets on the first floor, as well as the entrance from the mall. The fiction novels and children's sections were an escalator ride away on the top floor.

She could smell the fresh coffee brewing and specialty sandwiches being made in the café near the entrance. Before she could look in that direction to see if a seat was available for her and Mateo, Amirah was captivated by the display that featured one of her favorite authors' new books. She quickly grabbed a copy and continued in the store.

She readjusted the computer bag and quickly scanned the area to see if Mateo was snooping around, looking for a book or a magazine. She was definitely interested in finding out what the brother liked to read, and she knew that in a matter of minutes, she would get to find out.

As she got closer to the café, she found a corner table toward the back. It had two vacant electrical outlets nearby, meaning she wouldn't have to use the extension cord she carried with her.

God is good, she thought as she set up the laptop and within seconds, accessed Barnes & Noble's WiFi connection. Once she pulled up the His-Love.com profile, that's when she saw him.

Mateo's goatee was razor sharp. She could tell he'd just freshened it up, and his tapered haircut highlighted the slim shape of his head. He was wearing a red "Jesus is Lord" T-shirt with baggy black pants and some black work boots. As Mateo walked toward her, she could see he was hiking his pants up every so often.

Not a thug, Lord. Please, not a thug. I can't do another wannabe gangster, her mind pleaded as he finally made his way to the table. She noticed the MacBook that looked like it had just come off the shelf at Best Buy. She looked closer and noticed he didn't have any jewelry on, but the cocoa butter lotion had a thick but pleasant scent that worked well with the pastries in the café.

"Amirah." Mateo's thick Spanish accent was noticed and caused a few heads to turn.

Amirah stood up to shake his hand. She was used to taller men. The height requirement used to be at the top of the impossible list of standards she used to judge whether a man was good enough to be with her. Admittedly, most of the "ideas and standards" were superficial and had nothing to do with qualities that made for a good husband.

Mateo didn't work a professional job—strike two.

Mateo wasn't one hundred percent black—strike three.

Mateo looked and acted like the thugs she despised—strike four, five, six, and so on.

"Yes, Mateo, good to see you," Amirah responded as they shook hands.

Mateo put his MacBook down and quickly walked around to pull out the chair for Amirah and help her get comfortable at the table.

"Thank you." She showed her gratitude. It had been a minute since Amirah had been shown an act of chivalry, and she didn't know how to take it. *He's not getting in my panties just because he pulled out a chair,* she promised herself as he walked around to his seat.

"You're welcome." Mateo hiked up his pants one more time and sat down. "And God is good, because even though I couldn't find my belt, He made sure I was on time for you anyway."

Mateo was a Christian—check.

As Amirah matured, she found this quality becoming more important. As she reflected on his mannerisms, she realized she'd never been with a Christian man before. Mateo may have presented himself as a dope man, but she could tell the only drug he was pushing was the Word of Christ.

"Can I get you something to eat or some coffee?" Mateo offered.

Amirah smiled. "No, thank you."

Mateo was a gentleman—check.

He not only offered to get her some nourishment, but she didn't have to pay for it. Amirah didn't mind being with a man low on funds, but she avoided them at all costs. Last thing she wanted was a man who couldn't take care of himself. The other piece to that was that he offered; he didn't insist.

"How were the students today?" Mateo started the conversation as he set up his MacBook.

"They were good, actually," Amirah answered. "I'm teaching some of them how to build spreadsheets and how to use them to maintain household budgets, track spending, and other real-life uses. I'm enjoying it because I know what they learn in my class they can use for a lifetime."

"That's what's up. I just got a second job so I can make some moves and improve my situation." Mateo continued, "I just want my own space. It would be nice to own a house one day."

She liked that Mateo had goals—check, and check. Mateo worked an honest job—check. That meant no more looking over her shoulder or fighting random side chicks who thought her man was their man and everything he worked for came with a check stub.

Amirah didn't encounter many men who had goals beyond hustling in the hood or trying to take something from someone that they didn't work for. She could work with ambition, even if it was taking baby steps. At least she had something to look forward to.

Mateo eyed the book she had just gotten from the front of the store. "Is this the new Victoria Christopher Murray book?" Mateo asked. "I thought it wasn't coming out until next week."

Mateo read fiction—check, check, check.

The last man Amirah had only knew how to read the statements on his bank accounts or the stock quotes in the business section.

"No, it came out this week." Amirah handed her copy to him. Mateo read the back cover and smiled.

"My mentor has a few copies of her books on his bookshelf in his office." Mateo handed the book back to her. "You remember Minister Stan Hammer?"

"I have heard of him. He owns the Christian Cab Company, right?" Amirah asked.

"Yeah, I work for its sister company, Heaven's Inn," Mateo confirmed with pride. "I just started working at Burgers & Fries, too, but only part time. I appreciate all Hammer is doing for me, but eventually, I want to be independent. It's not like I freeload off of him, because he charges for the room. I help Hammer with Heaven's Inn as well, and he helps keep me on the right path. I'm trying to talk him into letting me drive one of the cabs, but that's a never-ending conversation. Anyway, you should come and hear him speak at Guiding Light Ministries."

Mateo not only attended a Bible-based church, but he was under the leadership of an incredible man of God and was making strides to getting his life with Christ right—check, check, check, check, check.

Hammer's reputation for working with guys from the streets preceded him, and wherever Mateo was at under his leadership, Amirah was willing to compromise to see if he was truly the one.

This date was off to a great start in her eyes.

"I'll have to come by and hear him speak. Usually when I visit, I hear Pastor Cummings," Amirah confirmed.

"You're a member of Gospel United Christian Center with Pastors Slate and Hughes, right?" Mateo impressed her.

And he knows of my pastor. God, you are moving incredibly fast, Amirah thought. Then she remembered that Mateo had visited her church a few times before. It wasn't a huge secret that most of the teachers of Shiloh Christian Academy attended the church where Pastor Ingles preached. It wasn't a prerequisite for their job, but it made praying together and working together and trying to live life as Christians together so much easier.

"I'm supposed to be doing some work with them soon. I just became part of this ministry group called Street Disciples. It's based in Winston-Salem, but the Asheville group is based at Guiding Light."

Yes, God! Amirah cheered to herself. *Yes!* "I didn't know you were a member of the Street Disciples."

"The group was founded by a man named Rahliem Victor, and he got the vision for the group while serving the last few years of his prison sentence. It was designed for the 'world's misfits' to come not only get the Word, but to in turn, *Go therefore and make disciples of all the nations, baptizing them in the name of the Father and the Son and the Holy Spirit,* as we are commanded in Matthew 28:19."

The more Mateo talked, the less she saw him in the thug image he portrayed and saw the future in him as the man of God he was destined to be. She thought it would be interesting to date a guy who was at the beginning of his spiritual journey. Even if that date didn't work out, she could see herself hanging with him long-term and studying the Word with him.

"So where do you teach?"

"I teach at Shiloh Christian Academy."

"I'm glad they did something positive with that place," Mateo interjected. "When I went to that school, it was Shiloh High School, and we had a rap for being the bad school."

"Really, when did you graduate?"

"I graduated with the Class of 2005, the best class."

Amirah chuckled and shook her head. She had started teaching during the 2011-2012 school year, only two years after Pastor and Mrs. Ingle applied for the charter and got grants from several churches to help take over the school.

"You want to get something to eat?" Mateo offered again. "I was going to get a chocolate chip Frappuccino and a cantuccini."

"A cantuccini?" Amirah was confused. She'd never heard of that treat before.

"It's another word for biscotti."

"Yes, I would like one. I've never tried the Frappuccinos here before, and I do like biscotti. Can I get a chocolate one?" Amirah asked.

"Coming right up."

As Amirah was getting ready to go into her purse and pull out a few dollars, Mateo was already making his way to the short line. She watched as he pulled his pants over his black boxer shorts. Amirah was willing to give him a pass on the pants today but trusted that Mateo would find a belt in time for their next date. Or she'd have to buy him one. She was willing to do that.

"I lost some weight since I got these pants about a year ago," Mateo offered as he returned and placed her biscotti and Frappuccino before her. "And I'm upset that I couldn't find my belt. This is embarrassing."

"No worries," Amirah assured him.

"You don't seem like the kind of a sister that would be into bad boys," Mateo suggested. "I used to be a thug's thug, but since giving my life to God, I still struggle with that. Changing twenty-seven years of attitudes and ways of life has been a huge adjustment for me, and sometimes I don't get it right, but every time I fall short, I find a way to get back up again. And if that doesn't work, I can always depend on Hammer to give me a swift kick on my bottom."

Amirah didn't mean to, but she chuckled at that last line. She could picture the minister flinging Mateo around like he was disciplining a toddler.

"I'm glad I get to see you laugh." Mateo laughed with her.

"I'm sorry. I really didn't mean to—"

"No," Mateo interrupted. "I'm good. I think it's sexy when a woman can smile and let her guard down. I may have been a player in my past life, but in this one, I don't bite."

Amirah almost struggled to down her Frappuccino. She hadn't expected him to reveal his experience. She wasn't a prude, but she wasn't used to men being frank without being vulgar in that regard.

"Well, that is good to know." It had taken a while for Amirah to respond. She looked Mateo over again and smiled. "So what books do you like to read?"

"I'm not going to lie; I read magazines mostly. I'm into fitness, so *Men's Health, Muscle & Fitness*. I also like *Money, Entrepreneur* and *Black Enterprise*. I read *Sister 2 Sister* and *Essence* too."

"I can respect that," Amirah responded. "I like faith fiction and some suspense novels."

"I get into ReShonda Tate Billingsley, Victoria Christopher Murray, and E. N. JOY, but when I was locked up, I started by reading John Grisham and De'nesha Diamond and K'wan too. Big fan of his."

The crime novelist's name was a shock, and interestingly, a guilty pleasure of hers as well. She was surprised they had favorite books in common. "*Animal* fan?" she asked.

"Of course."

Amirah and Mateo had an intense conversation about the series and found that they shared many common views. She was happy that she was able to talk to a man about books for once, not just asking him to buy one for Christmas, Valentine's Day, anniversaries, and birthdays.

After their conversation, they agreed to meet at David's Table. Mateo had never been there, and she figured he could benefit from meeting some other Christians their age that were handling their business. Mateo got up and helped Amirah out of her seat and it confirmed what she was feeling.

As they left the store, Amirah decided for herself that Mateo was a good man, and she'd be more than happy to give him another chance.

Chapter Eighteen

. . . of Terror

Amirah was surprised at how her date at Barnes & Noble went. It was clear that Mateo's primary objective wasn't to get in her pants, and that he wanted what she wanted, which was to take it slow and to feel each other out.

Amirah never had a man she could talk about Christ and books with before—check, check, and check. She was looking forward to conversations and revelations.

So what if Mateo looked like he was in the latest rap video and he probably smoked weed in his spare time? At least she thought he did, judging from the way his fingernails were trimmed and kept at the perfect length to hold a blunt at the tip. He'd only been saved for less than a year, so Mateo was allowed some passes. After all, God gave them all passes and forgiveness on a regular basis.

"Give me my computer, chump," she heard a booming voice yell behind her.

Amirah turned around and saw a six foot four, evenly stacked, French vanilla–colored man snatch the MacBook from Mateo's arm.

"Give me my laptop, Turner!" Mateo yelled as he got in his chest.

They weren't evenly matched, and Amirah noticed the height disparity between the two men. Mateo's imperfections were showing. He'd resort to violence to settle an issue, and he could curse like a sailor. Her ears thought her mind was playing tricks on her, because just a few minutes ago, the man fighting for his laptop was quoting scripture and having an intelligent conversation about books.

She walked toward the confrontation with intentions of pulling Mateo away. She was hoping that cooler minds would prevail.

"Yo, dawg, why you always messing with me?" Amirah heard Mateo ask.

She'd grabbed Mateo's arm to pull him away from the confrontation, and he snatched it back. She didn't like that.

Both men dashed outside, and Amirah was right on Mateo's heels.

Mateo got back in Turner's face and tried grabbing the MacBook from him. Turner used his height advantage and rotated the laptop between both of his hands while mean-mugging him. "'Cause you're always in my way!" she heard Turner's voice boom.

Turner continued to taunt him, calling him several curse words and offensive slurs that attacked both his dark skin tone and Hispanic heritage.

"Just give me my MacBook back." Mateo stopped trying to get the computer back. He stood there waiting patiently.

"I bought it!" Turner yelled as he got in Mateo's face.

Amirah could see Mateo clenching his fists at his side. She didn't like that either. The last thing she wanted was for Mateo to backslide. She didn't know what his deal was with Turner, and she didn't care. She wanted the man she had a wonderful date with back.

"Mateo!" Amirah yelled, hoping that calling his name might encourage him to give up the fight. The MacBook could be replaced; his life on this side could not.

Mateo turned to say something to her. Before the words could escape his lips, Turner took advantage of the distraction and sucker-punched Mateo, sending him flying a few feet back and landing him on his back. Turner quickly passed the MacBook to one of his cronies, who'd come upon the fray. Like a lion capturing his prey, Turner pounced on Mateo's frame and sent a few Floyd Mayweather—like blows to his head.

Amirah watched in horror as the beautiful picture God created was being destroyed. Mateo's head was bouncing like a basketball being dribbled. His blows were coming up too short and were no match for the much bigger and stronger nemesis.

Amirah ran up to them in hopes that she could try to save Mateo or help him in some way. Before she could get close, Turner scooped Mateo up and body-slammed him on the pavement. She heard a crack and saw Mateo's eyes roll to the back of his head. His body was shaking violently. The impact of his body hitting the pavement induced a seizure.

Amirah screamed, and within a few seconds she saw black 1995 Toyota Camry pull up and the passenger side door opened. Turner flashed them both the bird and smirked when he hopped inside. The violent rap music drowned out what she was sure were profanities being hurled in their direction by Turner. She pulled out her smart phone, hoping to capture a picture of the license plate, but the car sped off before she could snap the picture.

Several onlookers were rushing to Mateo, and she called 911.

"9-1-1—" the operator tried to recite her introduction but was hastily interrupted.

"We need an ambulance at the Asheville Mall right outside of the Barnes & Noble!" Amirah yelled, cutting off the dispatcher. "We just saw a man get brutally attacked, and it looks like he's having a seizure."

Amirah continued to fill in as much detail about Mateo as she could. She decided to wait until the ambulance arrived. When Mateo's body stopped shaking, she turned him to his side and looked for his wallet that she knew he put in his back pocket. When she didn't find it, she checked his front pocket. The wallet was missing too. Amirah didn't remember seeing Turner taking it, but she reasoned it could've fallen out of his pocket when Mateo paid for their order or when they started their conflict. Amirah had hoped that Turner hadn't snatched the wallet from him, but she didn't put it past him either.

Amirah didn't know what Mateo's dealings with Turner were, but clearly the two men had a violent past, and she felt guilty for her role in Turner getting the best of Mateo. When the ambulance arrived, she gave them as much information as she could, and she asked them to let her follow them, because if nothing else, she knew who Hammer was, and that would be the man who would be able to sort out this mess.

Mateo awakened to Bible verses and prayers being said simultaneously. At first, he was sure that he was in heaven; but he saw no sign of Jesus and had no flashback of how he'd lived his life. There were no voices praising God or heavenly sounds. And he knew he wasn't in hell, because his spirit wasn't on fire.

Then he heard Hammer's voice. He could also hear Pastor Cummings talking to his mother. Her sobs nearly broke his heart. Mateo hadn't kept up with her or his siblings the way he should have, and the last place he wanted them to see him was in the hospital.

Mateo cursed himself. He couldn't believe he'd let Turner get the best of him again. He could barely open his eyes, but he could feel the needles in his arms, and he could tell the hospital had him on some form of anesthesia.

Mateo struggled to open his eyes, and he couldn't move his arms or his legs. He vaguely remembered how he got into the hospital, but due its distinctive disinfectant smell and the beeping of the monitor, he was sure he was hooked up to a slew of devices.

Mateo was sure that the morphine he was injected with was sedating him. He felt higher than he did when he used to smoke weed. Mateo hadn't felt like this since he and one of his old friends did some nasty things with a group of women in the back room of a strip club.

He couldn't identify any other voices. Mateo figured he wasn't dead because he could feel himself struggling to breathe. He wondered if he had been connected to a machine that helped him to breathe. He hoped he wasn't paralyzed, because he did not want to live the rest of his life like this.

"Son," Mateo heard his mother ask, "can you hear me?"

Mateo nodded his head. He was happy that he could finally move a body part.

"Doctor, he's moving!" Hammer shouted.

He could feel the excitement in the room as he continued to shake his head. Mateo didn't feel strong enough to speak, and he couldn't move his lips. At least he didn't think he could.

Mateo could hear a lot of things ruffling and moving, and he knew something was going on. All of a sudden, he couldn't feel anything again. He couldn't hear God, but he knew that something was going down. And he wasn't ready to die.

Chapter Nineteen

We Are Not Ashamed

Amirah sat in a daze in her classroom. She had considered calling out but didn't have enough paid time off, and she couldn't afford to have a substitute's pay come out of her pocket.

Thankfully, her class hadn't started yet when Mrs. Ingle walked in. "Amirah," she called out in concern.

Amirah snapped out of it and turned her head to face Mrs. Ingle. "Yes, ma'am."

"Are you sure you are okay?" Mrs. Ingle asked. "I heard about what happened over the weekend, and I'm sorry that you knew the young man involved in that incident."

"We had a good date, too," Amirah answered. She couldn't play off her feelings for him if she wanted to.

Mrs. Ingle grabbed Amirah's hand without warning, closed her eyes, and bowed her head. Amirah immediately did the same. "Father God, we come before you now, praying healing mercy and grace on that young man—what's his name, dear?"

"Mateo," Amirah stuttered. "Mateo Valdez."

"We pray for healing mercy and grace for Mateo Valdez and his family as they go through this time of need. Lord, you are Jehovah Rapha, and we need you to heal Mateo's mind, body, and spirit in the way you see fit. Bring about the spirit of comfort and forgiveness for this family, and we pray for mercy and healing for the family of the young man who inflicted pain on Mateo. Help them know your love if they should not know you, and encourage them to stay strong in you and your Word if they do. God, we praise you, honor you, and magnify you, and it is in your Son Jesus Christ's name we pray. Amen," Mrs. Ingle prayed.

"It is well." The utterance of these three words caused Amirah's spirit to heal and to feel at peace. She smiled for the first time that day, and remembering what Mateo said about her smile made her want to smile even more. "I'm thankful you prayed with me." Amirah reached out to Mrs. Ingle for a hug.

"That is what we do, child," Mrs. Ingle replied when she hugged her back. "That is what we do. This is Shiloh Christian Academy, and in this house and at this school, we will praise and serve the Lord."

Amirah knew Mrs. Ingle meant that. She heard the bell ring, and she quickly grabbed some tissue to wipe away any tears. She did not want her students seeing her in distress.

"We are teachers," Mrs. Ingle said.

"Our duty is to teach the youth," Amirah replied when Xen walked in.

Mrs. Ingle found her exit as more students walked in.

"Ms. Dalton, I apologize for how my parents acted the other day," Xen offered as other students were putting their bags at their desk and logging into the computers.

"It's all right." Amirah accepted his apology.

"I also have this to give you." Xen pulled out an envelope and handed it to her. "I was saving this so I can get a car, but I feel responsible for my mother destroying the monitors."

Amirah could feel the weight of the money in the envelope and handed it back to him. "You keep this for now, and we'll talk with Mrs. Ingle and decide what she wants to do."

"I need somewhere to stay—after school—so I can study for my math class. I know if I go into the library, I'm just going to get in trouble, and if I go home, I'll be sneaking over to my girlfriend's house." Xen didn't need to paint a picture for Amirah to get what he was saying. "But if I can stay after school in your class while you are tutoring other students or when you conduct your FBLA meetings, I will have a safe place to study and no one will bother me."

"What about How—I mean Mr. Amber? What about his room?" Amirah suggested.

"It's football season, and he hardly has time. And the other math teachers won't help me."

Amirah found that hard to believe, but she'd deal with that another time. "I will say yes for now, but only temporarily. I'll see about getting Mr. Amber to help you too. But for now, bring your math books and whatever other classwork you are struggling with, and I will provide a safe place for you to study. Now go to your seat so I can start class."

"Yes, ma'am."

Xen walked to his computer and soon, everyone was logged in and she was ready to start class. She showed them the topic for the day, and she briefly explained how their lesson was going to meet the objective she had.

Xen wasn't struggling in her class, but he did need help keeping his fingers on the home row keys. The daily exercises were helping, and Amirah felt that by the end of the semester, Xen would be typing fast with a little practice.

"Did the little street boy get out of the hospital yet?" Marjorie asked as she sat at the table, pulling out the trade paperback copy to *After the Feeling* by T. N. Williams.

"That's cold, Marjorie," Amirah pressed as she pulled out her own copy of the book. She could see that she was not as far into the book as Marjorie and that Marjorie had already highlighted the book with pink and green highlighters so she could identify passages for their upcoming discussion.

"No, it's not," she continued as she turned the pages of the book, pulling out her green highlighter to cover another passage. "I'm not at all happy that the boy body-slammed him in front of the Barnes & Noble like that. I'm thinking about your health and safety and what else Turner Mustafa Spartenburg may have up his sleeve."

"Oh, thank God you are okay." Aja and a few other members of the book club rushed Amirah as if she had returned from a trial by fire. As crazy as Turner was, many in the group believe she had.

"I'm fine. It's Mateo who could really use your prayers right now. He needs to heal and get better so he can continue working on being the man God has called him to be," Amirah affirmed.

She had hoped that the other women weren't as judgmental as Marjorie. She knew they could be outright anal in their treatment of the characters in the books they read and the developmental skills the author used to bring their stories to life. Mateo wasn't a book, and she didn't want him analyzed like one.

"Well, before we start the meeting," Sarai said, "let us all touch and agree with Amirah and pray for Mateo right now." Sarai helped Amirah get situated in the chair. "Reach out to two women right now, and everyone else, grab a hold of our sister Amirah."

Amirah was amazed at how quickly the women banded around her and touched her shoulder, her forearm. A sister had her palm on the crown of her head.

"Father God, the ladies of the Essence of Prayer Book Club come to you right now with a Word of prayer for Mateo." Sarai interrupted her prayer when she realized she'd forgotten Mateo's last name.

"Mateo Valdez," Marjorie chimed in.

"Yes, Mateo Valdez, Lord. We are praying for Mateo Valdez, and we are not just asking for you to be the doctor and the Father we know you to be in the hospital, but we ask that you move his heart in kindness, so that he may forgive Turner for the damage he's inflicted on him. And God, while we're at it, we ask for healing for Turner as well, and forgiveness so that before he leaves this earth, he repents of his sins and comes to know you, oh Father God. We pray for all gangsters and heathens, be they behind bars or in the streets. Deliver them from the traps Satan has set before them, and it is in your Son Jesus Christ's name we pray. Amen."

"Amen," the group of women said.

"It is well," Amirah whispered as she wiped tears from her eyes.

"This is how a book club meeting is supposed to start," Sarai pointed out. "We read and heavily advocate for godly books on Facebook and Twitter, but who are we if we can't stand before our sister and let her know that we will pray with and for her in her time of need?"

"Amen," Aja chimed in.

"Let me turn this over to Marjorie before I start preaching a sermon in here." Sarai took a seat next to Amirah and pulled out her iPhone. "Y'all, I fell asleep in bed reading again, and my husband rolled over on my Kindle."

"Again?" Aja asked from behind them.

"Yeah, girl, this is the third one. I'm making him get me the Kindle Fire after we get our bills paid next month. I heard the device can do a lot of things, and I can keep up on His-Love.com as well."

"Speaking of His-Love.com . . ." Marjorie brought their conversation to the floor. "Anyone else besides Amirah and Aja have a His-Love.com update they want to share?"

"You mean I can't talk about my husband joining the networking group and trying to be everyone's friend?" Sarai asked, rolling her eyes but trying to keep from laughing.

"No," many of the women of the group responded and then busted out in laughter.

"Darn." Sarai snapped her fingers and joined in the laughter.

"Well, I'll go," Marjorie said. Everyone sat up quickly and leaned a little closer to hear what their leader had to say. "Y'all are dead wrong," she said, which made everyone laugh again. "I think I may have found someone. We are going at a tortoise's pace, but I'm all right with that. God's plan is God's plan."

"Amen," the group responded.

Amirah listened as Marjorie talked about her much older man, and she wondered who he could be. She noticed that more men were registering, to the delight of some of the women, but she didn't investigate. She'd enjoyed her time talking to Mateo via their chat sessions up to their date. She was making the most of things by spending time with him in the hospital.

Amirah felt good that they prayed not only for Mateo, but for Turner too. She didn't know Mateo well, but it was good to know that she was part of a group that cared for everyone's soul. Regardless of what he'd done, Amirah was praying for Turner too.

Chapter Twenty

Jesus to the Back

Mateo was out of the hospital in a matter of days, which was a blessing considering his injuries. He suffered a severe seizure, a broken rib, and other bruised internal organs and spine.

He was home resting, listening to Pastor Cummings' sermon on forgiving your enemies. He enjoyed hearing the older, Southern Baptist–style preacher deliver a fire-and-brimstone conviction that brought him to tears.

In the back of his mind, Mateo wondered if—no, when—he should get even with Turner. That body slam knocked him out, and he still couldn't remember what happened that caused the man to scoop him up and toss him around like a rag doll. Mateo never knew so much pain in his life. This was worse than being shot.

How was he going to pay for his second trip to the hospital in a matter of months? Turner and his boys were responsible for him being shot, and now he had to take two thousand milligrams of ibuprofen every four hours to attempt to ease the pain caused by the trauma to his back.

Mateo was angry and rightfully so. His MacBook was gone, and so was the three hundred dollars he'd given Sonic. He was happy that Sonic was able to put the money to use removing two more letters from that satanic bastard's name from his back. Still, that didn't ease the pain he felt.

His smooth stroll was now slowed down a few paces. At times, Mateo thought his mind was blanking out, and he couldn't control the sudden shaking of his arm. He knew what God said, but he would be lying if he didn't admit that he wanted to kill Turner and ensure that he'd die a gruesome death. The old him would've had the spirit to do it; but Pastor Cummings' message and God's strong but humbling voice were weighing on his heart, cautioning him that forgiveness was the best answer.

Mateo walked past the mirror, and he saw his slowly healing face. He could see remnants of the black eyes he had. His lips reminded him of a botched lip augmentation. Instead of nice and full, they looked like water balloons on the verge of bursting. His right cheek was still puffy and slightly red. The only thing Mateo thought looked decent on him was his hair—and the way Mateo was feeling, even that was in question.

I'm gonna kill that fool, Mateo vowed and cursed himself for not being the better man in the fight. He didn't care that Turner had a height and muscle advantage over him. Mateo cared about winning.

Mateo went under his bed and pulled out a small black box, one that was slightly smaller than the shoe box his size nines came in. He took out his keys, and the small brass lock key stood out like a sore thumb. He used that key to open the box, and he pulled out a shiny black Glock. He'd stolen it years ago from a wannabe thug, when he used to run a group trying to initiate locals into the MS-13 gang. They thought they'd get put on if they committed a rash of crimes and terrorized the city of Asheville, but they were no match for the city's police force and the county sheriff's department.

Every year he promised himself that he'd get rid of the gun, but someone or something would cause an anger to rise in him, and he'd keep it in the box . . . just in case.

"Ay, Mateo." Sonic burst in with his key, and Marvel wasn't too far behind. The thought crossed Mateo's mind to hide the gun, but what was the use? The expression on Sonic's face revealed that he saw it, and Marvel turned his eyes away quickly. He'd seen it too.

"Mateo, come on, man," Sonic voiced as he begged Mateo for the gun by extending his hand. "We've come so far on this journey with Christ."

"Relax. I'm not going to kill him today." Mateo checked the clip to see if it was full. "But I can't promise I won't try if I see him tomorrow."

"Mateo, think about Amirah," Marvel suggested.

Mateo thought about her. The horror he heard in her voice as she called for help. The agony he saw on her face for the brief second he was able to look her in the face before his body took that descent. Mateo thought about her long and hard. He wanted to be her man, and he wanted to be able to protect her.

Turner was a cancer, and he spread his filth to his victim's families, friends, and whoever else they loved. In the back of his mind, Mateo realized that in order for Turner to have known he was at the Barnes & Noble, he had to have been following Mateo or had one of his goons trailing him. They had probably been watching him for some time.

If they were watching him, who was to say they weren't watching Amirah? True, they'd just met, but did someone follow him inside the store and see him sitting with her? They'd been in Barnes & Noble for more than two hours, long enough for someone to take a few pictures of the two of them together and trail her to her house, or to the school where she worked. That meant the students she taught, as well as everyone at Shiloh Christian Academy, were in danger. Whoever was being paid to watch Mateo was probably watching the motel, too, looking to see who was coming to visit and how long they were staying.

Turner was the vindictive type. This past spring, he'd hounded Sonic for leaving him and harrassed Hammer for stepping in. Turner hunted both of them down until Mateo, Sonic, and Hammer ended up getting shot.

"This has to stop, and Turner needs to be stopped," Mateo finally voiced. All the thoughts battled in his head, and this conclusion for revenge won over his heart by a landslide.

"I know I can't stop you." Sonic lifted up his shirt and showed him his bullet wounds. "Let me remind you what revenge did to me. Think about that before you walk out of here with that gun."

Sonic pointed to each of the bullet wounds he had received over the years of being in Turner's company and when he tried to leave. Then he lifted his right leg to show off the one there. That did nothing but infuriate Mateo more and motivate him to find Turner and put an end to his breathing.

"You're not the only one walking around with miscellaneous holes in your body." Mateo brushed past Sonic as he put the Glock behind him in his waistband. "I got somewhere to be. Close my door when you leave."

The looks on Marvel's and Sonic's faces did not go unnoticed by Mateo. His plans weren't to shoot Turner at that very moment. For him, the Glock evened the odds and gave him leverage he didn't necessarily have. Mateo didn't want to admit that the odds of him beating Turner in a fair fight were slim to none.

In his mind, he felt that if he had to face Jesus and talk to him about the gun in question, he'd have the perfect answer: "Look at him and look at me."

Satan would've accepted that answer. God wouldn't, and Mateo knew it.

Mateo took out the keys to the Lincoln that he was still "borrowing" from Hammer and pressed the button to unlock to the door. He still couldn't get Hammer to let him drive one of the cabs, but after running an errand for the old man, he never asked for the keys back and told Mateo to keep gas in it until he needed it.

Mateo hadn't expected he confrontation between him and Sonic and Marvel. Now he knew it was just a matter of time before Hammer confronted him about the gun. Having the weapon was a direct violation of his rental agreement and could cause him to gct kickcd out of thc motel and lose his job. With a few more years before his felonies fell off, Mateo legally couldn't possess a gun of any kind either. Mateo knew the risks, but he couldn't afford not to bear arms. He was willing to risk it all, including the extreme possibility that he'd be right back in prison if he was caught with the Glock.

Mateo didn't have to go to work right away, and he didn't have a friend that would lead him into trouble that he could hang with. Finding a new place to hide the gun wasn't an option either.

And going after Turner wasn't a smart move, at least not without a plan.

Mateo needed time to decide what he was going to do and how he was going to keep the gun and everything he needed to survive. As he pulled out of the parking lot of Heaven's Inn, he didn't have a clear direction on where he was going, but he knew he needed to be on the road to somewhere.

Chapter Twenty-one

Provider . . . Comforter

Amirah was thankful that Mateo was out of the hospital. She was concerned because she could tell that Mateo's spirits were down. She offered to cook and clean for him, but he refused. Amirah didn't press trying to meet up with him because she knew he was recovering and figured he wanted some privacy. She did the only thing she could do for him: pray and check on him periodically.

The backlash from her show was dying down too, and she was thankful for that. The memes continued to be spread throughout social media. The good thing was that the outside interest from those who didn't seem to want Christ in their hearts seemed to vanish. Amirah couldn't remember who'd done something foolish in the past week, but between them and the prejudiced people slandering President Obama for filth, she'd been given a break.

Amirah surprised herself and others because she'd been able to do the show after watching Mateo's brutal attack. She used her platform to talk about senseless violence, and the heartwarming heart-to-heart talk with a paraplegic that used to think guns and violence were cool changed her perspective on life and God. She wished Mateo could've been at the taping, but Amirah told herself she'd get him a copy of the show and watch it with him later.

At the school, she lived up to her promise and let Xen stay in her room for a couple of minutes after school. She and Howard had been e-mailing back and forth throughout the day so that they could work out an arrangement where Howard would provide tutoring since he was Xen's math teacher.

Xen had made good on his promise to be a better student. He was more focused in class and sought out help from her and his classmates. Amirah got reports on how Xen was turning in his work on time in other classes and his grades were improving.

Once Xen left the room, she made sure all of the computers and laptops were secured. She pulled out her cell phone and called Mateo. It had been a while since she'd seen him, and previous attempts to reach him by phone were unsuccessful.

"Hey, Amirah." Mateo answered on the second ring.

"It's good to hear your voice. Where are you?" Amirah put her laptop in her bag and got her nightly papers to grade together.

"I'm on my way to work, but I wanted to stop by Shiloh and see you for a minute."

"Umm—" Amirah stammered, at loss for words because his request was unexpected.

"I'm not trying to stay at the school. Actually wanted to make sure you got home safely." Mateo offered, "Maybe I can tell you more about what happened when our date ended."

Deep down, Amirah wanted to know if Mateo was still a thug, and if he was, what he was into. She really wanted to believe that he'd left his past in the past and was walking forward in Christ. Everything on his His-Love. com profile and in their conversation indicated that he had. His run-in with Turner would suggest otherwise.

Amirah couldn't be around anyone like that. Not with the life she was living and the people she was involved with. She had her church family and her students and their families to consider. She couldn't afford to take that risk.

"Well, I'm on my way to my church's leadership group. If I leave now, we'll be an hour early. Why don't we meet there?"

"A'ight. I'll see you in a couple of minutes."

When Amirah made the suggestion, she was hoping that maybe a few people would be in the church. Once she got to the parking lot, she realized that she had forgotten the youth choir had rehearsal that day. They weren't just preparing for Sunday's service but for the youth conference that Amirah was taking them to in a few weeks.

She was pleased to see that Mateo was wearing his black-and-silver Burgers & Fries shirt and blue jeans and that he wasn't stopping to pull up his pants every time he turned around. The big *3:16* belt buckle could be seen from a few hundred feet away.

This is a start.

As she looked at him closely, she could see the scars on his face were healing; his limp, more pronounced. She wondered if the man would need a cane in the near future.

"Hey." He managed to smile.

She smiled back. "Hey, Mateo. I'm glad you came here."

"Come on now. I always make it to church." Mateo leaned in for a hug. Amirah obliged, and then she motioned for him to follow her to a side entrance to the church. From there, they entered into a small pre-school classroom. "Just have a seat at the table over there."

"Thanks."

Amirah made sure to lock the door behind her, and she walked to the other door and locked it too. She looked around and could picture the preschoolers she used to care for singing "Jesus Loves Me" and other songs. Their art projects decorated the room, along with scenes from the Bible.

"His name is Turner," Mateo said once Amirah gave him her attention.

Her mouth dropped open. "That's Turner Mustafa Spartenburg?"

Mateo nodded his head. Amirah had heard all of the stories about the infamous Turner and how he was trying to be the big man of the Smoky Mountains. Rumors of the dead bodies he left in Asheville, Hendersonville, Greenville, Spartanburg, Knoxville, and Johnson City made him a terror in three states. Turner roamed free because he had law enforcement agents on his payroll, and the region in general wasn't attractive enough for the real thugs in Winston-Salem, Charlotte, or Nashville to take over. It didn't help that he had access to his family's status on the other side of the law.

Up until that moment, Turner had been a legend in her mind.

"How do you know Turner?" she asked.

"He and Sonic used to be lovers," Mateo admitted.

Amirah had also heard of Turner's voracious sexual appetite. The pictures of him being naked with scantily-clad females were constantly talked about by the students in the school and the church. Videos of his sexual exploits frequently hit the net, and he was talked about so much that major gossip bloggers ran stories on him from time to time. Surprisingly, the rumors that he also messed with men didn't deter women from pursuing him either.

Admittedly, if Turner had been under the right direction, he could have been a highly pursued male model. He had the perfect height, and the way his muscles protruded through his clothes gave him an action figure–like quality. Turner belonged in the *G. I. Joe* and *Transformer* movies, or he could've been a WWE superstar. The combination made him dangerous.

Amirah admitted to herself that physically, Turner was more the type of man she preferred. While he wasn't dark, he was tall, and he had great facial features and the ideal body type; but when she thought about the baggage he was carrying, she wised up and realized why God had the man pursue the woman.

"Wow," Amirah finally replied, digesting it all.

"Sonic and I got saved around the same time. Hammer has been mentoring both of us, along with a guy named Marvel, trying to keep us in the Word and out of trouble. Remember when Hammer got shot?"

Amirah remembered hearing something like that, but she was not able to follow up on what happened. The discernment in her spirit let her know that Mateo was telling the truth. She remembered the members of her church praying for Hammer and taking up a collection to help cover his medical expenses a few months ago. "Yeah."

"Well, the reason Hammer got shot was because Sonic had had enough of Turner, and he no longer wanted to live the lifestyle he was living with him. Sonic wanted to live for Christ. Hammer helped Sonic get back this new green Kia Rio he owned, and when Turner confronted him about it, Hammer beat him up.

"So we helped Sonic trade in his old car for the Toyota he has now so that he could stay low key and of course, I was teaching him how to defend himself, because I don't believe anyone should be a victim of domestic violence.

"Turner and his crew caught us slipping at the motel one night, and while his goons jumped me, he confronted Hammer and Sonic and he shot them both. I got shot too; hence the reason I walk with a limp."

Amirah remembered them talking about the shooting at Heaven's Inn. It was a big story because of who Hammer was to Guiding Light Ministries. There were concerns about the ministry, but Pastor Cummings had put everyone's minds at ease at a private pastor's conference that she knew the Ingles and the Hugheses had attended.

"For the last couple of months, I've been helping Sonic sell some of the items Turner had given him during their *situationship* so that he could, in turn, use the money to pay off some of his hospital bills and remove the *Turner* tramp stamp from his lower back."

Amirah had seen the tattoo of Turner's name a few other men and women had on their lower back. She never knew why they'd gotten the same tattoo on their backside, but after listening to Mateo, it made perfect sense. Turner marked his territory well.

She was impressed by Mateo's desire to help Sonic turn his life around, and by the fact that the two of them were doing life together in Christ. She also knew it took a level of bravery to stand up to Turner and sell the items for ministry and to live life right. Amirah admired that.

"Is there anything I can do to help?" She surprised herself by offering. Amirah didn't want to get mixed up in whatever Turner had going on, nor did she want to get on his radar, but she couldn't stand by and watch Mateo get brutalized, or watch Sonic and Hammer do battle with this Satanic-bred militant alone.

Amirah trusted God would step in and help when the time was right. He'd already confirmed for her through visions that Mateo had been telling the truth.

"I'm good," Mateo replied confidently. When he stood up and turned around, Amirah thought she saw the imprint of a gun on his backside. A part of her wanted to ask him about it, but she listened to the discernment that God was in control and that by bringing it up, she'd only make things worse. "I felt that if Turner had tracked me down to the bookstore, there was a good chance that he was watching you or your students."

"So you came to make sure I made it home safely?" Amirah asked.

The smile on Mateo's face confirmed his answer. "That and to see if we can meet up at David's Table tomorrow."

"Yeah. Should I pick you up?" Amirah offered.

"Now, you know the man is supposed to pick you up." Mateo smiled. "I'd rather you not come to my motel room. How about this: I'll meet you at David's Table, and if I don't show up, go home."

Amirah nodded her head. "I can do that."

Mateo and Amirah hugged. Yeah, she felt the gun. She wanted to say something about him bringing a weapon on church grounds, but again, the spirit in her urged her to keep her mouth shut, and she chose to listen.

Chapter Twenty-two

Gimmie the Loot

Almost there, Mateo told himself as he hopped out of the car and walked briskly to his room. He could see the college students who were staying in two of the adjoining rooms near his going ape over the latest J. Cole track. The girls were scantily clad in bikini tops and Daisy Dukes even though it was only forty degrees. The guys partied, gambled, and talked trash even though they had exams that week.

He knew that Hammer had to be in the streets driving one of the Lincolns in order for them to be allowed to party with the door open. Fortunately the noise wasn't loud enough to be heard once the door was closed. Mateo figured that either no one complained about the noise, or the manager on duty must've been asleep. Or both. Normally, the patrons respected the noise ordinance because they valued their stay at Heaven's Inn.

"Yo, Mateo! You should stay out and party with us," one of the white boys yelled out as he raised a flavored malt liquor bottle in the air.

Mateo chuckled to himself as he recognized a co-worker from Burgers & Fries. "I'm good, man. I gotta study this Word and get ready for my meeting tomorrow."

Mateo could feel the temptation to get high and drunk. The girls were looking right, and he could stand to let one loose. He wanted to "pour it up" like Rihanna, preferably with her on his arm, but the God in him kicked in, and instantly, he was brought back to focus. No way was he going to stay outside any longer than he had to. He was dying to take the bandana from around his forehead and free his thin, curly hair to the free-forming Afro he usually wore when he wasn't at work.

He couldn't wait to cross the threshold of his front door to get out of his wet clothes, take a shower, and if he was lucky, relax for a little while before he had to be at the front desk of the motel in a few hours. It was a little after six o'clock in the morning, and Mateo wanted to get in some personal time before he went to sleep. He wondered how long their party would last.

Mateo was determined to eliminate the smell of fries and burgers from being in that fast food joint for the last seven and a half hours. Working for Burgers & Fries was stressful at times, and when they closed at four in the morning, he was part of the crew that cleaned the restaurant from top to bottom. Since Mateo held down the late-night cashier's spot, he cleaned the registers, wiped off the sauce display, and restocked the napkins, forks, and spoons. When he was done, he was the one to do the dishes.

The kitchen crew was responsible for cleaning the grills, the fry stations, and the sandwich boards, and when they were done, they hosed down the whole floor and mopped the store. Mateo would still be doing dishes and would always be in the way, so his feet always got wet when it came time for them to get to the back of the restaurant. Washing all the containers and utensils got his shirt wet too.

Usually, when Mateo walked in the door, he stripped butt-booty-ball naked so he could toss the day's dirty clothes into the hamper and make a beeline to the shower so he could get "Zestfully clean."

This early morning was no different. He walked in the door, took off the black hoodie and the long-sleeved *John 3:16* T-shirt that had the Burgers & Fries logo, and tossed both items on the floor. He stepped out of the cheap black clogs he got from Walmart that needed to be replaced, and he struggled for a full minute to take off the soggy socks. Mateo tore off the A-line shirt he was wearing and loosened the belt buckle as he pulled off his boxers, thermals, and slacks, with the intention of being steps way from hitting the bathroom.

As he reached for the doorknob, he heard a small clicking sound. He turned his head in the direction of the sound, hoping he was hearing things.

It had been almost a week since his confrontation with Sonic and Marvel about the gun, and this particular morning, he'd left the Glock in the desk instead of putting it back in the box under the bed. He'd figured that if they'd really told Hammer, he would've already confronted him about it. Maybe they'd kept his secret.

Or not.

He reached for the pocketknife that he'd placed on the desk before he went to work. That would've been closer than the gun. He felt hardwood and his calendar under his fingertips. The knife was gone.

"Who else do you know that has a key to this room besides me?" Mateo heard Hammer ask the question. Mateo bent down to pick up the shirt he'd just taken off, and he concealed his torso when he flipped on the light.

"Why you sitting in the dark?"

Mateo's senses were heightened when he heard Hammer's deep masculine voice boom from the far side of the room. Hammer had moved the chair from his desk to the window and looked out again briefly before facing Mateo, who felt his body tense up as his eyes adjusted to the light.

"You've been avoiding me." Hammer was blunt as he stood up and walked toward Mateo.

"No, I haven't," Mateo lied and turned away. He tried to see what Hammer may have been up to. He saw Hammer playing with the pocketknife, making the clicking sound before putting it in his back pocket. He was dressed in a black *Serve Them* polo shirt and some loose-fitting black cargo work pants. His work boots gave him an extra inch in height.

"You always trying to get hood on somebody." Mateo shook his head as he tried to figure out how he was going to get Hammer out of his room so he could get some rest.

"Look, man, let's cut the bull." Hammer's voice was sharp and commanding. "I'm here for the gun, and I expect to walk out of here with it."

Mateo looked at him. He knew Sonic and/or Marvel had told on him the minute they got the chance. He didn't know whether they told on him right away or after Sonic had confronted him again in his room earlier; and the truth was he had been avoiding Hammer. There was no way he was parting with his burner, and if that meant getting evicted from Heaven's Inn, then so be it.

"I'm disappointed in you," Hammer continued as he shook his head. "I thought we were past the point where we felt we needed to arm ourselves with the weapons of the world. It's apparent that you don't have the gun on you, because I don't see it on the floor or in plain view. I could've just walked in here, found it, and taken it, but that would be stealing, and I'm so much better than that."

Mateo didn't say anything. As bad as he felt the need to, he wasn't going to fight Hammer to keep the gun. For starters, he still felt grimy after working hard on third shift. He was surprised that Hammer hadn't put his hand up to cover his nose. Mateo was sure he reeked, and he knew Hammer could smell him. In the grand scheme of things, he couldn't punch and protect his midsection at the same time—and he didn't have time to put his drawers on.

"I didn't come over here to beef. I came over here to help you stay in line with the man *you* said you wanted to be. I can help you, but you have to give me the gun." Hammer tried to reason with Mateo. "When God called you to ministry, He called you to be a new man. He called you to be forgiving and to walk in forgiveness. As your mentor and as your friend, I'm not going to sit here and watch you backslide just so you can get revenge on someone who's hurt you."

Mateo smacked his lips. He didn't want to admit that everything Hammer said made sense. What he was doing that very moment, contemplating killing Turner, was a contradiction of everything he wanted to be as a minister.

Sure, he could ask for forgiveness if he walked up to Turner and smacked him in the head. He could even ask for forgiveness if he pulled the trigger and sent him to hell; but for that brief moment in time, the Spirit convicted Mateo. In that same moment, Mateo had to ask himself, *What if I'm the one who's to introduce Turner Mustafa Spartenburg to Christ?*

The thought made Mateo smirk, as he didn't think it was likely. He grabbed the gun from the drawer in the desk and slowly sat on the bed. He put the gun to his side. Hammer sat on the bed next to him. "Sometimes the hardest decision is to follow God and to do what's right. Killing someone is always the easiest way out."

Mateo looked away. He didn't want Hammer to see him with the tear falling down his face. "I failed the test."

"Maybe so." Hammer put his hand on Mateo's back and rubbed his shoulder. "But the best part about our God is that He gives second chances, and if we fail at our second chance, he gives us multiple chances until we get it right. With God, there's always a retest—another chance to get an *A*."

Mateo let what Hammer said marinate in his mind. He knew that his mentor was right. Just as sure as the day was long, Mateo would get his retest, and internally, Mateo vowed that he would be ready.

"Go take a shower, because I know you feel groggy and grimy. Get some rest and take the day off. I'll talk to you later on, okay?"

Mateo nodded his head. "So what are you going to do with the gun?" Mateo handed it to him. He watched as Hammer stood up and put the gun in his backside.

"You know I have a way of getting rid of things." Hammer smirked.

Mateo knew that within an hour or so, Pastor Cummings and his assistant, Emilio, would have disposed of the gun. In their past lives, Pastor Cummings and Emilio had ties to an old biker gang, and Emilio still had his disposal business. Word was that between Pastor Cummings and Emilio, they performed illusions better than Houdini. Hammer couldn't risk keeping the gun, because he himself still had a few years before he could legally own a piece. Mateo was glad that Hammer didn't ask him where the gun came from or how long he'd had it.

"The Lord is not slack concerning his promise, as some men count slackness; but is long-suffering toward us, not willing that any should perish, but that all should come to repentance." Hammer closed the door on his way out.

Mateo tried to remember the Bible verse Hammer's words came from, but it slipped his mind. He shook his head, wanting to take a shower, but he didn't have the energy to take the few steps to the bathroom or to turn on the shower. Mateo got up and tossed the shirt that he was concealing his nakedness with in with the rest of the dirty clothes and got under the covers. He knew he was going to wash laundry the next day, and he had a clean set of sheets to change the bed with. He was as content with that as he was with his soul feeling clean again.

Chapter Twenty-three

Do-over

"Amirah Dalton?" the waiter asked when she walked in.

"Yes." Amirah smiled when she heard her name. She was surprised because she didn't have a reservation. She looked into the restaurant and couldn't see Mateo anywhere.

"Right this way," the waiter said. "There is a gentleman waiting on you."

Bonus points, Amirah thought as she followed the waiter. As she passed the other patrons who were enjoying their dinner, she still couldn't find Mateo. The waiter made his way back to a secluded room. She was happy to see that Mateo was pulling out all the stops. She was greeted by a dove sculpture that pumped water. A fruit spread had been set at their table, filled with cut watermelon, mango, pineapple, cantaloupe, honeydew melon, and strawberries.

Mateo was waiting behind a chair that he had pulled out for her. He was dressed in a teal blue shirt with a purple-and-silver tie, black slacks, and well-polished dress shoes. Mateo cleaned up very well. Remnants of the scars he suffered still appeared on his face, but she could tell he was in good spirits and in a better place spiritually.

"Good evening," Mateo greeted her.

"Good evening." Amirah took her place before the chair. Mateo gently pushed her chair up to the table.

"I'll give you a few minutes to get situated," the waiter announced. "Then I'll come back to take your order."

"Thank you." Mateo nodded his head.

Mateo walked around to his seat, took the napkin off the table, and put it in his lap. "I hope you like."

"Of course. I'm still trying to figure out how you pulled this off. It takes forever and a day to get a private room at David's Table, and usually my book club has to get our reservations months in advance."

"Ask and ye shall receive, seek and ye shall find, knock and the door shall be opened unto you." Mateo quoted scripture. "I called and asked to see if I needed a reservation; they said no. Then I asked if anyone had canceled a reservation for one of the rooms, and it just so happened that the person who had this table booked had an emergency and had to cancel. So I did a little step and dance, and we are here."

"Wow," was all that escaped from Amirah's lips. She hadn't expected Mateo to be able to pull out all the stops. She expected this to be a low-cost affair where they would get a few snacks or a light meal and then be off to their next adventure.

"Plus, they didn't want all that food that had been prepared for the other party to go to waste, so we will be taking home whatever fruit we don't eat."

Amirah shook her head in amazement—not only at God's favor, but at the lengths that Mateo went to, to treat her special. "This is really nice."

"I do whatever I have to do to make sure that you are treated nicely. Hopefully, this will allow you to see a nicer, softer side of me."

Amirah's mind traveled. If Mateo did all of this during courtship, she could imagine what he'd be like as a husband. She hadn't intended to think that far ahead, but she could see romantic dinners like this in her future with him.

"After dealing with those children all day, I want you to enjoy yourself. No pressure. Enjoy the food, good conversation, and anything else you want, Amirah."

She smiled as she stood up and got a plate of mixed fruit and watched as Mateo did the same.

Beneath all of that hard exterior is a kind, gentle-hearted man, Amirah told herself as she returned to her seat. By the time they were finished with grace, the waiter had returned to take their orders.

"I just want the strawberry and chicken salad," Amirah ordered.

"Aww," Mateo expressed after hearing her order. "You can do better than that."

"I don't each much for dinner," Amirah defended. "I usually eat a heavy breakfast and light meals and snacks throughout the rest of the day. Plus, I had chicken and dumplings for lunch, and I don't want to eat anything else heavy for the rest of the day."

"Understood. I'll have the same, with a glass of lemon-lime sparkling water."

"A drink for you?" the waiter asked Amirah.

"Sparkling water is fine, something with a berry flavor," Amirah added to her order.

"Coming right up." The waiter finished writing the rest of their order and left the room.

"So how do you feel?" Mateo asked once the door was closed. "I want to make up for our last date, to make this one special and one for you to remember me by."

"I'd say you were doing a good job."

Mateo smiled and nodded his head. They ate in silence, and Amirah sat and took it all in. She didn't expect to find a man *this* nice on His-Love.com. Her original plan was just to make friends and to network. Getting close to a man or falling in love wasn't part of the equation.

Within minutes, the waiter brought in their food, and they enjoyed their meal in silence. Soft, classic R&B music made its echoes in the background. Babyface, Toni Braxton, Regina Belle, and Luther Vandross took turns crooning love songs.

"This is so romantic and tempting," Amirah spoke up.

"I'm sorry." Mateo picked up a handheld device and pressed a button. Within seconds, silence filled the room. "I guess I should have had them play Fred Hammond or something."

"No, it's not that either," Amirah said. "I just know me, and I know where that music can take me."

Mateo wiped his mouth with the cloth napkin. "I can respect that. Everyone has their boundaries. What you can handle, another person may not."

Amirah nodded her head. "Understood."

"You want me to play some gospel?" Mateo asked.

"No, I'm good."

They ate in silence. Once their meal was over, they bypassed desert. They ate more of the fruit and talked about the Word. As she listened to Mateo speak, she found that she had more in common with him than she realized.

Mateo tipped the waiter, and they each had a healthy box of fruit to take home. Amirah was really feeling Mateo and could see herself enjoying another date with him—and she couldn't wait.

Chapter Twenty-four

Home Run

Yes! Mateo thought as he had intentions to drive home. Dinner at David's Table was a success, and he was well on his way to making things permanent with Amirah.

The old him tried to make an appearance, to let Amirah know how he felt about her physically, but Mateo shut it down quick. Mind over matter, Christ over body. In his heart, he knew that if he followed God's plan, Amirah would be his as his wife.

Mateo decided to take a detour. No, he decided not to go straight home but to another place he once called home. He found himself getting closer to West Asheville, where I-240 crossed Patton Avenue and merged with I-26. He took I-26 east and got off at the Hill Street exit. He could see the lights on in the apartment complex.

Even as the day was getting later, several of the residents found something to celebrate. He turned onto the street that led to its entrance. Mateo felt the discernment that going into the complex was not a good idea, but he ignored it.

Before long, he'd driven over two huge speed bumps that had makeshift spikes built into them and nodded his head at the security guard, who was sitting down and fully engrossed in a T. Styles urban horror novel. His old self was reawakened and started to spit game at the beautiful lady whose sandy blond hair and caramel highlights emphasized the features on the right side of her face.

She was a beauty, but she wasn't Amirah. Their eyes met for a moment, and behind her irises he felt a spirit that would bring him nothing but trouble if he engaged her. As fine as she was, she wasn't worth losing Amirah over.

He made it past the entrance of the apartment complex and drove past the community center that greeted the residents and visitors at the entrance. Old memories of misusing its purpose came to mind, but Mateo knew he wasn't getting tempted by that.

He drove down the rows of two-story townhome-style apartments and could see the neighborhood children laughing and playing, not having a care in the world. They darted across the street without looking both ways for cars. The older ones cursed and said things he didn't have to courage to do when he was their age.

As he drove further in the hood, he could see a young man dressed in baggy clothes, his pants falling off of his behind to reveal the name of the athletic apparel brand that made the body-hugging orange boxer briefs he was sporting. Mateo saw a big, white masculine hand pass some folded greenbacks to the young man, who put them in a smaller pocket above his pants pocket. The young man looked in Mateo's direction, nodded his head, licked his lips, flashed his grill, cocked a grin, and got in the old-school white Buick.

Mateo knew what time it was as he watched the car drive off. He closed his eyes briefly to say a prayer for the safety of the young man and the driver of the car. Mateo prayed that no incurable impurities passed between them.

Ahead, Mateo was drawn to the old school Jermaine Dupri joint that he'd produced for Nelly. In the midst of it all, he could see Turner's huge, action-figure body sitting comfortably on the hood of a remodeled, dark-colored

Crown Victoria. While some of the ladies were scantily clad, a few looked just as hard, if not harder, than the men they pretended to be. From a distance, one couldn't distinguish one from the other. One guy, who was obviously high off that Molly, was dancing and stripping by the car. One of Turner's goons pushed the guy away from the group, and like a determined young buck who was fighting for his woman, the man went back into the group.

Mateo wasn't pleased that all of this was going on in front of his mama's house.

Mateo and Turner locked eyes as he cut off the car engine.

I'm not going to let this punk keep me from seeing my mama, Mateo thought as he stepped out of the car and walked toward his old residence.

The inner man wished he had listened to the discernment he had earlier, but he couldn't run. He wasn't about to provoke Turner any more than he had by showing up.

"What brings you here?" Turner hopped off the Crown Vic and walked toward him, his balled right fist being cover and massaged by his left.

Mateo did a quick scan of the area. He counted ten goons and fifteen drunks, all of them affiliated with Turner. He also noted about seven or eight women and a bunch of children who were still riding bicycles, bouncing balls, and playing basketball on nets fitted to the doors of the complex. Mateo felt he would be safe.

"I came to see my mama. What you here for?" Mateo walked closer to the crowd. He was going to have to get through them to make it to her house. The street lights were on, and if this was the mama he had back in the day, she'd have been standing at the door waiting for him with a belt.

"I guess that body slam wasn't good enough for you." Turner stood over him and tried to push him back. Mateo held his ground and looked Turner in the eye.

"I'm still here," Mateo responded confidently as he continued to walk around Turner and head to his destination.

"Well, you know, dead people walk and talk all the time," Turner bragged as he put his arm around Mateo. Turner leaned over and whispered in Mateo's ear, "I'd hate for your next trip to be in a body bag, son."

Mateo faced him and looked him dead in the eyes. "You will go to hell in one before I'm called home to my Maker." Then he grinned.

Turner was pissed off. Mateo held his guard and tried to find all of his nemeses discreetly without taking his eyes off Turner. All were still present and accounted for.

"You and that Hammer seem so sure of this God you're serving." Turner got in his face again. "If this God you got is so big, why do I rule the world?"

"You really think this world is yours?" Mateo replied. "Satan has your mind warped even worse than I thought. The evil-doer is only using you for a period of time. When he's done with you, you'll be disappointed in who your 'successor' is."

Turner chuckled and laughed, but he moved out of the way to let Mateo pass through the crowd. They parted on each side like Moses used the staff to part the Red Sea.

"I am Turner Mustafa Spartenburg," he bragged. His drunken nature became apparent as he slurred his last name. "I'm going to live forever."

"I pray that you do." Mateo made it to the front door of his childhood home. "I pray that forever for you means an eternity in Christ and not a lifetime of torture and pain."

Mateo knocked on the door. He could hear Turner mimicking and cursing him. Like the followers they were, his crowd of cronies and crowd pleasers gave their support by laughing and clapping. As Mateo knocked on the door again, he thanked God for getting him out of that situation unscathed, and that despite ignoring the warning from God to turn around, his Maker saw it fit to keep him in one piece.

"*Hijo!*" Mateo's mother was excited as she hugged her son.

"*Sí, Madre, es mío.*" Mateo entered her home safe from harm.

Not only was he being comforted by the arms of his mother, but he was being protected by the arms of God.

Chapter Twenty-five

La Casa

Inside Mateo's mother's home, he could smell the arroz con pollo that she had cooked earlier. The pot of red kidney beans made its presence known too—along with the jalapeño pepper. He couldn't tell whether his older brother had been over, but he knew his young sister was around the apartment complex somewhere.

He didn't even want to know what she was doing. Julio and Luisa were into mischief, which would explain why they were both MIA during Mateo's two visits to the hospital. In Luisa's case, she was still a teenager and was acting her age, but Julio had a few years on Mateo and should've known better.

"¿Quieres comer?" His mother led him into the kitchen. "I have some mango and pineapple juice in the refrigerator."

"No, I'm not hungry." Mateo answered the question his mother asked him in Spanish. "Where's Julio and Luisa?"

His mother smacked her lips and mumbled something in Spanish that translated to Luisa being a whore in someone's home down the street. She went on about how disappointed she was because she didn't raise her daughter to disgrace her name, nor did she honor her sons being hood rats.

"I should've kept y'all in the *iglesia*," his mother answered aloud, referring to the church.

"Madre, you can't fault yourself for how any of us turned out," Mateo commented. "And besides, I go to Guiding Light Ministries now."

That put a smile on his mother's face. It wasn't a Catholic church, but his mother was well pleased. "I can die an honorable woman knowing that at least one of my children is going to heaven." She gave him another hug. "This gives me motivation to continue to pray for the other two."

"Aw, Madre." Mateo hugged her back. "You know you love us."

"I do." She went into the refrigerator and pulled out the pot that Mateo was sure held the arroz con pollo. Even though he had just told his mother he wasn't hungry, she had fixed him a plate anyway, along with a smaller plate for herself. "You come to my house looking hungry, like you haven't eaten in days." She placed what he presumed to be his plate in the microwave.

"Naw, Ma." He noticed the past-due bills that floated across the dinner table. Mateo knew that ever since she'd fought off cancer when he hit puberty, money was always tight around the house. When Mateo and Julio ran the streets, they brought back what they could to help her out; yet they shared the same fate millions of families in America had, drowning in debt.

"I just came from a date with a nice young lady," Mateo told her. "I think I'll bring her by in a few weeks; let you meet her."

"I hope she's a nice woman." His mother placed his plate in front of him. Then she went to the other side of the table, across from him. "I hope she's better than that woman of the night Julio is probably entertaining upstairs, or that married woman I seen you chasing around like a dog in heat."

Mateo shook the guilt from his head. He hated that his mother hadn't thought good things about him and that he kept her worried. The last time he'd seen his mother was a month before he'd gotten shot at and met Hammer. The woman in question and his mother were arguing outside of the woman's husband's house, while Mateo was pulling the woman he was sleeping with back in the house so they could do more of the same.

After reflecting, he tried to recite, in Spanish, the small blessing his mother tried to teach him. He knew he'd said it right when the smile appeared on her face.

The last time Mateo had seen Julio was a few days after he went to prison. Julio was on his way out for good behavior. His sister still wore the uniform of the Catholic school their mother forced her to go to, hoping that she wouldn't turn out to be a hooligan like her older brothers. That hadn't worked.

"She teaches at Shiloh Christian Academy," Mateo boasted proudly, hoping to put a smile on his mother's face. "Her name is Amirah." Just mentioning her name brought a smile to his own face.

He smiled when he succeeded. His mother's face lit up like the sun, and Mateo took great pleasure in that. "I approve. You better not corrupt her," his mother warned as she waved a finger in his face. He hated how his mother could split personalities within seconds. "*Los profesores* there are good Christian teachers. If I weren't a devout Catholic, I would've sent Luisa there, but I didn't know."

"Ma, you can't hold on to how the three of us turned out." Mateo reached for her hand. He hoped a glimpse into his eyes would ease her pain. "Julio and Luisa will come around; I promise."

As if on cue, Mateo heard the stairs creaking. From the pace of the descent, he could tell that whoever was coming down the stairs was running.

"Julio! You better get that whore out of here!" his mother yelled loud enough for the security guard to hear her at her post.

"Ma! I just came down to use the bath—Mateo!" Julio shouted excitedly and hugged his brother in the chair.

"Boy, go put some clothes on!" their mother fussed. "Mateo come in here with a shirt and a tie, and you come dancing out of here with your little jalapeño dancing out of your boxers."

Mateo was shocked.

"Ma!" Julio turned away from Mateo and adjusted himself. That's when Mateo noticed that all his brother had on were some boxers. Mateo shook his head. "Why I gotta be a *little* jalapeño?"

His mother waved her hand and then pointed to the bathroom. Julio went to the bathroom to do what he needed to do, and when he came out, he had a white towel wrapped around his waist.

"See, Mateo? This is what I put up with." His mother scooped up the yellow rice. "Every day, Julio and I fight about him walking around the house naked or near naked and whatever woman he bringing over this house, thinking this is his house. It's the same three or four dumb girls who think my son is God's gift to them. If they only knew what I know."

"Ma, please don't do that," Mateo begged, knowing where his mother was going to take the conversation. Julio went upstairs, and he was calling out something profane to his guest in Spanish. Their mother shook her head.

"We know your brother gets one of them crazy checks ever since he came back from Iraq. Half the time he can't act right and forgets where he is. I wish the Army would take him back and fix him, but he refused to go to the VA. The two of you went in and out of jail and juvenile detention like it was your second home. At least he had an excuse."

"Why I gotta leave?" A random female interrupted their mother as she and Julio made their way down the stairs and to the front door. She was barely dressed, and Julio was stuffing her clothes in a plastic grocery bag.

"Because my brother is here and our time is over." They heard Julio trying to explain to the woman as he opened the door and sent the girl on her way. "I'll have to come to your house in a few days."

"You better," the woman replied.

"She nasty," their mother whispered in Spanish. "Now watch this."

"Hey, Ma. Hey, bro!" Julio shouted like he was outside. He came back in the kitchen wearing a tight, muscle-hugging shirt that advertised the fact that he worked out. He still had the towel wrapped around his waist and some brown sandals on his feet. "Ma, you cooked?"

"*Estuve haciendo arroz con pollo y frijoles por cuatro horas.*" She told him she'd been cooking for four hours.

"*¿Por qué no llámarme?*" Julio asked his mother why she hadn't called him down to eat.

"I did!" she shouted. She hated that her children's Spanish wasn't as great as hers, but she got was Julio was saying. "You were too busy entertaining that—"

"Ma, don't call her a name please." Julio fixed his plate and put it in the microwave. "That's the one I like."

Their mother turned her head to the side and raised her eyebrows. "What's her name?"

"I don't know, but she's the one I like. Them other two just occupy my time."

Mateo shook his head. He tried his best not to chuckle. His inner man told him that nothing he was seeing or hearing was funny.

Julio's plate finished warming up, and within seconds, he joined them at the table and dug into his food without saying grace.

"We can't praise God anymore?" their mother asked.

"God, watch and pray. Amen," Julio said and continued to eat.

"See? What I tell you?" their mother complained. "He got that DHAD."

"It's ADHD, Madre, and no, I don't." Julio defended himself. "The doctor said I got whatever it is that makes it hard for me to pay attention, and some obsessive-compulsive disorder—and I suffer anxiety from whatever it was that sprayed out of the bomb during that war."

Mateo watched as Julio finished his food, tossed the plate into the sink like a Frisbee, took the towel off from around his waist, and rushed upstairs.

"Can you take him with you?" his mom complained. "I need a break."

"Yeah—but Ma, I stay in Heaven's Inn now. And I work at Burgers & Fries."

"Yo, bruh, you gonna get me some more food?" Julio asked.

Mateo was pleased to see that Julio was dressed more appropriately in a loose-fitting, short-sleeved shirt, a pair of baggy black jeans, and some off-brand black work boots.

"We'll go out, but I don't have any money for food."

"I got money." Julio pulled out a knot full of bills and a few cards bound in the middle of the wad.

Mateo looked at his mom, and she nonverbally gave them permission to go.

"Oh yeah, homes. What I tell you about being around *mi madre's casa*?" Julio could be heard yelling as Mateo was closing the door.

Mateo knew it was about to go down. He didn't know that Julio and Turner had beef or that they'd thrown blows. He knew he needed to get outside and stop Julio from doing something crazy. Mateo got up and hugged his mother. He hated that he had to rush, but with Julio already out the door and Turner outside, he had to follow.

Once he got outside, he saw Turner and Julio getting ready to go toe to toe. The fight was still unfair, as Julio was only four inches taller than Mateo, but not over six feet.

"Mateo!" Turner barked. "You better get this runt out of my face before I do something."

"You just mad because I stomped your head in last week," Julio bragged as he pushed Turner. Mateo was amazed that Turner took a few steps back. "And if you don't step off my mama's front lawn like I told you before, I'm gonna stomp your head again."

Mateo knew he had to get his brother out of the way. He didn't know where all of Turner's goons were, and he didn't want to be taken by surprise. "Julio, bring your—" Mateo started the curse but thought better of it. He grabbed Julio's arm and dragged him in the direction of the car. He watched as Turner and Julio exchanged one-finger good-byes.

"You shoulda let me kick his butt," Julio complained as Mateo tried to shove his much bigger brother in the car. "I needed the exercise."

"You need to stay out of trouble," Mateo replied. "I can't afford to bail you out of jail."

"Ooh, where you get this car?" Julio played with the radio, listening to a little bit of every Mexican radio station on the AM and FM dials before he settled on the blues being played on 100.7 WRES.

"You done?" Mateo asked as he started the car.

"Yeah, man, I want to go to Burgers & Fries. Hurry up."

Mateo shook his head as he pulled off and left the apartment complex. He couldn't believe that Julio was still hungry after eating a full plate of their mother's Mexican cuisine, but then he remembered that Julio always had a voracious appetite and that he stayed so active, he most likely burned off any carbs as soon as he inhaled them. He thought about what his mother said about his brother and sister and felt guilty for not coming around, but he often hated how his mother constantly threw his past in his face. His mother was never too thrilled to learn that he was sleeping with "*su tía.*" Even though his uncle was his relative by marriage and technically, his wife wasn't his aunt legally, his mother had always viewed the relationship as incestuous. Then when she found out that Mateo and "*su tía*" were into group sex and went to sex parties, his mother would have liked to have had a heart attack.

However, Mateo hoped having Julio with him now would ease his mother's burdens just a little. He vowed to make the best of being around his older brother.

Chapter Twenty-six

Teacher Word Day

Amirah welcomed the smell of breakfast provided by Chick-Fil-A that filled the cafeteria. The spread featuring chicken biscuits, hash browns, chicken burritos, mixed fruit, muffins, and yogurt parfaits called out to Amirah's stomach.

The students were home for the teacher workday, and Amirah was amazed at how fast the school year was coming to an end. Xen's grades were improving in all of his classes, and Howard was spending more time with the boy as promised. For his part, Xen was growing and maturing, staying away from classmates who would bring him trouble, and trying to befriend those who not only would challenge him academically but encourage him to walk in the Lord. It seemed as if Xen was determined to prove to everyone that he could do better and act better than his parents did the day they came to the school.

This was what she enjoyed most about teaching— watching a student grow from troubled to greatness; participating in that change and doing what she felt and believed God called her to do; being an example of what a woman of God should be, or at least strive to be.

One thing about Shiloh Christian Academy: they knew how to feed their teachers. Pastor and Mrs. Ingle believed in nourishing bodies, minds, and spirits, and Amirah knew they shared their view of the school being a reflection of the Body of Christ. It was good that the janitors, cafeteria workers, and other staff members were not left out of the festivities. They mingled and sang along to the worship songs that were blasted from the radio.

Another thing she liked was that when Shiloh Christian Academy had teacher workdays, they tried to make them as fun and educational for the faculty as possible. The state mandated that the teachers took a minimum of fifteen continuing education credit hours for them to maintain their teaching licenses. Mrs. Ingle encourage her staff to work on many of the hours collectively, so that the group could bond. Amirah loved it, because all of the teachers got to let their hair down and be casual. Mrs. Ingle was Angela, but only a few teachers addressed her by her first name. Amirah appreciated it, because most of the administrators she'd run into felt that they were a few steps above her and would reprimand her more harshly than they would the students.

The best part was that Shiloh Christian Academy didn't just have the word *Christian* in its name or just pretend to be a faith-based organization. Pastor and Mrs. Ingle treated the school as a big part of their ministry. When Amirah worked for a public school system in the Charlotte metropolitan area, she remembered how she'd gotten in trouble for praying while on her break. The school system was horrible to its faculty, especially to the first-year teachers and those who were new to the Charlotte area. Shiloh Christian Academy hired teachers of different faiths, but they respected all teachers' rights and desires to respect God and put Him first in their lives.

In the background, Hezekiah Walker had finished encouraging everyone to give praise to God, and Donald Lawrence opened the training session by reminding everyone to encourage themselves. So when Tamela Mann's "All to Thee" came on, Amirah was caught up in the spirit, as the song always brought her to praise and worship.

"Girl, this song does it to me too." Sarai stood behind her, getting her food.

"I wasn't closing my eyes and singing, was I?" Amirah looked around, almost embarrassed that she may have been holding up the line.

"Girl, ain't nobody thinking about that," Sarai replied quickly, "but no, you weren't holding up the line. It's actually moving kind of fast."

Amirah and Sarai quickly got the rest of the items they wanted for their plates and then grabbed their seats closer to the front. Byron Cage's "Broken but I'm Healed" came on, and she thought about Calvin Rice, her Career and Technical Education Curriculum Coordinator and one of her mentors. He'd come from the same school that she had taught at, and she remembered how he once told her that the song was a big part of his healing. She looked around for him in the midst of the other teachers and office staff, but she couldn't find him. Normally, the department sat together so they could compare notes for their department meeting.

Once the song was over, the projector was rolled into place and being set up for their continuing education course that would help them improve their teaching methods.

After the teaching seminar was over, Amirah went to her classroom for a brief second to make sure the demo for the speech recognition program that she was teaching the students to use was working correctly. She was startled to see a man sitting at one of the student computers at the far end of the room.

"Come in and close the door," the voice commanded Amirah as she walked in from lunch. "Everyone doesn't need to hear our conversation."

Turner turned around and flashed a smile. Amirah looked behind her and then up at the camera that was in the hallway.

How did Turner get in here undetected? Amirah asked herself. *What does he want, and what will I say when Mrs. Ingle finds out?* She wondered as she looked outside to see who was walking past. There was not a teacher or a staff member to come to her rescue. She complied with the request and was about to have a seat.

"Naw, don't sit at your desk," he continued as he typed at least fifty miles an hour. "Any attempt to hit the H and END key on any computer will give me a reason to make sure you are in need of help," Turner threatened without looking up.

Amirah had no choice but to take a seat near him. She wasn't expecting anyone to be in the class after the seminar was over. Her plan was to come in, record some of the grades, and register for a few of the continuing education courses she would need to keep her teaching license current. She had canceled the tutoring she was going to do because she didn't want to be unable to make her commitments. She only had to be at the school for another hour before she could go home for the day.

Amirah's first instinct was to run, but she didn't want to risk the possibility of anyone else getting hurt. Her next was to face Turner head on and prepare for the worst. She tried to get her mind right and prepare to battle with Satan in her classroom, in the flesh.

"Calm down. I'm not going to hurt you." Turner seemed to close the gap between them. "I just want to talk to you for a little while."

"Talk about what?" Amirah demanded. "And why are you in my classroom?"

"I'm just here to deliver a message." Turner dug in his pocket and pulled out a card key to Heaven's Inn motel. "I got a room there now. Paid it off for the whole month."

Amirah was confused at first as to why he was giving her a key to his room, but then it made sense. Mateo also stayed at Heaven's Inn, and Hammer owned the motel. Turner was there to cause trouble.

"I need a new place to hang out, and I think you should join me," Turner suggested as he continued to work the keys on the keyboard in front of him.

"I think you're wasting your time," Amirah suggested as she got smart with her captor.

Turner moved closer to her. "What, are you too good to come hang with me?" Turner grew frustrated and suddenly grabbed Amirah's arm and brought her close to him. "Don't tell me you buy that goody-two-shoes act Mateo is putting on. He's a thug just a like me. Anyway, he has something I want, and I need you to make sure he returns my property."

Amirah started to rebuff his statement. She grew irritated as she rubbed her arm, hoping he didn't leave a mark. "So this is what you do?" Amirah asked. She had to admit, up close, Turner was a very attractive man. She also remembered they said Satan was beautiful beyond description when he was with God. The lavender and hemp oils he wore made for a masculine mix. "You scare and intimidate people to get them to do what you want?"

"Do I scare you?" Turner moved to face Amirah.

"Heck no!" Amirah replied sharply as she looked him in his eyes.

"Good. I'm not here to scare you." Turner turned away and continued typing. Amirah looked over his shoulder and could see a narrative being e-mailed through a Gmail account. "I'm here to warn you about your little boyfriend."

"Mateo."

"Did you have to call his name?"

"Only if that would make you remember."

"Look, girl, don't get smart." Turner faced her again, and this time he had a fire in his eyes. It was as if the presence of evil surrounded her. She quickly said a small prayer from the Book of Isaiah, and her uneasiness faded away. "I don't want you to get hurt messing with that little roach sucker."

"I'm not going to be hurt," Amirah replied confidently. She got up and walked to the door. Within a matter of seconds, Turner was on her heels, but she didn't care. He grabbed her arm, and she snatched away. She reached for the door, and Turner quickly shut it.

"You think this a game?" Turner asked as he moved into her personal space.

"No. I'm into card games, not board games."

Turner smirked, catching the double meaning. "So you're going to be my spades partner now? You got a lot of mouth. I like that in my women."

"What about your men?" Amirah threw his business out there. Curiosity made her wonder what he'd say.

"They serve their purpose." Turner confessed to the rumors she'd heard about him. "I think you can do better than rollin' around Asheville with a little thief."

"Who's the thief?" Amirah confronted him. "If you *gave* something to someone and they turned around and *sold* it to Mateo, I don't think that constitutes him being a thief."

"So you're going to take his side?" Turner acted as if he were offended.

"Are you going to body slam me like you did him?" Amirah responded back. "I never thought you'd be the kind of man who'd pick on someone half your size."

Turner rolled his eyes. Amirah had hit a soft spot. "Look, I hate to see you get hurt hangin' around Mateo. That's all I'm saying."

"I'm not worried about getting hurt. I serve a God who's bigger and stronger than you. That's all *I'm* saying."

Turner licked his lips and leaned in to kiss her. Amirah tried to push him away but found that she was no match for the giant. Turner leaned in and whispered in her ear. "It's okay to admit that I'm the bigger man, the better man. I see the way you look at me. You want me."

Amirah was appalled. She was half-tempted to slap the man. She thought better of it when she reflected on how she had witnessed Turner scoop Mateo up and body slam him into next week.

"I want you to leave," Amirah warned, "before I call the police."

Turner opened the door behind her, and Amirah stepped to the side. "I'm in room one twenty-four. At the end of the building. Tell him to come see me soon." They stared at each other for a few moments before Turner ended the showdown with a smirk and left her classroom.

As he was walking out, Sarai was walking in. Amirah watched as Sarai looked him up and down, and after a while, Sarai rushed to Amirah's side. Amirah exhaled. She didn't fear him, but she didn't want him to hurt her either.

She walked to her desk and pulled a bottle of purified water from her bottom desk drawer and took a sip.

"Was that who I thought it was?" Sarai asked as she walked in. "And are you okay?"

"I just want to finish my work so I can leave," Amirah confirmed without answering the question. She took a few sips, and then she turned her computer on so she could record grades. "I got to get in touch with Mateo."

"Do we need to call the police?" Sarai asked as she pulled out her phone.

"No, don't call the police yet," Amirah insisted. "I may have another plan that will work, but first, let me get in touch with Mateo. He needs to know that trouble just arrived on his doorstep."

Sarai looked at Amirah in disbelief, but she went along with her friend's request—for now. Sarai gave Amirah a hug as she was leaving. "I've finished my training for the day. Let me get my stuff and I'll come back and stay with you."

"Thanks."

Amirah watched as Sarai left the classroom. She looked at the clock. Thirty minutes later and she was ready to walk out the door.

Chapter Twenty-seven

Boxing with God

Mateo watched as Sonic finished the rest of his food as he entertained a female guest. He had just rung up one of the last customers he'd served before the end of his shift. He was covering for one of the teenagers who'd called off work, and Mateo could always use the extra money. Wednesday was the day he normally had off from both the motel and Burgers & Fries.

Sonic and the female were laughing as they ate cheese fries loaded with ranch, ketchup, and turkey chili. As they finished their meal, Sonic and the young lady got up and threw their waste in the trash. They stepped outside. Moments later, they hugged and the young lady got in a blue Kia Rio and drove away.

"Thanks for covering that shift for me." Doug came with a new cash drawer, relieving Mateo from his duties. Doug brought up the manager's screen and typed in a code to take Mateo off the register.

"No problem." Mateo smiled. "I appreciate getting the extra hours."

"Well, a full-time first shift position will be coming up in a few weeks. You'd only get paid a quarter more, but you would be guaranteed thirty-five hours a week, and if you do well after a few months, you maybe could move up to shift leader. Plus, they are opening a new store in South Asheville in six months. We could probably have you ready for management by then."

Shift leader. That meant a small management role and a chance to lead a small team. That also meant Mateo would be eligible for benefits. Mateo didn't want to jump for joy, but he knew this opportunity was a small step in the direction that could lead him back to school or being able to land steady employment. He inwardly praised God for this small favor.

"That first shift sounds nice," Mateo replied. "I probably could make that work. What about my felonies?"

In the back of his mind, he thought about the two hours overlap between that position and what he'd normally do at the motel. Mateo figured he could talk Hammer into working around his schedule, especially since he encouraged all of the employees to seek outside employment. The first shift position was a step toward independence and getting his own spot.

"You would have to wait four more years before you become assistant manager, but I wouldn't worry about that now. Even if you become shift leader, you know you could still pick up some overtime hours too," Doug pointed out.

"Anything that will keep me out of trouble."

A few seconds later, Mateo was logged off, and he followed Doug back to the manager's office. He watched as Doug poured the coins into a coin counter and ran the bills through a bill counter similar to the ones he'd seen at the bank. "Perfect drawer, that's what's up."

That made Mateo feel good. He didn't like his drawer short, and if it was over, he wanted it to be because a customer told him to keep his change or because he had a tip that was left for him. Mateo left the office and walked to the front counter where another manager was signing one of the night crews onto a new drawer. Mateo quickly clocked out and headed to the lobby. Sonic was standing on the side of the building.

"Who's that girl that you were just with?" Mateo asked as he walked up to his boy and gave him a pound.

Sonic chuckled. "That's Iesha."

"Oh, word? That's the girl who works at Wendy's, right?"

Sonic smiled and nodded his head. Mateo looked at him again. Something was off. It wasn't the fact that Sonic was talking to a woman. He looked again. "You trimmed the dye from your head?"

"Yeah," Sonic confirmed. "It's time for me to do something different."

Sonic looked different without the dark blue tips at the end of his hair. Instead of looking like a punk rocker, his African features really stood out and made him look like one of the college students who attended an HBCU.

"Well, if you like it, I love it," Mateo told him as they headed toward Sonic's car.

"I want to sell the car," Sonic said once they got inside and he turned the ignition.

Mateo looked at him like he was crazy. "Boy, you just got this car almost a year ago."

"I know. I need to do something different. I'm thinking about getting an older F-150 or another truck. Something different."

"That girl got something to do with you wanting a truck all of a sudden?" Mateo quizzed.

"Naw, Iesha has nothing to do with the truck. She and I are just cool. Seeing where things are going."

"Where'd you meet her at?" Mateo asked.

"His-Love.com. I told her about my past before we agreed to meet up, and she was cool with it. Told me everyone deserved another chance. She just got out of rehab and is looking for a fresh start too."

Mateo was proud of Sonic. He was happy his boy was meeting a woman who was willing to look past his past and see the God in him. His phone vibrated and he saw Amirah's number. He picked up the phone and read the text message.

Are you close by?

No. Mateo typed. Where are you at and do we need to come get you? I'm with Sonic. Just got off from work.

I'm at the school. I'll wait on you.

Mateo sensed that Amirah was in trouble. "Ay, can we go to Shiloh real quick? I think something is up with Amirah."

"Yeah, no problem."

Sonic left Burgers & Fries and turned on Patton heading toward the I-240/I-26 intersection. Fifteen minutes later, Sonic pulled up in front of Shiloh Christian Academy, and Mateo was leading the way to Amirah's classroom. Mateo and Sonic passed by a few high school students who were hanging around waiting on the basketball game to begin, or leaving club meetings.

When they arrived, they saw Amirah and Sarai sitting at her desk.

"What's wrong?" Mateo walked up to Amirah and gave her a hug.

"Turner came into my classroom today."

Mateo could feel his anger rise. His heart beat a little faster and his senses became heightened.

"Where is he now?" Mateo asked.

"He left a few hours ago," Amirah answered. "He told me I could do better than you, and that he had a room at Heaven's Inn."

"That dude . . ." Mateo walked around, slamming his fist in his hand. "He always wants to try me." Fuming, Mateo wished he still had his Glock.

"Naw, man, we can't do it like that." Sonic tried to get Mateo to a calm down. Mateo eventually took a seat. "Turner is just doing this so you can come looking for him—and he can have a reason to put his hands on you."

"Yeah," Sarai cosigned. "No need to chase the devil when you don't want his attention."

The words sank in, and Mateo realized that Sarai was right. It wasn't about wanting to kick Turner's butt. He was tired of Turner trying to bully him and Sonic and run their lives.

"What is it going to take to make that man stop coming after us?"

"I know what it will take." Sonic stood up and walked toward the window. "I don't want to do it, but I'm going to have to talk to him."

"Naw, I'm not with that," Mateo responded.

"I'll talk to him and make him understand that what we had is over. Let him know that I rock with Jesus now and that I'm happy with Him being my Lord and Savior." Sonic continued to stare outside.

"What is that going to do?" Sarai asked.

"It's not about what that's going to do," Sonic said. "It's about me standing up for myself and letting him go once and for all."

"Sonic, last time we tried to stand up for ourselves, Turner and his goons crushed us. We were the ones in the hospital, while he and his boys rode through the town." Mateo was agitated. He wanted another physical confrontation with Turner, but he didn't want Sonic in the middle of it.

"This time, we pray *before* we see him. He won't be able to surprise us if we bring it to *Him,*"— Sonic pointed upward—"first." Sonic was sure of himself.

"If it's any help, he's in room one twenty-four—but I don't want y'all to do nothing crazy," Amirah shared.

"I'm not going to do nothing crazy," Sonic promised. "I'm just going to talk to him. See if we could settle this like men."

"I don't think he's trying to talk," Sarai suggested.

"I agree," Mateo jumped in.

"He wants you back," Sarai continued. "And he's going to do anything and everything possible to make sure he gets you back."

"That may be true," Sonic admitted, "but Turner is just going to have to accept the fact that he can't have everything he wants."

Everyone in the room knew what Sonic said to be true. Equally, they knew how violent and possessive Turner could be about things and people he viewed to be his possessions. Mateo was furious because Turner brought the battle somewhere he'd hoped the man wouldn't step foot, but Turner just showed him how vengeful he could be. Next time, Amirah could be hurt or find herself with a couple of days at Mission Hospital courtesy of Turner and his goons. Or worse, they could be visiting her at Hart Funeral Home down the street from the hospital.

"Let's pray before we get out of here." Sarai stood up and motioned for everyone to gather around her. Everyone complied, and Mateo's face lit a smile as he grabbed Amirah's hand.

"Father God, we need your help. We have an earthly enemy that needs to know you and know that you, God, are in control. Please give us all safe traveling mercy as we make it to and from our destinations. And we trust that you have our backs in whatever we do—and that what we do will be in line with your Word and your will. The Lord *is* my light and my salvation; whom shall I fear? The Lord *is* the strength of my life; of whom shall I be afraid? He gives power to the weak, and to *those who have* no might He increases strength. That is your word,

God, and we are trusting and resting upon it. In Jesus' name we pray. Amen."

"Amen," they all said in unison.

Mateo gave Amirah a hug before he and Sonic left the room. He knew what he was going to have to do, and he was thankful that Sarai thought to pray for him to have the strength to do it.

Chapter Twenty-eight

Get out the Way

The students walked in and grabbed the test from Amirah as she stood at the door. During test time, her students knew what to expect. They read the instructions first so they could find out whether the test was going to be written, performance, or both.

Amirah learned to mix the test around to keep her students from guessing what they were going to be doing. She was notorious for giving her first class one type of test, her second class another type of test, and the third class a completely different test altogether. This was done to keep the students from cheating or discussing the test in between classes.

The copy of *Secrets and Lies* by Rhonda McKnight sat on the edge of her desk. She was tempted to pick it up and read it. That way she could be ready for the upcoming book club meeting, but during test time, she had to keep her eyes on the students at all times. Amirah made sure no one had answers written on a sheet of paper or on themselves, and that all electronic devices were put away. For the students who were doing performance-based tests, she made sure the students using the computers didn't have access to the Internet.

Amirah cared about whether her students learned and possibly could apply the material being taught, especially for the accounting class. Her goal for the accounting students was that they could gain a head start for those wanting to be business majors in college and/or gain jobs as bookkeepers for those looking for work.

The students sat at their computers and got to work. Soon, she could hear students reading passages and their words appearing on the screen. She was pleased as she heard some of the students dictate the user commands to correct errors and to fix other issues with what they typed.

Amirah got up from her desk and walked around so the students could see that she was watching them. From what she could see, the students understood the concepts and had a mastery of the speech recognition device.

Xen raised his hand as she approached him. "Can I go to the bathroom?" Xen stood up. Amirah pointed in the direction of the small clipboard that she used for a hall pass. Xen's smile said thank you, and he walked and grabbed the pass from the board.

After checking on all the students, she went back to her desk. There, she could no longer resist temptation, and opened the pages of *Secrets and Lies*. She looked over the pages of the opened book and found none of the students staring back at her.

A *ding* alarmed her that one of the students had finished their test early. Amirah clicked on the program to acknowledge receipt, and the student returned to his assigned seat and picked up the textbook so he could read the upcoming chapter on spreadsheets.

As each student completed the test, Amirah would stop and acknowledge receipt of their test. She moved through the pages of the book and began writing discussion questions for the literary group.

The knock on the door almost startled her. She knew it wasn't Xen knocking. Her class policy was that if you had a hall pass when you left, walk in and put the hall pass back on her desk. Amirah left her door unlocked so that she wouldn't be interrupted when she was giving instruction. Amirah put down her book and went to answer the door.

"The school is on lockdown," the school resource officer stated. "Is there anyone missing from your class?"

"Xen Anderson," she replied. "He's supposed to be in the bathroom."

"Keep an eye on your e mail and watch the school channel for updates."

"Thank you." Amirah received the instructions. She wanted to peep out of the window, but she knew she couldn't. As she had been trained to do, she reached into her desk and grabbed two yellow index cards and placed them on the window of the door and on the window facing the office. The yellow cards let police and administrators know that she was missing a student.

Amirah turned on the television, which she usually had off when she gave tests, and she turned it to the school channel. An announcement scrolled at the bottom of the screen that second period would be extended until further notice.

"We will be staying here for a little while after the bell rings," Amirah told the students. Some showed displeasure, but others were silent.

Amirah looked up and said a silent prayer for Xen and his safety. If Xen were to knock on the door, she wouldn't be able to let him in until lockdown was over.

"Where's Xen?" one of the students asked. Amirah looked around and noticed that all of the students had completed the performance test she had for her second period.

"He stepped out for a minute," Amirah answered. Not wanting to think the worst, she hoped that Xen was okay and that an administrator or one of the police officers had him in a safe place.

Thankfully, none of the other students asked questions—for a moment.

"Did one of the students get stabbed?" another student asked.

Amirah's heart raced fast. She wanted to avoid the feeling she'd gotten that something had gone terribly wrong with Xen. "I don't know. What makes you ask that?" Amirah questioned.

"My mother just texted me." the student said as she held up the cell phone.

Great! Amirah thought as she walked over and looked at the message the student's mother had sent. *The students will find out more from their parents and outsiders before we've had a chance to process anything.*

"We don't know what's going on." Amirah tried to keep a straight face, praying that the news she'd just received wasn't true.

"My aunt just sent me a message asking the same thing," another student offered. "I told her I was okay."

"Please don't tell them anything else," Amirah warned. "I'm not trying to be mean, and I understand your parents are worried about you, but we don't have any information, and the school will notify the parents and let them know what's going on once they have information they are allowed to send." Amirah hoped her students would heed her request. The last thing she needed was for the students to know any more about the situation than she did.

The bell rang and the students remained in their seats. "While we wait to be dismissed, go ahead and finish reading your chapters on spreadsheets. Tomorrow, we will review the information and start our unit. We may even get to try to operate the spreadsheet program with the speech devices."

The students continued to read their materials while she walked by and did a visual head count. Amirah walked to the door and stood. Not being able to resist temptation, she took a peek out of her window. She could see Xen's body being placed on a stretcher. From what she could see, he'd lost a lot of blood. She watched as the emergency crews held him in place so they could bandage around his wounds.

What in the world did Xen get into? Amirah wondered as she turned to face her students. There was no way she was telling them that one of their classmates had been injured. She knew they would talk about it and ask her a bunch of questions she wasn't ready to answer.

The emergency crew wheeled Xen's injured body past their door, and she could see his face. He strained to keep his eyes open and fight back tears. Their eyes met, and Xen quickly looked away.

Amirah said another silent prayer, hoping that no other students got hurt and that Xen would survive and make a speedy recovery.

"Good afternoon, students," Mrs. Ingle said over the intercom and on the television screen. "We are going to dismiss school in thirty minutes. We will be coming to each classroom to release you individually. Unfortunately, due to the events that took place, we will not be able to permit you to go to your lockers. You will be escorted by our school resource officer, Asheville City Police, and your teacher. We do apologize for the inconvenience.

"Parents and guardians have been notified and will meet you at a safe point away from the school. Those of you who ride buses will be able to get on your bus and arrive home from there. Please pray for your fellow students and get home safely."

Thirty minutes later, the television screen went blank and the end-of-school bell rang. A few minutes later, she heard a knock and saw the school resource officer along with four police officers. The students lined up and were dismissed.

A police officer pulled her to the side and asked her questions about Xen and what he had been dismissed for. After she answered all the questions, the police officer did confirm that Xen had been one of three students who were stabbed in the boys' bathroom.

When they were done, Amirah was escorted to her car by one of Asheville's finest. Once she got in her car, she got a group text from Mrs. Ingle telling her that there would be an emergency meeting held at David's Table, where they would meet within the hour.

"Any more news about why this happened?" Amirah asked after she rolled down the window.

"Ma'am, we don't know any more than what's been reported," the police officer replied. "We're praying like you that the boys who got stabbed get their healing."

Amirah nodded her head and started the car. She felt foolish for letting Xen leave her room during the exam. It wasn't her fault that he got stabbed, but she could've told him no. Then again, Amirah had never been the one to deny a student the right to use the bathroom. Her mother dealt with incontinence issues in her last days, so she was more sympathetic and willing to give the students the benefit of the doubt.

As she drove away from the school, all she could picture were Xen's eyes as he lay on the stretcher. The boy had made so much progress in avoiding being a troublemaker. She prayed that the stabbing didn't send him back a few steps.

Chapter Twenty-nine

I Can't Write Left-Handed

Praying that the injured students would be okay, Amirah headed to the brief staff meeting that was being held at David's Table. They needed answers for the stabbings that had just taken place a few hours ago.

Amirah was still shaken. She hadn't thought she would ever see one of her students become a victim of a violent crime.

"I see you brought your Bible." Amirah noticed as she welcomed Mateo and Julio to the part of the restaurant that had been closed off for temporary school use.

A few of her friends and some of the worshipers at Guiding Light Ministries decided to get together for an impromptu Bible study. The violence at her school left all of their souls vulnerable, and the prayer for Xen's and the other students' safe healing and recovery motivated the crowd to move closer to God.

Mrs. Ingle and her husband came in too, and soon brought the meeting to order. "Today, we learn to be prepared for the unfortunate and unexpected," Mrs. Ingle started. "The stabbings of three of our students could have happened at any school in Asheville, North Carolina, or in the country. Unfortunately, school stabbings and shootings are becoming too frequent."

Amirah noticed the weary looks on the faces of her fellow teachers. To think that when she was a little girl, teaching used to be one of the safest professions in the world. It seemed that when tragedy strikes, many lives are lost and a whole community is left to deal with the aftermath.

"What's the status of the students who were stabbed?" Calvin Rice asked.

Amirah hadn't even noticed Calvin step into the room. Calvin was also one of the original members of the Street Disciples Ministry that she'd heard so much about, and he spent a lot of his time mentoring young men in the area.

"Thankfully, all of the students are stable," Mrs. Ingle confirmed. "We decided that we are going to make tomorrow a teacher workday and let the students stay home. Administration will be meeting with the police department and strategizing a safe return for the students the following day. Most of you have the ability to work from home, so I'm only going to request that you come in for a few hours to record any grades you need to record."

Amirah felt good. Knowing that Xen and the other students were going to be okay made her feel at ease.

"What do you need from the community?" Pastor Cummings asked. "Guiding Light Ministries is prepared to offer the sanctuary and access to our small classrooms and library for students who may need to meet or have counseling to deal with what happened."

"That is greatly appreciated," Mrs. Ingle replied. "We want the students to return to having as close to a normal school year as possible, and anything that can speed up the process is good.

"I did want to commend everyone for doing a great job handling the lockdown situation. I know that some of you were put in a tight spot with students knowing what the media had reported about the stabbing. I also want to acknowledge the teachers who remembered to put up the yellow cards for the students who were missing. Aside from the stabbing victims, everyone else was found safely."

Hearing Mrs. Ingle speak renewed Amirah's faith in teaching and working at Shiloh Christian Academy. One thing she could always respect about Mrs. Ingle was that in addition to running a tight ship, she seemed to be prepared for every possible emergency imaginable.

Amirah felt her phone vibrate. She pulled it out discreetly and saw that Aja and Marjorie had texted her with concern for her safety. She made a note to get in touch with them after the meeting was over.

After a few more questions, Mrs. Ingle separated everyone by department. Calvin led the rest of the group to the opposite end of the room. Amirah could see Mateo, Hammer, and Pastor Cummings huddled up with the other administrators.

He smiled. She felt safe with him around. She smiled back.

"I'm glad to hear we all did well," Calvin congratulated the team. "Amirah, if you need any help with the students on Thursday—"

"I think I'll be fine," Amirah assured him, "Xen had asked to go to the bathroom and didn't return. Most of my students were taking their unit test when the school went on lockdown."

"Well, it's almost six o'clock now," Calvin pointed out. "Mrs. Ingle will give an official statement on behalf of the academy, and Lord willing, that will answer some of the questions the parents and students may have."

Amirah agreed. She prayed that her students would return ready to learn and move forward. She had decided to visit with Xen later on after she got settled in at home.

Most of the teachers started to disperse, and she was pleased she was able to meet with Mateo on her way out of the building.

"Sorry you had to go through that." He walked Amirah to her car.

"I'll be okay," Amirah promised.

"I thought about Turner and whether or not he could've been involved," Mateo revealed. "I wondered whether or not this had anything to do with me or Sonic."

"Turner may not have had anything to do with this," Amirah surprised herself by saying. "The police haven't named anyone publicly yet, so there is no telling who they may have in mind. For some reason, I don't think Turner would have his eyes set on a student at Shiloh."

"He may not, but I know he has his eyes set on you," Mateo warned.

"I'll put Mrs. Ingle on alert about Turner." Amirah attempted to ease Mateo's mind. "I'm just glad that the students are going to pull through and for the extra security we will have on campus when the students return."

Amirah appreciated the concern Mateo had for her safety. "You want me to give you a ride to your car?" she offered.

"I rode with Hammer," Mateo confirmed, "but thanks for the offer."

Amirah and Mateo shared a hug, and Amirah watched as Mateo walked away. She quickly responded to Aja and Marjorie and promised to call them both when she got home. Amirah's feelings for Mateo were growing stronger every day. He just didn't know it.

Amirah stayed in her car until she saw Mateo and Hammer get in their car safely. When they pulled off, she followed suit.

Chapter Thirty

Where They Do That?

"Bruh, how come you don't have this refrigerator stocked?" Julio pulled out water bottles and fruit that was packed in smaller plastic containers. "If I didn't know any better, I'd think a homeless person lived here."

Julio had overstayed his welcome. When Mateo brought his brother home from Madre's a couple of days ago, he only meant he'd take Julio out for a little while. Julio had taken to sleeping on the other queen bed and claiming half of the room. Mateo's room had become Julio's second home.

"Julio, chill." Mateo tossed his apron on the bed. He had just come back from working at Burgers & Fries to help out with the lunch shift. With the students being off for a teacher workday, he'd spent the bulk of the four-hour work shift making shakes and prepping the toppings and condiments that went into the shakes.

The new threat from Turner raised his stress level. The man was down the hall from them, plotting, waiting to strike again. Mateo accessed the records and was amazed to find that Turner had indeed checked into the room under his real name. He thought Hammer must've been slipping. When he asked Hammer why he didn't kick him out, Hammer said something about not wanting to move too quickly.

What kind of mess was that?

Hammer's view was that Turner had been at the hotel for a whole week without causing any ruckus, and without the restraining order he failed to take out on him, Hammer would need more than a "he didn't like him" to put Turner out. Hammer wasn't going to approach Turner and offer him a refund to leave. He would inadvertently become the aggressor of any physical confrontation then. When Turner paid for the room in advance, he became a tenant and not a guest, so they had to treat him as if he were renting an apartment instead of a room. The only thing Hammer could do was to inform the employees not to renew his room after his time expired, or else they would enter into another monthly leasing situation.

Mateo wondered whether Turner was responsible for the stabbings of the students at Shiloh Christian Academy. That was yet to be seen.

"And you didn't bring back no burgers either. See, you don't ever do right," Julio complained when he took cup of fruit to his mouth and let the chunks fall in.

"Man," Mateo complained, "you been here two days, and you could've bought some groceries or something. I work two jobs. You need to get you one."

"Aw, come on, bruh."

"Come on nothing," Mateo responded. "I gotta pay rent and keep money so that I can take the bus back and forth when Sonic can't take me to work."

"Look, don't kill my vibe." Julio tossed the empty container on the counter next to the refrigerator. "I applied at all these places that claim they support vets, but they want you to be white and lesbian in the process. If I could get my money up, I'd get my truck and my lawn equipment together."

"Wait a minute. What happened to your truck?" Mateo had forgotten that Julio had a black Ford F-150 that was paid for.

"Wanna take a guess how I lost it?"

Mateo shook his head. It was anyone's guess as to what Julio may have done to lose his most prized position. He was going to reply with something smart when he felt his phone ringing. He'd just taken his shoes off and was about to undress when he saw Amirah's name flash across the screen.

"What's up, ma?" Mateo asked as he swiped the ANSWER button to accept the call.

"You made it home safe?" Amirah asked, annoyed that she had yet to hear from Mateo.

"I love you too, girl." Mateo put the phone on speaker, placed it on the bed, and took off his shirt.

"This isn't going to be no strip show, is it?" Julio got up and grabbed his keys off the table. "I can leave."

Mateo shook his head and put his finger to his lips to ask his brother to be quiet.

"Who was that?" Amirah asked.

"That's my brother. Long story. But to answer your question, I'm in my room. I'm safe and Sonic is safe."

Mateo could hear Amirah's sigh of relief. "I need to come by and see you. I forgot to give you his room key."

Mateo could feel his adrenaline rushing. Immediately he got up and grabbed the shirt he'd just thrown in the hamper seconds ago, and rushed to put on his shoes.

"He gave you the key?" Mateo could see Julio poppin' his knuckles and getting ready for whatever was going to go down.

"Yeah, he feels like he can be a better man than you and offered me a chance to find out," Amirah said.

"You see him around now?" Mateo cut her off. He was worried that if Turner saw her, he would be planning to do some physical harm to her. He could hear Julio in the background venting and mumbling in Spanish about everything he was going to do to Turner when he saw him again.

Mateo went to the window and took a peek through the curtains.

"He said he stayed down the hall from you. What room are you in? I have his key and I want to give it to you before Turner arrives." Amirah's voice came in fuzzy over the speaker.

"I'm in room one sixteen. The dude is at the end of the building," Mateo answered.

"Where he at?" Julio was hyped up, interrupting their conversation.

"I'll be there in fifteen minutes. Are you going to call Hammer?" Amirah asked.

"I can't. Hammer said something about Turner creating a tenancy in the room by paying a month in advance. We couldn't put him out if we wanted to." Mateo shook his head as he picked up the phone and turned off the speaker.

"Okay. I'll wait in my room and I'll see you in a few minutes."

Mateo and Amirah said their good-byes and ended the call. Mateo cursed himself for giving Hammer his Glock, but then the Spirit warned him to calm down.

"Where that fool at?" Julio asked. "We can go settle this right now."

The last thing Mateo needed was for Julio's OCD to kick in. He knew that Julio didn't take his medications regularly, and he spent most of his "crazy check" on booze and women.

"Look, bruh, chill. I got this."

"How? Hammer got your gun." Julio was frustrated. "I still owe you a whooping for giving it to him. Who does some dumb stuff like that?"

"Who said I needed it?" Mateo quipped back. He'd had enough of Julio and was ready to send him back to Madre.

"Look, short man." Julio got in Mateo's face. "That big boy out there ain't gonna stop at nothing until he gets what he wants. Where's Sonic at?"

"He's at work. He's closing the restaurant tonight."

"A'ight, bet. This is what we need to do: You go get in the shower so you can be fresh and clean for your girlfriend to get here, and I'll make sure I'm ready to knock Turner out."

Julio dropped to the floor and did military-style push-ups effortlessly. He even did a few with one hand behind his back. Mateo shook his head as he got some underwear and an undershirt from the drawer. He hoped that the shower would ease his mind and prepare him to face Amirah and confront Turner if necessary. He didn't like the idea that Turner just popped up at the school, or the fact that he hadn't been there to protect her. Now Mateo knew where his enemy rested his head, and he knew he needed to be ready for whatever Turner had in store for them.

Amirah knocked on the door. When it opened, she was surprised to see a taller, darker version of Mateo staring back at her.

"Ameerah," Julio greeted her, putting emphasis on the "e" portion of her name. "Me llamo Julio. Nice to meet you."

"Nice to meet you too," Amirah responded as she gave Julio a look over. Good looks definitely ran in the Valdez gene pool, and for a brief moment, she could picture darker and lighter little Mateos hanging around their uncle.

Amirah stepped in, and she heard the shower turned off. She figured Mateo had come in from Burgers & Fries and was changing to go host in the lobby. She'd never been inside Heaven's Inn before and was surprised at how large the room was. Two queen-sized beds fit into the room comfortably, with plenty of room to spare. The flat-screen television had the DVD player on the side, which gave the option for watching cable or renting something from Redbox or whatever. The floor of the carpet was new, and the buff comforter set looked like they came out of the Neiman Marcus catalog. The black refrigerator matched the other appliances from Kenmore.

Mateo walked out wearing an undershirt and a towel wrapped around his waist. Amirah flashed a smile, and he flashed one back. She watched as he grabbed a pair of black slacks and his dress shoes that were in the closet.

"Y'all look like that's the first time y'all seen each other naked." Julio smirked.

Amirah frowned and shook her head.

"Julio," Mateo commanded.

"What? I was just saying—"

"Hush," Mateo interrupted him. "I'm sorry for my brother. He a got little problem. I'll be back." He went back into the bathroom to put on his slacks.

"I got a *big problem*. I don't know what you talking about," Julio responded to the door closing. "My brother is so rude. He didn't even tell me he had a girlfriend until five minutes ago."

"Well, Mateo and I are taking things slow."

"Don't move too slow," Julio warned. "I'll have to snatch you up if he isn't careful."

Amirah wanted to keep a straight face, but she failed miserably. A smile and laughter escaped her face. Julio was definitely a trip. She could tell the two of them could entertain some company.

"Man, if you don't back up off my girl," Mateo threatened as he came out of the bathroom, pulling her close to him from behind. He kissed her on the cheek. He loved the feeling of having her near him, and he realized that where he belonged was with her. For the first time in his life, Mateo was in love.

"My bad, man. My bad." Julio backed away with his hands up.

Amirah dug into her front pocket. "Here is the key. What are you going to do with it?"

"I'm going to give it to Hammer," Mateo replied quickly as he put the key into his back pocket. He saw Julio giving facial expressions that indicated he was making a bad choice.

"You're not going to try to go after him, are you?" Amirah asked as she sat down on the chair next to his desk.

"Not today," Mateo promised. "He'll get dealt with later. For now, I just want to make sure that you are safe and that we don't have to worry about Turner trying anything stupid."

Amirah got up and kissed Mateo on his forehead. He pulled her close, and she felt safe in his arms. She knew she was in love. She just wasn't sure if she was ready to say so out loud.

Chapter Thirty-one

Back at Home

Mateo got up and started what had become his Sunday morning ritual. He took a shower and handled all of his bathroom needs. Then he turned the television on to BET to listen to one of the televangelists give a sermon. While the sermon played, Mateo would iron two sets of clothes: One set was for what he wore during service, and another set was street clothes he wore when he, Sonic, and Marvel hit the streets to spread the Word.

"You go to church every Sunday?" Julio groaned when he got up.

Mateo was starting to regret letting Julio stay with him. Sure, he'd agreed to a couple of days here and a couple of days there to help their mother, but Julio was taking the stay to a whole other level. Julio was slowly trying to take over the room. It wasn't that he didn't like being around Julio, but he had outgrown his brother's immaturity. Mateo wasn't the party animal that Julio loved to hang with.

"I try." Mateo applied starch to his dress shirt. "That's one way I get the Word in."

Julio sat up. "You do a lot of studying of the Word. What do you get out of it?"

"I get basic instructions before leaving earth. I get a chance to find out what God wants, what Jesus has to say. I feed my mind and the spirit of God in me, so that the

Holy Spirit can continue to apply the Bible's applications to me. It is by studying the Word that I find ways to solve problems that are more godly." Mateo looked at his brother to see if he understood.

Julio nodded his head. "You know some of those people were just in the club last night, or they were partying hard with other sinners the night before."

Mateo put down the iron. "I am accountable for my salvation. That's all I can work out with myself. I was once told that the church is like the hospital. God is the doctor. We nurse each other to health by working together to find the solutions God has for our problem. For some people, that solution may be as simple as going to God for the answer. For others, it could be Him working through me to accomplish something for someone. Either way, I allow myself to be used."

"And you said Pastor Cummings was some biker dude?" Julio got up. "Mom would flip if she knew that the man wasn't wearing a shirt and a tie. Which reminds me—why do you dress that way?"

"I dress because it's the only time in the week I get to dress up." Mateo chuckled. "No, I'm playing. I dress up to give my best presentation to God. Even when I don't wear a shirt, tie, slacks, and dress shoes, I make sure my clothes are presentable. I can't walk in there butt naked. I might cause a distraction."

"Or let someone know you're tempted." Julio laughed.

"But seriously, all jokes aside, I realize church is not a fashion show. I dress up sometimes because on nights where I have to work at the front desk, like tonight, it's easier for me to just change my shirt and go from church to work. Also, I do want Hammer to take me seriously when I tell him that I want to drive for the Christian Cab Company. I think of it as an opportunity to show that I am serious about the job I want to have. One day, I'll ask him to drive the cab and he'll say yes." Driving for the Christian Cab Company was so significant to Mateo because it would mean that Hammer saw that he was maturing and could be trusted.

Julio thought about what Mateo said. "How long before service starts?"

Mateo picked up his phone and looked at the screen. "I got about thirty minutes before I leave."

"Well, let me go with you."

This was a first for Julio. Mateo watched as Julio got out of the bed and made it military style. "You serious?"

"Of course, homes," Julio replied. "I wouldn't have gotten out of bed if I wasn't serious. I want to see this old biker dude preach."

"Oh, gosh," Mateo said. "Please don't let that man hear you call him some 'old biker dude.'"

Julio grabbed his personal bag, some towels, and got his clothes ready. In the time it took Mateo to get dressed, tie a Windsor knot, and brush his hair down, Julio was in and out of the shower, freshened up, and put on his slacks.

"Now, are we listening to Wiz Khalifa after service? I brought my CD," Julio said as he pulled out the CD from his carrying case and put it on the bed.

"No." Mateo smirked. "They is going to have 21:03 or somebody crunk that we can listen to on the way back. Hammer and a few of the other stewards transport us back and forth to service. Normally, he rotates one of the *WOW Gospel* or *Gotta Have Gospel* CDs. Every now and then we get to listen to a rap CD. We may end up going to Corner Stone or David's Table."

"Wait a minute. There's such a thing as gospel rap?" Julio asked.

"Yeah, we listen to LeCrae or Trip or The Revelation. The Revelation is Hammer's son."

Julio finished getting dressed and both men left the room. As they stepped outside, they could see Emilio pulling up with the church van. Michelle Williams' "If I Had Your Eyes" was blasting from the stereo.

"I could get used to this," Julio said as he stepped inside the van.

"Today, we are going to have a special guest speaker," Pastor Cummings announced. "He is a man who some of you have met before. After serving time in the state prison, Rahliem Victor founded the Street Disciples Ministry group that some of our members work with."

Mateo didn't remember seeing Rahliem walk into the church. He missed the men's Sunday school and normally, when Rahliem visited, he stopped by and participated. Mateo didn't see Rahliem or his wife and family in the front row or in any of the guest sections.

"Rahliem has been a role model and a leader and continues to expand his ministry, as he's looking to do programs in Tennessee and South Carolina at the beginning of the year. Ladies and gentlemen of God, it would be a great pleasure to introduce you to Rahliem Victor."

The audience clapped as Rahliem made his way from the back of the church to the stage. Rahliem wore a Carolina blue button-up shirt, some black slacks, and work boots—definitely not typical attire for a pastor or leader of God to wear.

Rahliem's message was short and effective as he spoke about the full armor of God. Rahliem reminded them that they were supposed to remember their salvation at all times, to live righteously, and to share truth. He also talked about how they had to carry their faith and let it be seen even in the direst of circumstances. Staying in the Word would be their weapon and their mission as they continued to spread the gospel to all they met.

Rahliem also shared a personal story about a young couple he met near the start of his ministry. They were a young married couple who decided they wanted new experiences within their marriage. Rahliem talked about how one of his bravest street disciples ministered to them without thought of what they were doing or how he was dressed. He pointed out how Abednego always answered the call and was ready to serve, and while on the outside, he looked like the street pharmacist he used to be. Abednego showed his true clothing in his work with God.

Mateo felt the message was for him, because he didn't always feel comfortable wanting to share the Word of God. He was still getting to know God and trying to be a good shepherd himself. Listening to Rahliem speak made him feel like he had nothing to be afraid of.

After service, Mateo introduced Julio to Rahliem.

"I've never met a minister quite like you before." Julio shook Rahliem's hand. "I always thought preachers like you couldn't exist, but after hearing your message and your story, you make it seem like anyone can go into the streets and spread the Word."

"Everyone is supposed to. The question is whether or not we choose to do it, and what determination drives us to save souls," Rahliem responded as he continued to shake hands with other parishioners.

Mateo let Julio and Rahliem have their conversation. He was happy that his brother was getting along with someone he'd looked up to. The thought crossed his mind to invite him to a Street Disciples meeting, but he wasn't sure Julio was ready for it.

"I didn't know you had a brother until he got in the van with you this morning," Hammer said as he caught up with Mateo.

"I'm the middle child between the three of us." Mateo volunteered the information. He didn't talk much about his family but felt comfortable enough with Hammer. "My younger sister is sixteen."

"You'll have to invite your sister and the rest of your family to our services. Do you and your brother need a ride home?" Hammer asked.

"Naw, we're good, but thanks." Mateo turned down the offer. "I'll see about getting my sister and mother out here. Remember, she's Catholic."

"And she's still welcome to our services," Hammer reminded him.

Mateo was glad that Julio came and enjoyed himself at service. He looked for Amirah, but after not seeing her, he decided he'd go home. He figured she went to her home church this week and that they'd catch up another time.

Chapter Thirty-two

Secrets and Lies

Aja and Marjorie walked into Amirah's classroom as she was getting straightened up for the day. Copies of *Secrets and Lies* by Rhonda McKnight were in their hands.

"Hey, ladies," Amirah responded excitedly as she hooked up the projector to her computer monitor. Soon, they could see the author's Web site and Skype being pulled up so they could do a live chat with her.

"Hey, Amirah." Aja and Marjorie greeted her as they gave her hugs.

Mrs. Ingle walked in with a copy of the book in her hands as well. "Ladies, I appreciate you allowing me to participate in this meeting."

"We appreciate you allowing Amirah to host this meeting in her classroom." Marjorie set up some of the items for the book club on the table next to Amirah's desk.

"I love supporting Christian works and ministry, and I can't wait to Skype with an author." Mrs. Ingle took a seat near the front. "I missed the one y'all did with Shana Burton, and I said never again."

The other ladies from Essence of Prayer Book Club found their way inside. One of the older ladies brought a meat and fruit tray, and another had drinks to serve.

Marjorie made her way to the front so she could start the meeting. "While we wait on everyone to finish setting up, I want to get feedback on the His-Love.com Web site. How is that working out for you?"

"I'll go first," Aja said. Amirah noticed how everyone got excited when Aja volunteered information. "All right, all right—it's nothing juicy, but Terrell and I have been spending a lot of time together. We went to service at The Lord's Church of Asheville a few weeks ago and really enjoyed the pastor and the sermon on remaining fully committed to God.

"Terrell is taking Alyssia to a birthday party this weekend and keeping her at his place for a while."

"Y'all managed to stay away from mistletoe this go 'round?" Marjorie put her business out there.

"Yes, we have." Aja tried to hide the fact that she was blushing. "Terrell and I are really working on making sure we build a strong and solid foundation before we walk down the aisle. He's picking up extra hours at the nursing home he works in, and I've been busy with some of the corporate accounts that I manage."

"That's really good," Marjorie said. "Amirah, tell us about Mateo."

"Marge, you are so messy." Amirah shook her head.

"Well, I don't have a man right now. The older gentleman and I didn't work out, so I get to live through you guys for the moment. So come with it. Tell us about your bad boy."

"Oooh." Some of the women chuckled.

"Mateo is not a bad boy." Amirah confided, "Not exactly. I think like most people who are new to Christ, he is on his way toward making a relationship with Him. He has great mentors in place, and when you look past his hardened image, you find that Mateo is really kindhearted and gentle."

"I'm glad you saw that in him," Mrs. Ingle spoke up. "My husband wasn't always on the straight and narrow.

When he came back from Vietnam, we had a fight to get him clean and off of drugs and alcohol. Once we got over that hurdle, he went back and finished school, and now he's an administrator for Henderson County Schools and a pastor. So you hang in there with Mateo if that's who you were meant to be with."

"I appreciate that." Mrs. Ingle's words of encouragement warmed Amirah's spirit. She knew that Mateo wasn't exactly who many people had in mind when it came to suitors for her heart.

"No problem. I know Hammer and Pastor Cummings. One of the things I've liked and respected about Guiding Light Ministries is that they really reach out into the community and go after those whom some would say are undesirable, and they bring them to Christ and let God show out in their lives," Mrs. Ingle continued.

"And that's the way it should be," Marjorie encouraged. "Anyone else?"

Some of the other ladies talked about some of the dates they'd had or their networking with some of the other men and women of God to find jobs or socialize platonically.

"Hello?" they could hear a young woman say on the screen. Amirah made some quick adjustments on the Skype program and soon, they were face-to-face with Rhonda, but even she enjoyed listening to the ladies talk of their experiences with His-Love.com. More than an hour had gone by before they got back on track and began discussing Rhonda's debut novel.

Chapter Thirty-three

Stop

The sun was beaming brightly as Mateo and Julio sat on the lawn chairs they put on the parking space designated for his room. Mateo didn't have to work the front desk of the motel for a few more hours, and he was enjoying the scenery. Cars sped up and down Tunnel Road, and he had nothing better to do than to text Amirah on the His-Love. com app and try to figure out what he wanted to do with the rest of his life.

Julio had brought back some Mexican food from Papas & Beer down the street. Mateo could smell the enchiladas, nachos, and other delicacies. Ever since his visit back home, he had developed a taste for more authentic Mexican food. He was craving all the foods he grew up with that Madre and Abuela cooked.

Mateo could also see the blunt Julio had rolled up and put behind his ear.

"If I were you, I'd put that away before Hammer sees you with it and flips," Mateo warned as he took out his food.

Julio looked at him and shook his head. He lit up the blunt, took a few puffs, and blew out some air and admired the smoke he was able to produce. He passed the blunt to Mateo, and when he saw Mateo put his hands up indicating that he didn't want any, Julio took the blunt back and smoked on it some more.

"I can tell you are really becoming a Christian." Julio blew out some more smoke and inhaled deeply.

"What's that supposed to mean?" Mateo looked up from the chicken quesadilla that had been occupying his mouth and his time.

"You praying before meals now, thanking God when you wake up, and saying prayers when you go to sleep." Julio continued to indulge.

"We used to do that before we grew up to be hardheads." Mateo wiped his hand on the napkin and took a sip of the soft drink.

"Y'all need to get back to doing that," Hammer warned. "How y'all gonna come to my house and blow some trees and not leave some for me?"

Mateo was surprised when he saw Hammer take a few puffs, blow out some smoke, and then put out the tip of the flame with his fingers and put the rest of the blunt in a gum wrapper he had in his pocket.

"You just going to steal my blunt?" Julio quipped as he kicked back on the chair he was sitting in. "If I had known you wanted some, I would've brought enough for you to have your own."

"Number one, I don't allow smoking of any kind in my establishment. Number two, back in the day, the rule was puff-puff-pass. You're supposed to bring enough to share if you are going to smoke out in the open."

Julio conceded and exhaled. He knew he couldn't argue with what was right.

Mateo thought back to a year and a half ago when he and his boys were caught smoking at one of the city park playgrounds after hours. In addition to being arrested and charged with loitering, Mateo served a few days in jail, paid a fine, and attended a few drug abuse classes.

The three men heard a fire truck blaring down the street, and they all rushed up to see where the truck was going.

"Man, just think: this time next year, I'm gonna be hanging off one of those trucks and I'm going to be putting out fires and all kinds of stuff." Julio's voice drifted in the air as he watched the firemen speed by with pride. His dream to be a fireman burned just as brightly as it had when he saw firemen putting out a fire at his old neighbor's house when he was five.

Hammer gave him the side-eye. "You ain't gonna be no fireman. I'm going to be a rapper before that happens."

"You always trying to clown somebody's dream, man. That's why I don't even mess with you like that."

"Young man, you don't even know me," Hammer replied. "I'm not trying to clown, but look at you. Nothing about you says fireman."

Mateo could see that Julio was uncomfortable with the eyes being on him. He wasn't exactly overweight, but he wasn't the cut-up army man Mateo remembered. Julio talked about it, but in practice, he didn't hit the gym like Mateo and Hammer did. Julio wasted his days drinking and smoking and talking to women he wouldn't have entertained before he fought in the war. Plus, he was bumming off of his mother and brother. Nothing said trifling more than that.

"So," Julio retorted as he snatched the weed from Hammer when he pulled it out of his pocket. "All this weed smoking and lounging around that I'm doing now is temporary. In fact, I'm counting down to about five months from now to do everything I want to do . . . then I'm going to get serious, give up smoking and excessive drinking, and I'm gonna lose this beer belly and get down to business."

"Why don't do you it now?" Hammer pressed the issue.

Mateo could see where this was going, and because it was for Julio's good, he did nothing to stop it.

"I'll be a fireman come this time next year. You'll see. And I'll have more muscles than you too," Julio bragged as he put his blunt back in the bag he had pulled it from, and then put it in his pocket.

"Dude, you don't even go to the weight room," Mateo pointed out.

"Why go to the weight room when I can lift my body weight anytime I want?"

"Good luck with that," Hammer replied as he reached in his back pocket and pulled out a pocket Bible. Mateo recognized it as being similar to the one he received when he first ran into Hammer a little over a year ago when he was dodging bullets for sleeping with and possibly impregnating another man's wife. Hammer had stayed on top of Mateo and Sonic as they took the first steps toward accepting Christ in their lives. Mateo could see that Hammer was getting ready to do the same thing for his brother.

"Since you are staying with your brother or at least visiting, I want you to take a look at this book," Hammer offered.

"Mi madre got plenty of these laying around," Julio responded and attempted to hand the small Bible back.

"Now you have one of your very own," Hammer responded. "Read it, and if you need help, come and see me or ask your brother. Either of us will be able to help you."

Julio cocked his lips and was two seconds away from saying something slick. When his eyes met Hammer's, he backed away and decided that the confrontation wasn't worth it.

"A'ight, old man," Julio finally said as he flipped through the pages of the Bible. "I'll give this one more shot." He leaned forward and faced Hammer. "But I'm gonna hold you to your word to help me with this Jesus thing."

"I'm a minister. That's what I do."

Mateo watched as Hammer got up and left them sitting in the parking lot. "You really going to give Jesus a chance?"

"Muhammad and Buddha already had their chance," Julio said. "I can at least give Jesus a try."

Mateo smiled. He was happy to hear that Julio was going to take his walk with Christ more seriously and possibly begin a walk of his own.

"Yo, has Hammer always been a minister?" Julio got up and put the Bible in his back pocket. "I get the feeling he's spent a lot of his time in the streets." He lifted his chair and carried it back into the motel room.

Mateo stood up too. "That's where he started. He's been in prison just like we have." He picked up his seat and followed Julio inside and they put the chairs back around the table. Julio sat on the bed and pulled the book out. "Do I read this thing from the beginning or what?"

"You should start with Proverbs," Mateo suggested as he looked in the mirror and checked to make sure he was ready. He knew that once he left the room, he wouldn't be able to come back until his shift at the front desk was over. "It has a lot of wise sayings and stuff to live by. And you don't have to read the Bible in one day. Just find a passage and meditate on it. When you spend your time in silence, just listen. The spirit will speak to you."

Mateo went to the sink and freshened up. He sprayed fresh body spray and applied some deodorant. After applying a new coat of lotion on his skin, he brushed his teeth and gargled again.

When Mateo got ready to go, he saw Julio laying on the bed and getting into the Word.

Maybe tough love was all he needed.

Chapter Thirty-four

This Is How It Should Be Done

Amirah was excited to have Achelle Sampson, the founder of His-Love.com, as a guest on her show. She was equally excited that most of the guests for the show had His-Love.com profiles and that some of them were couples who met on the site.

"I started His-Love.com as a Christian alternative to many of the dating and networking sites and to create an environment where those of us who worship the Lord can pray together," Achelle highlighted as she stood next to a screen that showcased the Web site. She moved to the opposite end and highlighted the site's links to Facebook, Twitter, Google + and other major social media sites.

"I know what I did when I went to the site," Amirah started her next question, "but what do new members typically do when they sign on to His-Love.com?"

Achelle touched the screen and a new page came up. "Believe or not, even though we are mainly a dating site, we have a large number of churches, book clubs, and other religious organizations who use the site as an alternative to the popular social media sites to connect with their members. They also contribute to the ads that are found on the top and the sides of the pages. Some of the organizations host dating parties where members can mix and mingle with each other in their local areas."

Amirah could feel the positive energy from Achelle and the Web site. She saw Mateo in the audience and smiled, knowing she'd made her connection on the site. She was feeling the grunge shirt that highlighted Isaiah 40:3. She made a mental note to find out whether it was an exclusive shirt for the Burgers & Fries employees or if it was a shirt they were selling on their Web site.

After the director yelled "Cut!" Amirah relaxed a little bit. She felt good knowing she wasn't dealing with any foolishness on her show.

"Amirah, can I ask you something?" Achelle left the stage and walked with Amirah as she headed to a table that had vegetable and fruit trays.

"Sure." Amirah wasn't used to answering questions on her show. She was used to spending the time comforting her guests and helping them get over being nervous.

"Have you met someone on the site?" Achelle seemed intrigued.

Amirah was surprised that Achelle didn't know the answer to that question. She assumed that Achelle knew of all major connections or activity on her Web site. "As a matter of fact, I have. See that guy standing over there?" Amirah pointed to Mateo, who seemed to be engaged in a conversation with some of the members of the crew. "We're trying to see where we are going. I really like him, and I can deal with his flaws, and he can deal with mine pretty well."

Achelle smiled. "I always like to hear things like that. I think it's good when people find what they are looking for—or what God may have in store for them."

Amirah and Achelle enjoyed a few snacks before they were called back to the stage. With the live-streaming of her show, Amirah had to work hard to keep things going at a fast pace. Cue music from Joshua Rogers broke through the air, and within seconds, Amirah was back to work.

"For those of you just joining us, we have with us Achelle Sampson, the founder of His-Love.com. His-Love.com is a Christ-centered dating and networking site that emphasizes and promotes mixing and mingling with those of like-minded faith. Achelle, I have question for you. Have you met anyone from His-Love.com?"

"No, I haven't." Achelle stunned Amirah and the audience. "I'm not opposed to meeting someone, and sometimes I look at the new profiles created and I wonder if he's the one, but no one serious has hit me up."

"Y'all hear that, single fellas? Achelle Sampson is available," Amirah said.

"Sometimes I think it's me, because I spend a lot of time as a mom first and foremost, and then making sure the site runs smoothly. We have a small staff, so I work with them on moderating our discussion boards, reviewing profile pics, and other day-to-day maintenance for the site," Achelle explained.

"What type of man would you go for, if given the opportunity?" Amirah asked.

"First and foremost, he'd have to be a man of God," Achelle started, which got a few confirmations from the crowd. "And I guess after that, a job, his own place to stay, some form of stability. I think I can ask for that, because I bring that to the table."

"That's fair," Amirah pointed out. "What advice would you have for someone entering the realm of online dating?"

"I think with any relationship you have to take it slow. Get to know one another on and off the boards. But you should ask and seek God's discernment. Marriage is a lifetime commitment, and while it's popular, and necessary for me, divorce is still frowned upon within the faith."

Amirah took all that in. She looked for Mateo in the crowd and was pleased to still see him in the front. She chose not to put their relationship out in the open just yet.

As they closed the show, Amirah was pleased with the outcome. She also had material to bring to the next book club meeting. She could relate to Achelle's struggle because just like it took time and struggle to build and maintain a Web site, she put that time and energy into getting the show together behind the scenes.

When Amirah got to her dressing room, she said a silent prayer that the man God had for Achelle would find her, and that His-Love.com continue to be prosperous not just financially, but spiritually, as she saw the site becoming a permanent fixture in her day-to-day routine.

Chapter Thirty-five

Lawd, Not This Again

Mateo was lying in the bed with the sheets covering his bare chest and the black-and-red jersey shorts he was wearing. With his hands behind his head, he was listening to and reciting the words to a Drake song about fear, even though he lived his life in the total opposite. The old melody encouraged him to nod his head as he remembered The Revelation's cover of the song, and soon, he was replacing the secular lyrics with spiritual ones. The alarm buzzed, letting him know it was time for him to get up.

It didn't take him long to remember that he and his brother had taken an impromptu trip back to Madre's house. Mateo hadn't slept in the bed of his youth in more than five years.

Realizing this was the fifth R&B or rap song that he was moving his head to and reciting, he looked at the clock and grew furious when the clock struck eight o'clock. He could hear the water in the bathroom being turned off finally, after having been on for about thirty minutes.

Why do women take so long to get in and out of the bathroom? he questioned angrily as he sat up to get out of bed. He grabbed the red Chicago Bulls T-shirt off the floor and put it on. The shirt used to be his brother's from when they won the NBA Championship in 1992. This was his third trip getting up and going to the bathroom, and he'd hoped that this time he wouldn't be turned away. He grabbed his red shower basket that was the temporary home for his personal hygiene products and headed to the only bathroom available for him to use. He turned his nose up at the sour-apple fragrance coming out of the bathroom.

And it's not just this *woman who takes forever in the bathroom. All of my ex-girlfriends acted like the bathroom was a field trip. Trying to impress guys who really could care less. All that makeup and hair glam stuff is a waste of time. If I thought she was ugly, I wouldn't be with her.*

Mateo furiously banged on the door again, making it bounce against the frame as the person occupying the room on the other side had yet to open the door. *Even my own mama takes forever and a day to get in and out of the bathroom.* He shook his head after being ignored for the past few minutes, as he banged on the door again. It sounded as if he was punching it with all of his might, trying to huff and puff and blow the door down like the Big Bad Wolf. *And that's exactly where my sister gets this mess from, our mama.*

To his utter disgust, his sister Luisa forcefully opened the door, and the anger on her face matched his. Mateo glanced at the feminine version of his reflection, wearing nothing but a salmon-colored head wrap and an apple green–colored towel that matched the nasty apple fragrance coming out of the bathroom.

"Eww . . ." Mateo did a horrible job of hiding his disgust. He could feel the two bean burritos and the cinnamon twist he had last night at Taco Bell starting to make their way up from the bottom of his stomach to the tip of his esophagus, threatening to break the dam in his throat and burst out like a waterfall. His anger returned. "Put some clothes on and hurry up. You know I got to use this bathroom too, and you being all inconsiderate."

"Wait a minute," Luisa snapped and rolled her head just liked the other young girls her age do when they are getting ready to go off on someone. "I know *you* are not rushing *me* out of *my* bathroom?"

"I said hurry up!" Mateo yelled at his sister, looking her at eye level. *I can't stand her*, he told himself. *Gosh, she gets on my nerves.* A trail of expletives and other mean-spirited words danced in his mind as he contemplated telling his sister how he really felt, even though Madre was downstairs and would surely chastise him for such behavior.

"Let me tell you something!" Luisa stepped out of the bathroom and put her day-old manicured index finger on Mateo's forehead, which he impolitely pushed off. "If you and that fast-tailed hussy hadn't broken the toilet seat trying to be grown, you would have your own bathroom to do your thing in. But this is *my* bathroom, and if I want to take thirty, forty, eternity minutes in *my* bathroom, then I will do as I please."

"Dang, Ma ain't fixed that toilet yet?" Mateo pressed his point. He remembered that the toilet had been broken years ago. He was tempted to yank his sister out of the doorway and end her bossy diva moment, but he knew that if he put his hand on her, Julio wouldn't be too far off on his behind, so he thought better of it.

"No, Madre had the toilet fixed, but the seat cover doesn't stay on, and it stopped flushing right a long time ago. You need to give Madre the money for it since you're the one that broke it. You know these trifling people who manage this place charged her to fix the plumbing y'all managed to pull out of the wall, but they still won't do anything with the seat."

"Why don't you fix it?" Mateo was heated because he really needed to get inside and handle his business. "I'm sure I wasn't the only one rocking back and forth on that thing. I know I had some help breaking it!"

"What is this?"

Mateo and Luisa stopped their argument at the sound of the inquiry being shouted. Madre was leaning against the wall behind Mateo in her dark navy business suit with the Bible under her arm, preparing for another morning mass at her Catholic church. To everyone's surprise, Julio was struggling to finish his black-and-gold tie on his shirt that still needed to be buttoned up.

"Ma, Luisa is taking forever in the bathroom again. She only does this 'cause she knows I got to share this bathroom with her."

"Well, maybe you should wake up earlier," Julio told Mateo .

Mateo exhaled but didn't take the disrespect much further because he knew Julio would light into his behind like he was his father if he thought that Mateo was thinking about bucking up to him. Plus, Mateo still had an issue he needed to take care of. Julio had a good four inches and fifty pounds of muscle over his brother.

"Have you come up with an answer or the money for how the toilet seat in your bathroom broke and how you managed to flood the bathroom?" Julio asked.

"Okay, I admit it. Five years ago, I had me a chick in there and I wrecked shop." Mateo could see the look of disappointment in Madre's eyes. He knew it was more so the fact that it took him so long to tell the truth than what he actually did. "I'm no different than you and Luisa using that spot to do your dirt, so we all need to put in for the toilet."

"Well, at least you didn't tell a lie this time." Julio finished buttoning his shirt. "I'm proud of you."

Mateo remembered telling the lie that he grabbed the toilet seat to keep it from falling. Julio had told him that neither he nor Madre bought that story when he had told it to them. Yet, Mateo refused to admit that he'd snuck a girl into the house, or what they were doing when they broke the seat, causing a flood. Mateo glared at Luisa, and at that moment, he realized that his younger sister was good for not snitching, because she helped both of them clean up the mess and hasn't said a word yet she knew what her brother and his girl of the moment were doing.

"Yeah, but at the same time, Luisa, you do need to be more considerate and spend less time in the shower when you know your brother has to use this bathroom too," Madre said, wiping the smile off of Luisa's face that appeared when Julio chastised Mateo. "I swear, y'all act like you're one, nine and eleven all over again."

"But I'm still a kid," Luisa said, "at least according to you."

"Now both of y'all need to hurry up because, Mateo, you need to catch a ride to go to work." Julio looked at his phone. "Luisa, you go to your room and change in there and let Mateo use the bathroom real quick."

"Yes, sir," they both replied sarcastically. Luisa grabbed her basket with all of her products in it and the outfit that she was going to change into. Mateo was rushing to turn the water on so he could jump in and jump out of the shower. He knew they would really have to book it if they expected to get to work and school on time. Mateo glanced at his sister, and they each rolled their eyes at one another.

She makes me sick, Mateo thought. He couldn't believe that she was still pushing his buttons like this after all these years, and he was beginning to wish that he'd gone back to Heaven's Inn. At least that way he wouldn't have had to share the bathroom with anyone.

Once Luisa was completely out of the bathroom, he quickly locked the door, hopped out of his clothes, and let the warm water soothe his body.

Chapter Thirty-six

It's Getting Late

Amirah could see Mateo waiting on her as she stepped out of another taping. As the weeks went by, their relationship flourished. It had gotten to the point where they saw each other almost daily. Amirah had come to appreciate the routine they developed.

"I can't believe you waited on me until seven-thirty." She pulled out the keyless remote to her car and unlocked the doors. "Don't you have to be at work?"

"Doug is cool with me making sure you get home safe." Mateo smiled as he opened her door and shut it once she was safe and secure in the driver's seat.

Amirah watched as he walked around the front of the car and entered the passenger's side. *Could I see his face every day?* she wondered. Amirah hoped she hadn't come off as vain in the Lord's eyes.

"What time does third shift start for you?" Amirah asked as Mateo fastened his seatbelt.

"I'm only going to be on third shift for a few more weeks, but I work from nine p.m. to six-thirty a.m., four nights a week. Then when I go to first shift, I'll work eight a.m. to three-thirty p.m.," Mateo confirmed.

"Those sound like long hours," Amirah suggested when they pulled off the church's parking lot and got on the highway.

"I make it. Third shift can take a minute to get used to, but right now I don't have the best record to keep or maintain a job. Heaven's Inn and Burgers & Fries are helping me achieve that. Maybe one day I'll own my own Burgers & Fries franchise."

Amirah nodded her head. She admired his ambition and wished that more people their age had the same goals or at least aspirations to do something.

"I like that about you," Amirah told him. "You know what you want and you don't mind going after it."

"I'm not in a position where I can afford to sit on my tail and do nothing. Let the State of North Carolina tell it, my story begins and ends with the fact that I'm a convicted felon. Let my God tell it, He can turn the same skills I used to scheme and steal from people to edify his Kingdom. You know how many thieves Jesus rolled with?"

Amirah smiled. "I got that chain e-mail about all the sins different men in the Bible committed. Speaking of which, how is the Street Disciples Ministry going for you?"

"It keeps me busy," Mateo replied. "Between working with those guys, Heaven's Inn, and Burgers & Fries, I stay tied up in ministry in some way."

"I feel that way about school and my television show," Amirah confessed. "Not that that's a bad thing, because living for the Lord is supposed to be a joyous occasion. Sometimes I'd complain because I used to think I was in church seven days a week. Then I think about the trouble I'm not in."

"When I'm at work, all I think about is the bills I got coming, the restitutions I'm almost done paying off, and moving toward the future—one that hopefully you'll be in." Mateo looked out the window and noticed they were pulling into his motel.

"And what about the threat from Turner?" Amirah was concerned.

"Turner will be here until God decides his time is up," Mateo answered as he leaned forward for a hug. "I just have to make sure that my interactions with him don't put me in a position where I won't be able to see Him face-to-face."

"Good point." Amirah watched as he closed the door. She saw the stragglers in the streets and she could hear one of the guys preaching the Word of God to anyone who would listen. Suddenly, any reservations she had about Turner disappeared, and she felt confident that everything between the two of them would be all right.

Chapter Thirty-seven

Teenage Love Affair

A smile appeared on Mateo's face when he saw a text from Amirah. He knew she was still at school and was most likely doing this on the sneak tip.

The message read: So what are we going to do next?

Mateo looked around. Julio was out of the room, and he was waiting on Sonic to pick him up so he could go to Burgers & Fries. The night would be short, as he was leaving at nine so he could rest for the double shift he'd work the following day.

There was peace and quiet, something he hadn't had in a while. Mateo loved his brother, but having him around every day put a cramp in his style.

"You should meet my family," Mateo spoke as his fingers moved to keep pace with his voice.

I can't wait, Amirah replied. Mateo could picture her smiling on her end. When do we make this happen?

Mateo thought about his response. Soon, was all he could think of. After pressing SEND, Mateo heard a car horn honking. He looked outside and saw that Marvel had pulled up and was waving for him to come out.

"Sonic does not follow directions," Mateo mumbled to himself as he got his backpack and checked to make sure his work boots were tied. As he stepped outside, he noticed the wind blew gently and the flow of traffic was light and mellow. Mateo thought to go back inside and grab his jacket, but he knew how much he would be sweating after work and decided against it. Mateo wanted to find out what was going on with Sonic and why Sonic hadn't called him to let him know he was changing plans.

At that moment, his phone buzzed with a message from Sonic that was sent ten minutes earlier. "Did I miss the message, or is there a problem with my mobile data?" Mateo wondered out loud as he closed the door.

Mateo started typing a message and by not paying attention, he bumped into Turner before he could make it anywhere near Marvel's car.

"So we meet again." Turner brushed off the spot on his arm where they had made impact. He looked Mateo up and down and snickered. "You not strong enough to handle me. I'm not giving you a rematch, but that old man who owns this joint . . . I'd put up the money myself to go toe-to-toe with him."

"Yeah, the last time y'all went one-on-one, he gave you a good ol'-fashion country butt-whooping." Mateo stopped in the middle of his message to Sonic. "I don't think you ready for all that."

Mateo's lips slowly twisted into a smile. Seeing the flashback of Hammer throwing down, which had been broadcast on WorldStar and on YouTube was enough to wipe the smile off Turner's face. Mateo remembered cracking up with Sonic and Marvel at some of the comments, then having to repent when Hammer chastised them for inappropriate use of the computer lab.

"I'm ready for that old buzzard." Turner cocked his head up and nodded. "Name the time and place and I'll be there. The question is, will he be there?"

The thought crossed Mateo's mind to set up the whole thing. What Mateo really wanted to do was knock him down a few notches himself. Turner had too much mouth. He also had too much brawn and had a good ten inches and almost a seventy-five pounds of muscle on Mateo, who wasn't trying to jump up to land a good punch on him.

"I see you decided to show your face?" Hammer asked as he turned the corner of the building. "I thank you for not being on the property for most of your stay."

Mateo couldn't believe the shade. Normally, Hammer was cool, calm, and collected. Mateo wanted to ask where he'd come from and how come this was the first time Hammer had run into Turner.

"I waited for you in the lobby," Turner replied. "Where've you been?"

"This is my motel, and out there is my fleet of cars." Hammer pointed to fleet of black and cream-colored Cougars and Continentals that graced the side of the building. "I've been minding my own business. What are you doing?"

"Well, you know, old man," Turner replied, "I roam this place much like Satan roamed the earth, to and fro. Wherever I lay my hat is my home."

Hammer smirked and shook his head. "You do realize Satan loses the war, right?"

Turner got in Hammer's face. Neither man budged. Mateo saw how Hammer maintained his composure, and he was sure that Hammer was going to come out on top again. Mateo felt his heart beating faster and his adrenaline rushing, ready for a fight.

Turner picked at one of Hammer's loose locks from his shoulders, rubbed it between his fingers, lifted it up to his nose, and inhaled deeply. "I've always loved a good fight, in and out of the bedroom. And as I stand here before you now, I can't lie. I feel like—" Turner paused and inched his face closer to Hammer, barely missing his lips. "I have to admit, old man—" Turner licked his lips, closed his eyes, and bit his bottom lip in lust and whispered, "You are beautiful."

Turner let Hammer's lock go and turned his head toward Mateo. They glared at each other for a hot second; then Turner curled his lips up and faced Hammer again and flashed his pearly whites. "I wish we were not enemies. I could show you how I can be your best friend."

"Those lines must work on so many dudes." Hammer smirked and stepped to the side. "I don't want your friendship. And if I were into men, which I can assure you that I'm not, I wouldn't want you."

Mateo almost felt guilty for wishing for the setup in his mind. He could see that Turner kept his emotions in check. It was known that Turner didn't take rejection well, and he didn't want the hellion to flip. Mateo gave Turner a look-over, and from what he could tell, Turner wasn't strapped, so if a rematch went down, at least it would be a fair fight.

Turner got in Hammer's face. "I paid for this room for a whole month. I got another two and a half weeks left." Turner poked his lips out and imitated a kiss, hoping to tick off Hammer. "After I do what I'm going to do, I'm bouncing."

Hammer lifted up his arm and slowly guided Turner out of his personal space. "You do that again, and you are going to force me to explain to Jesus why I wasn't meek or gentle with you."

Turner licked his lips. "Maybe I won't be *meek* or *gentle* with you. I like guys that like it rough."

"I bet you would like 'em rough." Hammer surprised Mateo when he smiled again. "I'll be sure to tell my boys that when you get locked up. They'll let me know how long you lasted before you became someone's girl."

Mateo shook his head. Turner scowled, as he couldn't come up with a comeback. He put up his finger and shook his head and a few seconds later, he returned to the end of the building and entered his room.

Hammer shook his head. "I'm going to have to talk to my receptionist about not taking money from just anyone."

"Wait a minute. Didn't we just have the talk about being more welcoming and less judgmental? Isn't that why I got in trouble for letting that drunk couple spend the night?" Mateo asked as he looked toward Marvel's car. He was still waiting on him.

"You got in trouble for not making sure that the drunk couple's credit card processed before handing them the keys to the room," Hammer reminded him.

Mateo thought about it, and Hammer was right. He also remembered the hard time he spent getting the couple out of the room, and how he had to pay Hammer back for their three-night stay.

"Don't worry about Turner, man." Hammer continued on his way to the other end of the motel. "He'll be out of here before you know it."

For both of their sakes, Mateo hoped he was right.

"I stopped honking when I saw Turner get in Hammer's face." Marvel sounded like an excited elementary school kid who'd just seen his first fight. "Tell me it wasn't about to go down."

Mateo shook his head and fastened his seatbelt. "Hammer was a good one, because if that had been me, Turner would be out on his tail."

"What makes you think he's not working on that?" Marvel asked as he drove off.

Mateo felt his phone vibrate at his side, and he picked it up. He'd missed four messages from Amirah asking about their next date, and one from Sonic asking him if he'd gotten his message about Marvel picking him up.

I appreciate you wanting to meet my family, Mateo typed as he watched Marvel drive in rush-hour traffic on I-240. You already met Julio, but Luisa is a fast-tail and mi madre is very old school. How is your Spanish again?

Isaac Caree was belting out the lyrics to "Clean This House," and Marvel found himself singing along with the lyrics. Mateo looked over.

Dude can blow, Mateo thought as he sneakily turned down the radio. Marvel continued singing and driving. "I wish I could write songs, man. I'd have a couple written for you."

Marvel looked and sounded nervous. "I don't sing often, but I don't mind letting the Lord use me whenever."

Asi-asi, the text from Amirah read. I'm still learning but maybe you can teach me.

I will. Mateo replied.

By time Mateo thought of something else to add, Marvel was pulling into the parking lot of Burgers & Fries. They could see teenagers sitting at all of the tables and a line building outside the door.

"I got to go." Mateo reached into his wallet to pull out a five.

Marvel put his hand up and pushed Mateo's hand back. "I don't need the money."

"You sure?" Mateo intended on insisting that Marvel took the money. He knew what Hammer charged for a ride from Heaven's Inn to where the restaurant was located on Smokey Park Highway. The ride was worth at least fifteen dollars, but five was all he had.

"I'm good." Marvel smiled. "I'm just glad you are trying to do something to better your life, and I'm happy that I play the role God wants me to in that."

"Thank you." Mateo put his money back in his wallet and his wallet in his back pocket. He put the fitted cap with the Burger & Fries logo on as he got out of the car.

He made sure his black apron was tied as he made his way to the front of the restaurant.

"Thanks for coming in," Doug said as he met Mateo at the door. "Clock in, and then I need you to help me unload this delivery we got an hour ago."

Mateo walked inside with a sense of urgency. He knew he'd spend at least an hour unloading the truck and then another hour helping to sort and stock everything so that the cooks could get to the items with ease.

For the rest of the shift, Mateo would rotate between keeping the restaurant clean and working one of the inside registers. With the crowd that continued to grow, he knew any kind of break would be quick and fast, so there'd be little to no time to really call and hear Amirah's sweet voice; but he knew that he wanted to do something really special for her as soon as possible. Mateo smiled as everything about her filled his thoughts as he started his shift.

Chapter Thirty-eight

Meet the Crew

"I'm a little surprised that Sonic didn't come along, Mateo," Amirah said as she turned to look at him with love in her eyes.

"I can't believe you talked me into taking them with us," Mateo vented while he started Sonic's Toyota. "Plus, with Sonic still resting, he gave me the okay to drive his car."

"What's wrong with us?" Julio reached in the front of the seat and moved the mirror. He fixed his hair and his eyebrows.

"Yeah," Luisa jumped in. "Don't act all brand new because we here with your girl."

Amirah reached across the console and grabbed Mateo's hand. "I'll be fine."

She smiled and instantly she melted Mateo's heart. He fixed the rearview mirror and looked at his siblings. Mateo loved his brother and sister, but he would've rather spent time alone with his girl.

"I'm glad that Sonic was staying on top of his health," Amirah pointed out as Mateo made his way to the Interstate. "He needs his rest after having those tats removed and getting rid of those piercings."

"I still can't believe he did that," Julio butted in. "If that were me—"

"Julio, chill." Mateo's agitation slipped through his voice. "I promised Sonic I'd make this trip to Dandy's to get rid of the last of these clothes. The only reason y'all are even with us is because I promised Madre I'd keep the two of you out of trouble."

"And we promised Madre that Amirah wouldn't turn up pregnant before you put a ring on her finger." Luisa smiled as she stared back at Mateo. "Aw, don't look at me, homes. Madre *diga*,and I follow."

"My gosh," Mateo let out as he shook his head. "If the two of you were coming with us, when would Amirah and I have time to do what we need to do to make a baby?"

"Well, unless God intends for Amirah to be the new Virgin Mary, you not getting any panties," Luisa quipped as she pulled out the latest street fiction novel and flipped the pages. "And you aren't either," she addressed Julio as he laughed.

"Look." Mateo tried to set a firm tone. "We're going to Dandy's, and then we are coming back here. I don't have the money to make any pit stops to any motels, and I wouldn't ask Amirah for any either." Amirah seemed slightly annoyed, but Mateo appreciated her allowing him to handle his mouthy sister.

Mateo turned up the volume on the stereo and picked up the speed on their route to Greensboro. He was furious because he wanted to spend more time with Amirah, enjoying some quality time with her. Between working at Heaven's Inn and Burgers & Fries, he hardly had a day off; but Mateo didn't complain, because if he was working, that meant he was staying out of trouble. Staying out of trouble meant staying off the streets.

In record time, Mateo made the trip to Greensboro. Luisa and Amirah were reading books, and Julio listened to the music on his phone and wrote in a composition notebook throughout the trip. Very seldom did any of the four passengers speak to one another.

Mateo pulled up to Dandy's and smiled when he could see the woman from the window. She and an older man were talking as they waited at the door.

"Okay, everyone grab a bag," Mateo instructed as he pushed the buttons to unlock the doors and the trunk.

Mateo reached into the glove compartment and pulled out the Green Dot card and a copy of Sonic's information so that the payment could be processed.

"I see you've brought friends." Dandy opened the door as she and the older man helped relieve them of the bags.

"The younger girl and the dude who look alike are my brother and sister." Mateo introduced them.

Julio and Luisa mumbled hello, dropped the bags on the counter, and headed back to the car. Mateo shook his head. Mateo put his arm around Amirah's waist and brought her closer to him. "And this is my lady, Amirah."

"Nice to meet you." Dandy extended a hand from across the counter.

"Likewise," Amirah responded, shaking her hand before turning her attention to some of the Afrocentric pieces closer to the front of the store. She picked up a purple-and-gold kente and brought it closer to her body. "My mother would've loved this."

Mateo's ears perked up. He so rarely heard Amirah make a reference to her mom. He knew she had passed on a few years prior, but that was all he knew. The one time Amirah tried to talk about her, she broke down. The only thing she said about her father was that he'd been locked up for a double homicide since she was three.

Mateo followed Amirah as she draped the kente over her arm and looked through a hat and scarf rack. It didn't take long for Mateo to find a matching hat for the kente. He picked it up and offered it to her. "You think she would have liked this one?"

Amirah's face lit up, and she shone brighter than the lights in the store. "She would have *loved* this one." Amirah hugged Mateo and kissed him on the cheek.

Mateo started to ask her a question about her mother but decided to let Amirah open up on her own terms. He noticed that she picked up another multi-colored kente head wrap, and she went back to the rack to see if she could find a matching kente.

"My mother was really big on Afrocentrism." Amirah picked up the dress she was looking for and laid it on top of the rack. She matched the two outfits and smiled. "It would surprise her that I became a believer."

"Your mom wasn't saved?" The question disturbed Mateo. He always assumed that Amirah was one of those girls brought up in the church. At least that was how she carried herself.

"No, my mother wasn't saved." Amirah exhaled as she picked up the garments and made her way to the counter. There was a sadness in her voice. "I don't like to think about it. I mean, no one wants to picture their mother or their father burning in hell, but the truth is the truth. My mother was spiritual. She believed she had her own relationship with God and she didn't need a relationship with Jesus or to get to know the Holy Spirit."

"Wow." The revelation shocked Mateo.

"I'm okay." Amirah sounded relieved as she got to the counter. She paid for the garments and smiled at Dandy once their transaction was finished. "Nice meeting you." She shook the woman's hand again, took her bag, and left the store.

"We finished the inventory on Sonic's stuff. We are putting $735.08 on the card." Dandy moved on to the next transaction.

"Thank you," Mateo replied when he took the card back from Dandy.

That's more than he thought he was getting, Mateo admitted to himself.

"You sure he doesn't have any more pieces?" Dandy asked as she started putting the clothes they'd brought in on hangers.

"As far as I know he's sure."

"If he finds more pieces, have him bring them to us."

"We will," Mateo promised as he made his way to the car. Luisa and Julio were already in the backseat of the car, and Amirah was laughing with them. He was happy that Amirah liked his family, no matter how crazy they seemed to get.

When Mateo opened the door, Karen Clark Sheard and Mary Mary let it be known that they weren't ashamed of the gospel. It was at that moment that he remembered how close his mother was to their father's sister and what a huge gospel fan she was. Growing up in their house, they listened to Spanish music, hymns, and gospel. As he listened closely, he could hear Luisa and Julio singing along as if they'd picked up on the tune instantly. He didn't even know his brother and sister could sing.

"Y'all got to sing this for Madre one day." Mateo complimented them once he stepped in the car. "This was always one of her favorite songs."

"We will when you sing it with us," Luisa insisted.

"He up there acting like he don't be singing sometimes." Julio continued the embarrassment. "You can't sing them Keith Sweat and Jodeci songs for Mom, but the old school gospel songs by Richard Smallwood and Andrae Crouch, you can throw down on them."

"I do not sing Keith Sweat. I like the songs, but I don't sing them."

Julio started singing the lyrics to "I Want Her," and Mateo shook his head and chuckled.

"Don't act like you don't know this song," Julio said.

"I didn't say that." Mateo got back on the highway and headed back to Asheville. He looked over at Amirah and smiled as he noticed her smiling and getting into the book she was reading. He looked back and noticed Luisa and Julio were doing their own thing.

Mateo would have to wait until they had some time alone and she was ready. The last thing he wanted to do was compromise what they were building by not being careful with a sensitive subject.

Chapter Thirty-nine

The Verdict

Amirah couldn't believe how well dinner with Mateo's family was going.

She was surprised that she enjoyed the meal of entomatadas, refried beans, and rice. Amirah had more fun watching as Mateo's mother made the entomatadas from scratch. She showed Amirah how to boil the chicken breast that she seasoned with garlic and onion powder. Next, his mother put chopped onions, diced tomatoes, chicken bouillon powder, and chipotle pepper in a blender with a cup of water. The flavors were attacking her taste buds and made her yearn for the meal. Then they warmed the tomato sauce for a few minutes.

Heating the tortillas was even more of a challenge for Amirah, as she didn't usually fry the food she cooked. His mother was patient every step of the way. Folding the shredded chicken into the tortillas and then arranging them on the plate made Amirah feel like an artist.

She loved the final results. Mateo, Julio, and Luisa did too, as they voiced their approval and patted their stomachs. The food went down well with Jumex mango juice.

At the table, Amirah told Mateo's family more about herself. It seemed that every time Amirah opened her mouth to speak, Mateo's mother grinned. Amirah thought it was safe to say that she had his mother's approval.

His mother told a few embarrassing stories about Mateo and Julio growing up, and then she talked briefly about Mateo's father. According to her, his father had been murdered chasing another man's wife. Amirah noticed that Mateo, Julio, and Luisa were uncomfortable as their mother talked about their father's philandering ways.

After their mother finished, Luisa changed the subject by talking about her favorite topic—*her*. Amirah admired the fact that the sixteen-year-old was rather feisty and very outgoing, the opposite of Amirah when she was Luisa's age.

As the two women conversed, Amirah was happy that she actually got along with Luisa. She understood being young, going out seeing the world, and the temptations that Luisa was finding along with it: Trying to please one's mother; saying no to boys and meaning it. Amirah hoped that she would be able to sit down with Luisa and talk to her about some of the trials and temptations she was facing. Maybe hearing solutions from a woman closer to her age would do the trick.

As always, Julio acted a fool. The stories about serving in Iraq and Afghanistan were surprisingly filled with humor. Julio made bullets flying over his head while looking for mines and staying in barracks seem like the place to be.

A part of Amirah wondered if Julio was really hiding the pain from war in his smiles. She knew from another teacher she worked with that all the killing and crying was enough to make anyone have a mental breakdown. Julio was very blunt about suffering from post-traumatic stress disorder. To hear him tell it, the bigger struggle was to laugh to keep from crying.

After dinner and a dessert of crème caramel, Amirah tried to help their mother with the dishes. She scooted her away and encouraged her to enjoy her time being a guest in her home.

Mateo and Amirah stayed for a little while longer after watching a Mexican soap opera, then Mateo drove Amirah home.

"Your family is nice," Amirah complimented as they pulled up to her apartment. The ride had been nice and quiet, with contemporary R&B music playing in the background.

"Thanks." Mateo smiled as he turned off the ignition and unlocked the doors.

Mateo walked around and opened Amirah's door and helped her out of the car. They walked hand in hand until they reached Amirah's apartment.

Mateo started to walk away, but Amirah tugged at his hand, inviting him in. He happily accepted.

"This is my small piece of the world." Amirah showed off her flat with pride.

She saw how Mateo walked around and was in awe, especially at the paintings and other fine collectibles. "This is bigger than my place."

She watched as Mateo took off his shoes and let his covered feet touch the plush carpet. Amirah noticed that Mateo seemed to enjoy the slight descent of each cushioned step. "Lavender, right?" he asked when he walked around and admired her soft couch and loveseat.

"Mom always said it soothes the spirit." Amirah surprised herself by bringing up her mother.

Mateo turned around to face her. "Your mother was right."

Amirah watched as Mateo sat down for a minute and then hopped up and walked toward her mantle, which held small, African tribal figurines. "Mom was a big collector," she explained. "She was particularly fond of the Ashanti tribe in Ghana. We almost got to go one year, but something came up with one of her businesses."

"You mother was a businesswoman?" Mateo encouraged as he smiled at her and then picked up another figurine and looked at it. The miniature warrior intrigued him, and Mateo touched the tip of its spear to see how sharp it was.

"Yes." Amirah let out a light chuckle. She got a kick out of watching him rearrange the figurines on the mantle like he was playing with action figures. "What are you doing, playing chess?"

"I can't remember how I found the pieces," Mateo said as he continued to move the pieces around.

"That's okay," Amirah confirmed. "I was saying that my mother owned several businesses here and in Liberia. In Liberia, she was a private investor in a few farms and fruit stands. She went a few times a year. I didn't go with her, because she wanted me focused on my studies here and to explore Liberia and the other countries in Africa when I got older.

"In America, my mother owned a few daycares and rental properties in Winston-Salem, and she hosted several programs for women who were interested in taking on jobs as teachers. We stayed in the projects because my mother never liked to advertise her wealth, and she liked to be closer to the women she mentored."

"Is that why you became a teacher?" Mateo asked.

"Yes and no," Amirah answered. "I wasn't fond of the toddlers and pre-kindergarten students, but as I got older, I was a bad girl who was attracted to bad boys."

"Oh, really?" Mateo challenged. He sat down, and Amirah made her way to the kitchen. She opened the refrigerator and grabbed a pitcher of strawberry Arnold Palmer, which was half strawberry lemonade, half ice tea, and placed it on the counter. Amirah grabbed two tall glasses from the cupboard and filled each glass half full with the drink. She put the pitcher back in the fridge and then picked up the glasses and gave one to Mateo. She took a sip from the other.

"I liked them bad," Amirah continued, talking about the boys. "I liked the ones that could fight, but I didn't mind a drug dealer every now and then. My mother warned me about those kind of men, and thankfully, I finally listened.

"As I got older and was a student at A&T, I found that I had a passion for working with teenagers. I thought it was interesting being at the cusp of adulthood. Hence, the reason I teach high school."

Immediately she felt guilty. Amirah hadn't meant to boast. "I'm sorry. I didn't mean any harm or any comparison of your place to mine. I realize you may not have had the same opportunities."

Mateo walked to Amirah, and then he got behind her and wrapped his arms around her. "I'm not harmed." Mateo held her tight. "I'm proud of you, ma. You're doing this thing by yourself and still holding your own. You give me something to aspire to."

Amirah's guilt gave way as she looked at her apartment. While she always considered her retreat a humbling place, she could see how it appeared that she had more in someone else's eyes.

"And you will get there." Amirah felt comfortable in his embrace. Everything about being in Mateo's arms felt right, and she leaned her head in for a kiss.

She meant for a peck, but as their tongues intertwined, Amirah got more than she bargained for. And she surprised herself by being just as aggressive as he was.

As Mateo and Amirah continued breathing into each other's souls, Amirah's mind sped off into a thought of being the future Mrs. Valdez. She felt a desire to be able to share with a daughter or daughter-in-law how to make some of her own favorite dishes. She could see the children she wanted to have with him. Their little boys and girls learning to play soccer and excelling in academics, and growing into fine, respectable men and women. Mateo coming home from work while the children learned from the best teacher in the world.

Amirah felt him, and she felt herself slowly merging her world with his. She was so lost in her kiss and her dreams that she didn't realize that she and Mateo were undressing and that they were *dangerously close* to how God created Adam and Eve.

Looking at his bare chest, Amirah quickly backed away. Putting her hand to her face, Amirah felt embarrassed that she led Mateo on and took things too far. He was exposed and she was almost there, and she felt guilty.

"I'm sorry, Mateo," Amirah apologized through tears as she quickly looked away.

She couldn't believe she had let a kiss lead her to a moment where her head fell off her shoulders. This carnal, inner woman that she kept at bay was about to make her break her vow to God to stay pure until marriage.

"It's okay." Mateo rushed to put on his clothes. She could tell that he was embarrassed enough for both of them.

Amirah apologized a few more times as Mateo dressed in silence. A few moments later, Mateo was out the door, and she was sitting at the edge of her bed, praying to God and repenting for entertaining lust and for tempting Mateo.

Amirah prayed that she hadn't pushed Mateo away by not giving herself away too soon, but she had to stay true to her vow and her promise to herself and God. And by repenting, she aimed to please Him.

Chapter Forty

The Sentence

As the last student left her classroom, Amirah couldn't wait to sit down. She'd been standing for most of the ninety-minute class block, showing the students how to use speech recognition to operate the spreadsheet program. Amirah felt like she was back at the call center she had worked at while in college, sitting and standing for long periods of time.

Her grades were already in the computer. She decided to take the tests home that she had just given her students in the previous class period, so that she could look over them after her date with Mateo. He was on his way to the school, and she was excited. It been a week since their slip-up, and both felt it was best to meet in a public place. Even though they had been dating for almost four months, Amirah and Mateo knew the attraction was there, and when that moment happened, it needed to be within the blessing of God.

Besides, they couldn't get it on like Marvin Gaye if they were in her classroom.

Amirah's after-school duties required that she stand at the hallway and monitor the locker rooms on her hall to make sure to students weren't doing anything obscene. The lovebirds knew the most they could do on her hall was hold hands and maybe share a hug. Amirah watched the students as they congregated at their lockers, getting ready to go home. She almost wished she was that age again, with no major responsibilities, just homework, soccer, and a part-time job at the local Burger King.

Once the hallways were clear, she closed the door and went back to her desk. Sitting, she slouched in her chair and tilted her head back and exhaled. Amirah could finally relax for a minute.

Thinking about Mateo still gave her shivers. She couldn't believe that the peck on the lips almost led to sin. They'd gotten too close to each other. Hands weren't where they needed to be, and neither were their minds.

Amirah felt wrong for lusting after Mateo. As much as she would have wanted to say that she could avoid the temptation, she wasn't convinced that she would be strong enough. She loved God, but she also loved Mateo's touch. She felt guilty for not wanting it to end and wanting to feel it again, but she had made a vow not to have sex until marriage. She was thankful that Mateo respected her and God enough to help her keep it.

Amirah got up to stretch, feeling good that she had a few seconds to relax. She walked to the other end of her classroom and closed the blinds. Once that was done, she turned off the printer and the projector, and she visually inspected the room to ensure that all the computers were turned off too.

Completing her task, she walked back to her desk to grab her book bag and some books so that she could get ready to leave. Amirah felt someone pushing her up against the wall.

"Miss me, baby?" Turner whispered in her ear.

She hadn't heard that voice in weeks. No, she didn't miss him. Amirah gasped as she wondered how Turner had managed to sneak into her classroom again.

As she struggled, she turned her head in the direction of the door adjoining her classroom and her neighbor's classroom, and she found her answer. It was open. While checking to make sure everything else was done, she didn't check the closet space she shared with the other business and marketing teacher. Turner had been in the closet the whole time.

"How long you been here?" Amirah decided that if she was going to be harmed, she could at least get the answer to a question.

"Long enough to know that I can give you passion better than Mateo can." Turner turned Amirah around and reached in for a kiss.

Amirah realized that Turner had been on her tail and observing her comings and goings in and out of the classroom. After the first run-in, Amirah quickly changed her routine and made sure she was extra cautious of her surroundings. She tried to keep Sarai or Howard in the know of where she was to be at all times. The resource officer promised to pay close attention to the cameras in the school to monitor the doors. With that, Amirah had everything taken care of—or so she thought. No recent signs of Turner and spending more and more time with Mateo had allowed her to drop her guard and what little bit of street sense she had.

"Stop, Turner!" She tried to push him away, but she was unsuccessful. She started beating on his chest. "I said no!"

"Don't fight me, baby." Turner tightened his grip on her. She could hear him unzipping his pants while moving his hand inside of her blouse. "I always wanted to make love to a teacher."

"It's not love if you have to force it." Amirah tried to lift her knee up so she could pry herself away from him.

Turner was too strong.

"You want to do it against the wall or on the desk?" Turner shoved all the neatly stacked papers and books off her desk. The ceramic apple that one of her students had made for her a few years ago broke in huge chunks.

Turner scooped her up and carried her by the waist. He moved swiftly to force Amirah onto the makeshift bed.

"I've wanted to make love to you since I saw you with that chump," Turner whispered as he applied his weight on top of her. He kissed her on the neck and pressed down on her even as Amirah was punching at his back and trying to shove him off of her.

Her efforts were in vain. Turner was just too strong. Fear of him harming someone else kept her from crying out for help.

As Amirah felt Turner trying to force her skirt down, she prayed to God for help. She felt a tear and wondered how she was going to escape. Amirah couldn't believe she was about to be raped in her own classroom.

"Get off of me, please," Amirah begged. She stopped fighting. She needed to find another tactic. "If you stop now, I'll let you get what you want at my house."

Amirah was desperate. She didn't want to be a victim of rape, and she didn't want what she was saving for her man of God to go to a man she detested; but if it had to be done, Amirah at least wanted a say about when and where.

Turner hummed. "You gonna hold out?" He moved his hips and grinded on her.

Amirah could feel Turner pushing her panties to the side and trying to impale her. She was thankful he missed.

"I won't make you wait long," Amirah promised as she gave one last effort at verbal persuasion. "Just let me get to the house. We'll be alone, and no one will walk in on us."

She could feel Turner easing up—at least that's what she hoped he was doing. Then she heard Turner yell, and he fell on top of her hard.

"You're not getting nothing!" she heard Mateo yell.

Amirah looked to the side, and she could see Mateo swinging a chair across Turner's backside again. When Turner fell, she saw him swaying the chair across his head. Blood splattered everywhere. Turner reached for his gun that had fallen out of his pants when he fell, but Mateo managed to kick it out of his hand. Cracking bones could be heard, but Mateo didn't care. He could overlook a lot of things, but Amirah being hurt wasn't one of them.

Amirah was scared. She thought Mateo had killed him; she was also thankful that he had saved her life. She was a bag of mixed emotions. Her heart was beating so fast that she was certain she was having a heart attack.

"He's a dead man walking!" Mateo vowed as he moved Turner's unconscious body off of Amirah. "Are you okay?" Mateo checked Amirah for any signs of injury.

Mateo saw that Amirah was visibly shaking. He felt bad, because he didn't mean to frighten her. His goal was to stop Turner's assault.

After a while, Amirah nodded her head.

Mateo wanted to be relieved, but he wasn't convinced that Amirah was okay. Still, he went along with it.

"I wasn't trying to kill him." Mateo stepped over Turner to help Amirah off the desk. He looked behind Amirah to see that Turner was still laid out on the floor, unconscious. "I just wanted him to keep his hands off of you. Stop means stop."

Mateo prayed that Amirah didn't see him as a monster. The blood leaking from Turner's head, however, indicated otherwise. The fact that he had no remorse for what he did to Turner made him begin to feel that way too.

"Thank you." Amirah hugged Mateo.

"Oh Lord!" Mrs. Ingle came and looked at the scene by Amirah's desk. "Amirah, are you okay?"

Amirah nodded her head. "I'm fine, Mrs. Ingle." She looked at Mateo and smiled. "I'm glad my hero got here in time."

"We called 9-1-1," Mrs. Ingle said. "We saw Mateo rush into action, and we knew something was wrong."

Mateo, Mrs. Ingle, and Amirah looked down at Turner's body. He still hadn't moved, even though he could be heard faintly breathing. Mrs. Ingle took off her jacket and placed it over Turner's waist, concealing his nakedness.

Mateo still felt the adrenaline rush from jumping into action. He remembered what had happened the last time he and Turner squared off and how things had been going well for him. As the sirens made their presence known, he knew his freedom would be short-lived. He knew where he was headed, but to save Amirah, he'd do it again.

Amirah hated violence, especially seeing it up close and personal. Normally, she tried to encourage her students to seek a peaceful resolution—talk things out, seek mediation before conflicts escalated.

Seeing Mateo and Turner gave her a flashback of what happened the last time their conflict got out of hand. Mateo shaking and twitching violently and his eyes rolling back was the exact reason why she avoided tension.

Amirah watched as Turner was escorted to the back of the police squad car. He yelled a bunch of profanities and obscenities directed at law enforcement. She looked toward the sidewalk where Mateo was sitting with his hands behind his back. The cuffs looked tight, and his hands were red. She walked to him, wanting nothing more than to hold him in her arms. Amirah took a seat next to him.

"You think I'm a failure because I hit him?" Mateo looked deep into her eyes. He wanted to see if she'd lie to him.

"I don't think you are a failure," Amirah responded as she knelt down at his level.

"Yeah, but when was the last time you ended up in handcuffs?" Mateo leaned forward and strained to lift his arms so that Amirah could see the cuffs.

"I'm not going to pretend like I know what you are going through." Amirah saw the officers coming their way and knew their time was over. She lifted her frame and stood off to the side. "I am committed to doing this thing with you, whenever that may be. I'm loyal. My mom raised me right."

Mateo smiled.

Two of the police officers stood at Mateo's sides and helped him to his feet.

The female officer turned to face Mateo. "Mateo Valdez, you have the right to remain silent. Anything you say or do may be used against you in a court of law. You have the right to consult an attorney before speaking to the police and to have an attorney present during questioning now or in the future. If you cannot afford an attorney, one will be appointed for you before any questioning, if you wish. If you decide to answer any questions now, without an attorney present, you will still have the right to stop answering at any time until you talk to an attorney. Do you agree that you know and understand your rights as I have explained them to you?"

As they walked him away to a separate vehicle, Mateo turned to face Amirah and blew her a kiss. She felt it. Though their lips didn't touch this time, Mateo had a way of making Amirah feel as if she'd blossomed like a flower. Her flesh caused her to bite her lip. He mouthed the words, *I love you.*

Amirah wanted him. No doubt about that.

Mateo was folded and tucked like he was a T-shirt and placed into the car. Mateo pressed his face against the window separating him from the outside world.

She blew him a kiss back. "I love you too," she whispered.

Amirah watched as Mateo eased off the window. The flashing lights came on, and that was when it hit her: Mateo was going to jail for saving her life. Amirah felt in her spirit that even though the situation didn't look good at that moment, she was making the right decision to stand by her man. Mateo had put himself in harm's way to make sure her virtue would remain intact. The least she could do was stand by him as Mateo went downtown and answered charges that could send him back to prison for a long time.

Chapter Forty-one

If He Did It Before

Yeah, it was worth it, Mateo told himself as he got ready to go before the judge to enter his plea. The flashback of Turner on top of his woman, trying to push himself inside as if Amirah was his, had set off a rage he didn't know he had in him. While it was a good thing he didn't have his Glock, the chair he picked up had served its purpose, and he didn't regret one swing.

Mateo knew he needed to atone and apologize to God for losing his cool and for striking Turner with a weapon. *But God saw what was about to go down,* Mateo figured. *I was at the right place at the right time, and I was protecting my wife.*

My wife.

The words made him smile as he walked into the courtroom. He looked at the judge. She was an older black woman who reminded him of his paternal grandmother. Her glasses looked like they would slide off the bridge of her nose if it weren't for the glasses holders keeping them in place.

He looked at the defendant's side of the courtroom as he made his way down the aisle. Amirah sat right next to Julio, Luisa, and his mom, right behind where he and his lawyer would be sitting. Marvel, Sonic, and a few of his coworkers from Burgers & Fries were in the next row. Behind them in the next row were Hammer, Pastor

Cummings, Rahliem, Donte Speaks, and The Revelation. A few members of his church and some of the other men and women Hammer was helping filled out the rest of his side of the courtroom, but it was the two men sitting in the far corner in the last row who caught his eye.

He'd heard the legend of King and Othello, but he couldn't believe they'd traveled all the way from Houston, Texas just to see him stand trial. King nodded his head toward him, and Mateo nodded his head back. Mateo remembered that King served as The Revelation's bodyguard and personal assistant. He got to speak to the man when Donte and The Revelation appeared as guests on Amirah's show. Mateo wanted to ask if all the rumors about him murdering rapists, child molesters, and abusers were true, and if so, how he'd gotten away with it for so long.

Mateo almost felt sorry for what he was sure would be a long road to hell for Turner Mustafa Spartenburg. Rape was a sin, and Mateo knew King was notorious for murdering rapists and child molesters, and if the legend was true, Turner deserved what was coming to him for less than that. Mateo knew he hadn't done anything sick or twisted to end up on their radar. Of course, King had given up that lifestyle to be The Revelation's bodyguard and personal assistant, but in the back of Mateo's mind, he wasn't convinced that King kept his hands completely clean.

Mateo got to his seat, and just when the judge was getting ready to bang her gavel, he turned around. He knew he had counted the faces of all the people who'd made it to support him. He was equally happy and shocked to see who was willing to stand by his side and who'd fallen off the wayside.

The judge called the court to order, and even the formalities seemed long and drawn out. For Mateo, the back and forth between the judge, his prosecutor, and his lawyer bantering back and forth moved at the pace Venus and Serena went when they played against each other.

"How do you plead?" The judge looked Mateo in the eye. It was almost as if she was scolding him for being in her presence.

"Not guilty," Mateo said.

Mateo really didn't want to drag this out in a trial, but there was no way he was willing to go to jail for saving someone's life. His *wife's* life. They weren't married now, but Mateo felt in his spirit that the day would be coming and soon.

Mateo looked back at Turner and had no regrets for picking up the chair and swinging it down Turner's back like he was using it as a fly swatter, trying to kill the elusive fly. *He did that.*

Mateo sat and listened to the police officers and some of Turner's cronies turn his trial into a circus. Turner's men painted Mateo as a violent offender who'd threatened them every chance he got. LeMarquise testified that Mateo had threatened him on a recent trip to his job at Burgers & Fries. Amazingly, LeMarquise was able to produce a restraining order that Mateo didn't even know the man had taken out against him.

Santos's testimony took the cake. That man got on the stand and said that he had witnessed Mateo violently beating Turner a few weeks ago. Apparently, Santos had Julio's fight with Turner confused with Turner attacking Mateo, but his recollection was damaging, because it corresponded with the testimony Turner's doctors made about the injuries he'd sustained during his battle with Julio.

Then Turner took the stand and acted a fool. Turner painted the picture that even though he had a good ten inches in height over Mateo, Mateo was the one who bullied him. Turner made it seem like Mateo coerced Sonic into selling all of the things Turner had given him during their relationship, and he alleged that Mateo was pocketing the profits. Turner made it seem like they had fights over women, and that Mateo used Julio to terrorize him. Only under cross examination did Turner admit that he "got the best of Mateo" one time, but he still insisted that Mateo and Julio roughed him up.

When asked directly if he had tried to force Amirah to have sex with him, Turner flat out denied it. Let him tell it, Amirah led him on, and she was encouraging him to please her at the moment Mateo found the two of them on her desk. Turner implied that Mateo's jealousy of him had to do with the fact that he was bigger than him in more ways than one.

When Mateo's public defender came on board, Rahliem, Donte, The Revelation, and Marvel testified to the model citizen Mateo strived to be and how active he was in the Street Disciples Ministry. Doug testified about his strong work ethic and being a reliable employee.

Sonic contradicted everything Turner testified and even stated on multiple occasions that Turner had abused him during their *situationship*. Under cross examination, Sonic admitted to not going to the hospital every time Turner beat him. Sonic also confessed to admitting himself under an assumed name several times when he was treated. Sonic was also forced to admit that he used to enjoy the lavish lifestyle Turner provided when they were together. The most damaging information was the admission that Turner had saved Sonic from an abusive relationship from his parents when they found out he was gay.

Hammer's testimony unraveled the same. The prosecutor nailed him for allowing Mateo to have residency and employment after he engaged in a brawl on his facility. The prosecutor questioned Hammer's judgment to knowingly let Mateo drive his personal car without a license. Hammer had to admit that he and Turner had gotten into a physical altercation on more than one occasion. That definitely did not look good.

The most damaging was the testimony from Amirah. First, the prosecutor attacked her credibility. Clips from the circus show featuring Armaad and Thursday Honesty Denyla Jackson were replayed for the judge. Even though Amirah tried to explain why the show hadn't gone as planned, she had to take responsibility for allowing the show to continue in the first place. That played into the prosecutor's attack that she had led Turner on and provoked his lust-filled emotions.

The prosecutor then asked questions about her dealings with Mateo, making it seem like Amirah would hook up with anyone who showed interest in her online. The prosecutor then dug up her past and some of the questionable boyfriends that she'd had, some of whom were locked up for violent crimes.

The final straw was something Mateo hadn't expected. He found out in front of his friends and family that before Amirah was saved, she had filmed a few sex flicks with Donte Longstocking. The prosecutor took great joy in highlighting how many films she'd done and some of the scandalous places where they'd filmed.

What hurt the most was watching Amirah cry. She tried to explain that the films were of bad judgment, but the prosecutor wasn't trying to hear that. Mateo wanted to bust the man in the face, but hitting him would only make it worse.

The public defender had advised Mateo against testifying, and Mateo went along with it. If the prosecutor was able to dig up Amirah's sex tapes and massacre Hammer's and Sonic's testimonies, who knew what the prosecutor had on him. Mateo wondered if the man knew he'd had a gun hidden under his bed, or worse, if the prosecutor would somehow produce the gun and turn the scenario into something completely different. Mateo didn't want to take that risk.

After a few days, the judge came back with her verdict.

"Mateo Valdez, I find you not guilty for the felony assault with a deadly weapon. However, I do find you guilty of the Class A1 misdemeanor assault which, carries a maximum of two years, including time served," the judge stated as she looked at some papers and shuffled them along her desk. "Case dismissed."

He'd gotten off easier than he thought, and he looked up and thanked God for it, but two years was still a long time to go without seeing Amirah or any of his family. He'd only served forty days, which meant he had six hundred and ninety days left.

Mateo held his head up high as he walked back to his jail cell. He looked at his family and friends, and that was when he saw her. Amirah was subtle and plain in a black blouse and pantsuit. She stole a quick glance at him, and then she turned her head away, tears rolling down her face.

Mateo nodded his head. He wanted to smile this time, but he couldn't. He was glad that Amirah had come for him. The punishment he was about to endure would not be in vain. Knowing that gave Mateo something to look forward to. He prayed that he would get to see Amirah again. He didn't expect her to come visit or to accept his collect calls. Truthfully, he couldn't fix his lips to ask her to do these two years with him.

Epilogue

He Can Do It Again

Two Years Later

After being released from spending almost two years in Buncombe Correctional Center, a minimum security facility, Mateo got down on one knee and asked Amirah to be his bride. Amirah accepted his proposal after letters back and forth every week, numerous collect and prepaid calls, and the occasional visit. In Mateo's eyes, Amirah was a true ride or die chick, and she did this bid with him without ever entertaining the mere thought of another man.

Mateo's sentence was longer than it could have been considering he had previous felonies on his record. North Carolina law could be brutal, especially when it came to habitual offenders; however, the stay at the state prison was short in the grand scheme of things. Mateo could've gotten seven years in addition to the two for his crime if the judge had decided to do so.

Rahliem and Hammer had sent a lot of printed worship materials to occupy his mind. He read daily devotionals and Christian fiction books. As he read and took notice and did his work release, Mateo discovered a passion for writing that he never knew existed. Julio and Luisa put their money together to get him a JP4 player, which was a mini-tablet so he was able to download gospel music, rap, and sermons. They paid close to eight hundred dollars for a fifty-dollar tablet, but they were willing to do anything to help keep their brother on the right track. Listening to The Revelation, Mali Music, Erica Campbell, Lecrae, B-Wise, and the Counter Culture Crew helped keep his mind in perspective.

True to her word, Amirah stood by his side. Sometimes, just seeing the stamped envelope with her name on the return address was enough to make him smile and get through the days.

He learned so much about Amirah as they continued their love affair.

Turner Mustafa Spartenburg managed to beat his attempted rape charge. Even though several people saw his near naked behind as he was lifted off the ground and arrested, it was his word—and money—versus hers. The fact that Mateo beat him senseless did Amirah no good when pleading her case, and when it came to him, Mateo almost got the Class E felony charge for intent to kill, which would have locked him up much longer.

During the rape trial, Turner's attorneys were able to use all the information from Mateo's assault trial against Amirah's character. The sex tapes only did harm to Amirah's reputation. Amirah was made to look like a harlot before the courts. With this information, Turner was able to cast doubt that he'd attempted to sexually assault Amirah. Because he did not actually penetrate her, it was not considered rape.

With all of this, Amirah still held strong. She was able to keep her teaching position, and she used her new platform to help rape victims stand up and speak out about the crimes committed against them. She led a new ministry that helped women in crisis, and her television show raised money for these victims quarterly.

***

Mateo knew in his heart that Amirah was the right woman for him and that she'd be the one to help him lay down a Christian-based foundation for his household. It was better to marry than to burn with passion, and Mateo knew that while the love was real, so was the passion they felt for one another.

In the men's bathroom of Guiding Light Ministry Center, Mateo, Julio, Sonic, and Marvel were getting ready for Mateo's big day.

"Bro." Julio was tying his orange-and-purple speckled bow tie in the mirror. "What Jedi mind tricks did you play on Amirah to get her to walk down the aisle with you?"

"I didn't know you were a Star Wars fan," Marvel said to Julio.

Mateo could see Sonic shaking his head out of the corner of his eye. "He ain't no Jedi." He smirked as he barely spoke above a whisper. "He's just moving in God's time, even if it seems too fast for him."

"Thanks, man." Mateo appreciated the compliment. He leaned in closer to the mirror to make sure his face was right and to make sure his boys weren't taking too long getting ready. He couldn't believe that within an hour, he was going to be marrying the girl of his dreams. "I don't believe in Jedi mind tricks. She warmed up to me, playa."

The crew was almost finished making sure they were looking right for the festivities. In a few minutes, Mateo was going to be standing next to Amirah Dalton Valdez, and he couldn't have been a happier man.

"You should have waited until I got married first, bro." Julio took a rag and wiped his shoes clean.

"You find the woman God has for you, and I'll give you marriage advice," Mateo offered as he stepped away from the mirror. He shook off his nervousness and was happy to see that once he stood up, Sonic and Marvel indicated they were ready too.

Julio was stalling. He shook his head. Mateo could see he didn't like that answer. "But on the real," Julio said, "I know I didn't say this when Sonic and I kidnapped you the other day for your bachelor party, but I do love you, bro, and I'm happy you found what's yours."

Mateo held back a tear. He didn't want Julio to see him losing his edge. The tough boy had to remain present at all times. "I'm happy I found her too."

"Y'all ready?" Hammer asked as he stepped into the room, cloaked in a white robe with dashiki trimming in the front and the sleeves. Mateo couldn't believe that his mentor would be the one marrying him.

"I'm always ready." Mateo looked himself over in the mirror once again before stepping away. He started to walk out of the room, but Hammer reached out to straighten his bow tie.

"I'm proud of you, man." Hammer put his hand on Mateo's shoulder. "I feel like I'm watching my son become a man."

"Thanks." Mateo gave Hammer a hug.

The two of them had been through a lot during the past few years. Mateo knew and trusted that Hammer would continue to lead and guide him in the right direction. All he had to do was follow and trust in God.

Hammer released him from the hug. "We gotta get you in there, man, so you can get ready for your bride."

"Yeah," Julio butted in. "Save the mushy-mushy stuff for Ma and Luisa."

Mateo shook his head. "Bro, you a mess."

Julio rushed to the door and opened it before Hammer could reach for it. "Married men and ministers first."

Hammer quickly put Julio into a headlock and rubbed his knuckles across his head.

"Y'all stop playing," Mateo directed. "I gotta get to my wife."

Hammer let him go. "Yeah, let's make sure the man gets to his wife."

Mateo watched the two men walk out, and he looked up. He felt proud to be taking another step toward Christ and fulfilling his duty as a man of God.

Thank you, he mouthed before he crossed the threshold of the door and started the first day of the rest of his life.

UC HIS GLORY BOOK CLUB!

www.uchisglorybookclub.net

UC His Glory Book Club is the spirit-inspired brainchild of Joylynn Jossel, Author and Acquisitions Editor of Urban Christian, and Kendra Norman-Bellamy, Author for Urban Christian. This is an online book club that hosts authors of Urban Christian. We welcome as members all men and women who have a passion for reading Christian-based fiction.

UC His Glory Book Club pledges our commitment to provide support, positive feedback, encouragement, and a forum whereby members can openly discuss and review the literary works of Urban Christian authors.

There is no membership fee associated with UC His Glory Book Club; however, we do ask that you support the authors through purchasing, encouraging, providing book reviews, and of course, your prayers. We also ask that you respect our beliefs and follow the guidelines of the book club. We hope to receive your valuable input, opinions, and reviews that build up, rather than tear down our authors.

What We Believe:

—We believe that Jesus is the Christ, Son of the Living God.

—We believe the Bible is the true, living Word of God.

—We believe all Urban Christian authors should use their God-given writing abilities to honor God and share the message of the written word God has given to each of them uniquely.

—We believe in supporting Urban Christian authors in their literary endeavors by reading, purchasing and sharing their titles with our online community.

—We believe that in everything we do in our literary arena should be done in a manner that will lead to God being glorified and honored.

We look forward to the online fellowship with you.

Please visit us often at:

www.uchisglorybookclub.net.

Many Blessing to You!

Shelia E. Lipsey,
President, UC His Glory Book Club